AN OUT OF TIME THRILLER

THE GIRL WHO KNEW DA VINCI

AN OUT OF TIME THRILLER

THE GIRL WHO KNEW DAVINCI

BELLE AMI

www.belleamiauthor.com

Published Internationally by Tema N. Merback
Calabasas, CA USA

Exclusive cover © 2018 Fiona Jayde Media
Inside artwork © 2018 Tamara Cribley, The Deliberate Page

PRINT ISBN 978-1-7322071-0-3
EBOOK ISBN 978-1-7322071-1-0

Editor: Joanna D'Angelo
Copy Editors: Patricia Grasso, Brenda Heald

This book is dedicated to artists who dare to follow their dreams. Some of us dream of achieving great things while others just do them. Leonardo da Vinci never ceased his exploration of every facet of life, and his paintings often took second place to his other endeavors. He was the quintessential Jack of all trades, but in his case, he was a master of all of them. Imagining what it would be like to know one of the greatest of minds in history, to call such a man friend, was rapturous and inspiring to me. It has led to a whole new journey in my life and the creation of a cast of characters that I hope will fill the pages of many books to come.

Thank you, Maestro.

ACKNOWLEDGMENTS

Thank you… Writers do not work in a vacuum, nor are their books created in a vacuum. Every person they have ever met, every person they have ever known contributed in some way to the pages plucked from their heart, soul, and mind. This book would not have been possible without the devotion and effort of my editor, Joanna D'Angelo, who worked tirelessly and held my "fingers" to the fire. She is a blessing and has brought out the best in me, and I thank her with all of my heart.

Also, thanks to Fiona Jayde, who created one of the most artistic and beautiful covers I have ever seen. *The Girl Who Knew Da Vinci* cover is a masterpiece and I believe Leonardo would have been pleased.

Thank you to my family who is so supportive of my journey as an author and encouraged me when others poo-pooed my efforts.

Thanks as well to my copy editors Patricia Grasso and Brenda Gayle, talented authors in their own right, who applied their keen eyes to my book. Thank you to Renata Coppola, an elegant and artistic Italian woman, who edited the Italian translations in my book.

Finally, I want to thank my readers for the pleasure I derive from your reviews and support. You make the hours spent alone in front of a computer screen worth it.

Things that happened many years ago often seem close and nearby to the present, and many things that happened recently seem as ancient as the bygone days of youth. ~ Codex Atlanticus, fol. 29v-a

~ Leonardo da Vinci

PROLOGUE

Florence, Italy
Uffizi Gallery
August 3, 1944

Sophia Caro was scared, but not half as scared as she should be. The world was at war and she was in love with a German officer. She covered her ears as another explosion rocked the building, pressing closer into the arms of her lover, Gerhard Jaeger. Had it only been a few hours? It felt like the Germans had been bombing for days.

"Florence will never be the same," she whispered brokenly. After each detonation, the Uffizi Gallery strained and shuddered as if struck by an earthquake.

Gerhard held her tighter, shielding her with his body. "It will my darling, you'll see."

They planned to escape from Florence. Gerhard, who was no Nazi, would desert. If captured, he'd be lined up before a firing squad. Adding to her worries were her brothers who were partisans fighting the Nazis. She and Gerhard were set to flee back home to her family vineyard in the Tuscan hills. She'd be lucky if her brothers didn't shoot Gerhard first and ask questions later. Time had run out and the man she loved with her heart and soul was prepared to risk everything for her and their unborn child.

Another round of blasts shook the building. Huddling in the long central gallery of the Uffizi, dust and pieces of the frescoed ceiling rained down around them.

"The ceiling! What if the building collapses?" Sophia couldn't control the panic that seized her. Blistering heat and falling debris made it impossible to breathe.

"We'll be fine Sophia. The Uffizi has stood for nearly five hundred years. It will stand for another five hundred, I'm sure." Gerhard kissed her forehead. "Longer than that bastard Hitler. It makes me ashamed and sick to be a German."

Sophia laid her hand against his cheek. "You're an academic, an art historian, not a soldier. You'd do anything to protect Florence's art treasures. It's one of the reasons I fell in love with you."

"Have I done enough?" Deep lines etched his face.

A massive blast brought another shower of plaster, covering them in a fine veil of white dust.

"Heaven help us. When will it stop?" Sophia buried her face in his chest.

"It won't stop until the bridges are demolished. Even for the industrious Germans that could take most of the night."

Sophia covered her ears to muffle another round of successive blasts. "In the name of the Father and of the Son and of the Holy Spirit, Amen." She crossed herself, wondering if God would listen to the pleas of a now-and-again Catholic. She felt a trickle of sweat roll down her cheek. Gerhard pulled his handkerchief from his pocket and wiped it away.

"*Amore mio*, I promise you it will end by dawn. My contact, Deiter, assured me that the Ponte Vecchio will not be destroyed. When they've finished bringing down the rest of the bridges the explosions will cease. Then you and I will leave this nightmare of a war behind."

A series of booms echoed again through the city and the reality of their situation returned. She held her stomach, protecting the small bump that protruded.

He covered her hand with his. "I hope you packed something substantial for our journey, my love. You need to keep up your strength for our child's sake. Besides which," he said, "I'd hate to be arrested for a grumbling stomach."

"This is Italy," she said with a quirk of her lips. "We aren't going to die of starvation." She looked around. "What have you done with the painting?"

"I had to cut it from its frame," he said with a grimace. "I wrapped it in tissue paper and rolled it paint side out. Then I rolled it in lamb's wool and fit it in a thick cardboard tube. I think it should be safe from the elements. My backpack is waterproof."

She knew he'd do anything to keep her and their unborn child safe, but the painting worried her. It seemed to her an unnecessary risk to take a painting from the Uffizi, even if he meant only to keep it safe. It was a bone of contention between them.

"It's twenty-seven kilometers south of Florence to my family's vineyard in Montefioralle. I'm afraid much of it is uphill."

"We're young and strong, Sophia. If I have to carry you up a mountain, I will. It should take us about six hours to walk twenty-seven kilometers; we can manage that. Didn't you say the area is famous for its Chianti?"

"The best Chianti and the most beautiful village in Italy. You will never want to leave."

"Sounds like a good place to wait out the war, a glass of wine in hand, a *bambino* on my lap, and a goddess in my bed. The perfect place for us to begin our new life." He drew her close and caressed her abdomen.

It seemed impossible that amid the chaos of war their child had been conceived. She hadn't meant it to happen and feared he'd think she'd entrapped him. But when she told him, he was overjoyed, professing his excitement to be a father. She knew, then, that his love for her was true.

Sometime after dawn, the explosions ceased, and the Uffizi Gallery grew quiet. Gerhard had kept his military uniform on until the last second. But now the die had been cast and it was time to escape. He discarded his uniform and donned the clothes of a civilian. Sophia straightened his collar while he stuffed the fake identity papers into his pocket.

"Well, Giorgio Bandini, accountant from Pisa, are you ready to begin the next phase of your life?"

He grabbed her around the waist and kissed her. "So long as I'm allowed to make love every night to the most desirable woman in the world. Shall we go, *angelo mio*?"

Sophia knew the Vasari Corridor like the back of her hand. If need be, she could walk it blindfolded. The concealed passageway above the bridge would be their escape route. She gave silent thanks to the clever Duke Cosimo I de' Medici who, in 1565, had ordered Giorgio Vasari to build the secret corridor. It allowed the Medici family to travel from the Palazzo Vecchio to the Palazzo Pitti in safety and privacy. During the five years Sophia had worked at the Uffizi, instead of walking the crowded Ponte Vecchio below, she'd chosen to walk the three-quarter mile from the Uffizi to the Pitti in privacy, just as the Medici family had.

Holding a candle for her, Gerhard followed her through the unmarked secret door near the Botticelli room and down a flight of stairs. She unlocked another door and, after he passed through it, she locked it behind her. The minute the door shut, it was as if the air changed. The eerie silence was disconcerting after the hours of continuous bombings.

"Don't worry, it always feels like you've entered another world," she said.

"Cooler. I'll take it." He shifted the heavy backpack to his other shoulder.

Taking his hand, she led him through the twists and turns of the corridor. "Before the war these walls were hung with Medici portraits. Now they're hidden in storage vaults. The war has altered the world forever."

"Not forever, *amore mio*."

They continued through the corridor until she paused and whispered, "We've reached the Ponte Vecchio. The corridor is built above the bridge and invisible, but we'd better snuff out the candle now. There are too many windows where we might be seen. Besides, we won't need it, the sun is rising. There will be plenty of light."

Gerhard blew the candle out and again took her hand, kissing it. "Where you lead, I will follow."

When they reached the center of the bridge they came to a series of large windows where the rising sun shed enough light through the panes of glass for Sophia to see across the Arno. Gerhard had warned her it was happening, but to see it made her gasp in horror. What had been one of the most beautiful sights in the world, the Ponte Santa Trinita and the Ponte alla Carraia bridges, had been destroyed. All that was left were piles of rubble, much of it submerged beneath the Arno River.

"Look at what they've done," she said. "How could they be so callous?" She turned to him. "This is so hard. So much needless suffering, and to destroy bridges that have stood for over four hundred years. Truly, the world has gone mad."

"*Tesoro*, we cannot save the world." He took her hand and kissed her palm. "We must protect our unborn child."

They left the bridge behind and continued until they arrived at the façade of a church. They walked past a large window over the balcony that gave a dramatic view of the central aisle toward the nave and the main altar.

"Where are we?" asked Gerhard.

"Santa Felicità Church. The Medici family often watched the Mass from this vantage point."

With a heavy sigh, she turned and followed the corridor's path as it cut through rows of houses. Whenever they passed a window, they could see tons of concrete and rubble below. The Germans had mined Oltrarno, decimating the neighborhood.

Gerhard blew out a breath. "It will take the Allied forces weeks to find a way through this devastation."

She nodded. "We could exit the corridor at the Boboli Gardens, but I think it's better we exit through the secret door in the Pitti Palace."

"Agreed." He smiled, brushing his knuckles against her cheek. "I think this will be a story to tell our children and grandchildren. *Si, amore mio?*"

She returned his smile. When he spoke of their future, it filled her with hope. She cradled her belly and walked ahead.

CHAPTER 1

Los Angeles, California
Getty Museum
Present day
August 3

If she didn't get a good night's sleep soon, she would go mad.

Angela Renatus sat at her desk and stared with bleary eyes at her computer screen. Headaches and insomnia had kept her up night after night for weeks. It had all started when she began her internship at the Getty Museum six weeks ago. She'd always been a sound sleeper, but now her nights were plagued with vivid dreams that left her wary and unsettled.

The intercom on her phone lit. Extension 212. *It's him.* She shuddered. "Yes, sir."

"Angela can you come into my office, please."

The pounding in her temples accelerated.

"I need your research on the Botticelli in ten minutes."

"Yes, sir. I'll print what I have so far."

"Don't bother. Just email it to me and I'll read it before you get here."

Trembling, she hit send, then picked up her cup and took a sip of water. The dream job of a lifetime had become a nightmare. Landing an internship at the Getty Museum had been a coup, but she couldn't stomach working with Dr. Alberto Scordato, the director of the museum. She'd begun to dread being called into his office, trying to come up with ways to avoid being alone with him. It sucked up a lot of her mental energy. What little she had left, given her lack of sleep.

She needed coffee before facing him, and she needed a minute to collect herself. In the employee kitchen, Kathryn Hayes, Scordato's administrative assistant, was refilling her coffee cup.

The woman turned to her and must have read her distress. "Angela, dear, are you all right?"

Recovering herself, Angela forced a smile. "Just tired, I guess. Haven't been sleeping lately. I have to meet with Doctor Scordato in a few minutes."

Kathryn's smile faded. "I've worked for that man a long time and I know how difficult he can be. Don't let him get to you."

"It's just that I fought so hard to get this internship. This is supposed to be the gold star on my resume, my paved-with-gold path into the art world. Instead, I'm struggling to survive."

Kathryn tilted her head. "I've seen many interns come and go over the years, but you, my dear, are putting them all to shame with your long hours and coming in on weekends. Too much work and not enough fun isn't healthy."

"I've been doing that for years. I'm not sure I know any other way." Angela shrugged.

"Honey, this isn't the end for you; it's just the beginning. It will all work out, you'll see." Kathryn stared at the coffee in her cup as if she were trying to decipher tea leaves. "He's done this before, Angela."

"Done what?" Angela said, a chill skittering up her spine.

Kathryn hesitated. "He has a penchant for the ladies. You know how men are. Just be careful when you're alone with him."

Angela gripped the counter, watching the coffee flow into her cup. "There are too many jerks in this world. My dad taught me how to fight. I can take care of myself."

"Is Scordato the reason you haven't been able to sleep?"

"No, not him, although his behavior is far from professional. I'm not sure why I'm having trouble sleeping. It's strange, really. It's been so disruptive that I'm keeping a journal to help track of my dreams and how often I wake up throughout the night. So far, it's only shown me how vivid my dreams are."

"Are they nightmares? Do they frighten you?"

"No, not really," Angela replied. "They're about Leonardo da Vinci and his friendship with Fioretta Gorini." Her lips quirked. "Isn't that odd?"

"Maybe the dreams are a message," Kathryn suggested. "Believe me when I say, there's life after the Getty. I can assure you, a qualified academic like you will have no problem doing well in the art world."

Angela thanked Kathryn and made her way to Scordato's office. A recent conversation with her thesis advisor, Dr. Hoffman, flickered through her mind. A private investigator who specialized in retrieving stolen art had contacted Hoffman, asking if he could recommend a Renaissance expert. Hoffman relayed the offer to her, encouraging her to look into it. The detective had followed up with her and set up a meeting for that night. Alexander Caine was his name. Could this be a way out for her? Could she somehow bow out of her miserable internship and avoid risking her career in the art world?

Angela knocked lightly on Scordato's door.

"Come in."

Scordato's corner office was filled with light from the border of windows that looked over the hills of Bel Air. The silver-haired director was in his fifties, and known to be exceedingly charming, except to her. Besides being a brilliant art historian, he was a master in the art of siphoning donations from corporations and wealthy patrons, and of wrestling artwork from prospective donors. Because of his position, he held a lot of power and could make or break a career.

"Angela, my dear." His smooth smile assailed her from across the room. Seated at his desk he stood and approached her. Standing just inside the threshold, her hand gripped the doorknob. *You know what he's going to do. Leave. Now. Quit.* Her feet were frozen to the floor. *I can't. Can I?*

As she continued to battle with herself he reached her side, his hand landing on the small of her back. The pressure of it propelled her forward, forcing her to let go of the doorknob. Bile rose in her throat as his hand roamed up her spine, her back ramrod-stiff at the unwanted intimacy. She sunk into the leather-upholstered chair facing his desk. Shrugging his fingers off her shoulder as she leaned forward to lay a file on his desk.

He cleared his throat and strolled back to his chair opposite her. Impeccably dressed in a silk-blue suit, his right hand smoothed down the front of his jacket. She suppressed a shudder as she watched his fingers preening the cloth. "Angela, I've gone over your analysis of the Botticelli and I'm afraid it's lacking in historical context." He leaned forward, his hands palms down on the clear glass top. "Why don't you and I have dinner and go over your findings—brainstorm a little?" His charming smile didn't fool her for one second.

"I'm sorry but I have plans this evening." She crossed her arms over her chest, unconsciously shielding herself from his bold perusal. "But I should have a more detailed outline for you tomorrow morning."

The director frowned. "I'm sure you know how busy my schedule is. The fact that I'm willing to make time for you, to help you through this muddle is all but unheard of, especially for an intern."

Well, the thought of fending off your advances makes me sick. "I'll give it some thought, sir. I hate to deprive you of your free time."

"Please, Angela, I'm only concerned for you to do well in your position."

She stood, eager to make her exit. "Thank you. Perhaps we can arrange some time soon."

"I have a better idea." He stood and came around his desk, his hands reaching for her shoulders.

She wanted to push him away and get the hell out of there. But something kept her rooted to the spot—Fear. Uncertainty. Worry about her future.

"Plan on having dinner with me tomorrow night." The pressure of his fingers cemented his words.

It wasn't a request, it was an order.

She didn't reply. He dropped his hands and stepped back, allowing her retreat.

She hurried out the door and bee-lined to the library in the research center where she'd set up a temporary workstation. *I can't do this anymore. I can't take this anymore.*

Scordato picked up his phone and punched in a number.

"Security, Charles speaking."

"Bring me yesterday's video from the red gallery where the Botticelli is hanging."

"Yes, sir."

Ten minutes later Scordato loaded the video into his computer, steepled his fingers, and waited. The video image showed Angela walk into the gallery, sit down on the bench in front of a Botticelli portrait of Giuliano Medici. Her shoulders relaxed and her breathing became deep and even, as though she were sleeping. Except her eyes were open. He turned up the sound when she began to speak in Italian...

His beautiful, young intern was carrying on a one-sided conversation with a painting of a man who'd been dead for nearly five-hundred years.

It had been going on for weeks. Charles, one of the security guards, first brought it to his attention, asking if he should approach Angela about her "problem." Scordato had vetoed that idea, telling him he would keep an eye on matters and to tell no one. He made a point of slipping the security guard a crisp hundred-dollar bill. Subterfuge and bribery served Scordato well.

This business with Angela was unusual. Unbelievable really. If Scordato hadn't been privy to the conversations himself, he wouldn't have believed it. The intern had some kind of connection to Giuliano Medici and, more importantly, Leonardo da Vinci. Somehow, she was tied to the mystery of the missing da Vinci painting. It had to be the same painting Max Jaeger was after.

Scordato had spent the summer in Florence searching for the elusive painting, but every road led to a dead end. Frustrated, he returned to Los Angeles, only to have this little gem fall into his lap. Rather than telling Jaeger, he decided to keep the information to himself. The German billionaire was only interested in trying to clear the name of his uncle from the Nazi taint. A noble cause to the international philanthropist.

If found, a da Vinci would be worth a fortune and the prestige priceless. Why share the golden egg with Max when the painting could be his alone? He'd already hired someone to watch Angela and follow her. But Scordato needed more. He needed to get into her head, to control her and have her lead him, and only him, to the painting. Disposing of her was not past his machinations. Whatever it took was well worth the risk. One way or the other, he would use her to find the painting and then he would get rid of her.

It was nearly closing time, and there were few people left in the North Pavilion where pre-1700 paintings and sculptures were displayed. Natural light from the ceiling cast a warm glow, washing the precious masterpieces in a filtered luminosity. Alex Caine entered one of the gallery rooms and noticed a young woman sitting by herself. Something about her stillness drew him.

Her midnight hair, secured in a bun atop her head, and her black-framed glasses couldn't hide her beauty. The prim accoutrements enhanced her high cheekbones and full mouth. He moved closer to get a better look at her. She was oblivious of him and showed no sign that her private sojourn had been intruded upon.

With her hands folded in her lap, the young woman sat like a statue. Her dark eyes were riveted to a painting. A portrait of a young man captured in eternal contemplation. The subject's eyes were hidden from the viewer. Why Botticelli had chosen to paint the young man with his eyes downcast was a mystery. The youth was handsome, almost beautiful. Thick dark waves of hair framed his face. He wore a stylish red velvet tunic that distinguished him as a man of royalty or rank. However, wealth could not dispel the overwhelming sadness imbued in his face. In three-quarter profile, his finely etched brows portrayed a man of extreme sensitivity, his face and demeanor more of a poet than a man of commerce.

He recognized the painting of Giuliano Medici—he'd seen it before, in Berlin. But never had he witnessed such a visceral reaction to a painting as this young woman had. The woman was so deep in contemplation that he could have broken out in song and she wouldn't have flinched.

He hovered for a few moments, inexplicably drawn to her serene beauty. She began to whisper as if she were speaking to the painting, but he couldn't hear what she was saying. Peculiarly, the lights dimmed, and an encroaching darkness descended upon him and the young woman. Looking up, he noticed the skylight showed a clear, blue sky.

What the hell is going on?

A fog swirled up from the floor, forming a cloudy curtain, separating them from the other visitors to the museum, who seemed completely oblivious.

A sudden flash of light over the painting propelled Alex to protect the woman. He rushed to crouch in front of her, but she continued to stare at the painting as though in a trance.

"Are you all right?" he asked her with concern. He felt compelled to protect her, but protect her from what?

What happened next made him doubt his sanity.

Her eyes changed color, turning from dark brown to forest green. Her gaze fixated on the young man in the portrait as though he were alive and standing before her. Her expression reflected radiant, passionate, love. Intense. All consuming.

It took his breath away.

Alex's eyes shifted back to the portrait and what he saw sent his pulse racing.

The young man in the painting came alive, turned his face, opened his eyes and stared at the young woman, his dark eyes mirroring the same intensity as hers.

Alex was stunned. Never in his life had he witnessed such intense love in just one look, let alone directed at a portrait of a young man who'd died more than five centuries ago.

He shook his head, trying to clear his vision. Any minute he expected to hear Rod Sterling's voice.

Another flash of light, like a lightning bolt, shot out from the painting toward them. Reacting on pure instinct, Alex covered the woman with his chest and arms, feeling the jolt hit him in the back. Not pain, exactly. But, certainly a shock.

He pulled away from the woman, hoping she was okay. And then something remarkable happened. She looked him straight in the eyes, laid her hands on either side of his face and spoke to him.

"*Ti amerò per sempre.*" *I will love you forever.*

He couldn't take his eyes off her as she spoke.

"*Sei l'unico uomo che amerò mai.*" *You are the only man I will ever love.*

Alex had lived most of his life in Europe and was fluent in Italian. He understood every word she said.

She leaned in and pressed her lips to his, provoking him to respond. Desire seized him, his fingers tangled in the silk of her hair, pulling it free from the confines of her bun. A waterfall of dark waves cascaded down her back. Their tongues danced together and for long, breathless moments, he lost himself in her kiss.

Regaining his composure, he pulled away from her luscious mouth. The woman gazed at him with the same intense love she'd directed at the painting only moments before. Her eyes, still the color of forest-green moss. He was mesmerized. A yearning flowed through him, the likes of which he'd never felt before. He wanted this woman with every fiber of his being. Shocked at his own visceral response, he let go of her and leaned back, his gaze straying to the painting of the young man. He was relieved to see the portrait had returned to "normal" and the young man's visage was turned away once more.

The young woman turned his face back to hers. "*Siamo insieme in questo,*" she whispered. "*Devi aiutarmi. È il nostro destino.*" *We are in this together. You must help me. It is our destiny.*

And without another word, she got up and left, walking through the swirl of gray mist.

The gallery filled with light again, the cloud lifted and the buzz of visitors walking by filled his ears. There was nothing to indicate anything out of the ordinary had occurred.

His heart was pounding, and he got up from the floor and sat on the bench. His face felt hot and feverish. The surprise kiss had unglued him. Hell, the entire experience had unglued him. He sought to find a plausible explanation.

He hadn't had a PTSD attack in about two years. It had taken a year of intense therapy to mitigate the effects of four deployments in Afghanistan, capped off by a compound fracture that had nearly cost him his left leg when the Humvee he was driving was blown up. He closed his eyes, breathed deeply, and focused his mind until the raging storm passed. This didn't feel like PTSD. This was something completely different.

Inanimate objects don't come to life. It must have been the light playing with my imagination. And the kiss? Yeah, it's been too long… This case must be getting to me.

The case was a conundrum. He'd been hired by Max Jaeger to find a painting that might not even exist. Max's claim was based on letters from an art historian who disappeared off the face of the earth seventy-three years ago, during the evacuation of Florence in World War II. Max's uncle, Gerhard Jaeger, had written to his mother in Germany of a great discovery—a misattributed Leonardo da Vinci wedding portrait.

It was a meeting with Alberto Scordato, the director of the Getty Museum, that had brought Alex to Los Angeles. In a surprising about-face, Scordato, who'd been a consultant on the case and an avid proponent of the painting's existence, had soured and declared the painting a fraud.

From what Max had told him, Alex suspected the director was on his own treasure hunt to find the painting first. Ironically, Alex had already been investigating Scordato, hired privately by a Getty board member, who also happened to be a close family friend of Alex's mother. The board member mentioned odd financial discrepancies concerning Scordato, especially in regard to his expense account.

He glanced at his watch, noting the time. He'd ponder the extraordinary encounter with the mysterious young woman later. Right now, he had to keep his wits about him for his meeting with Scordato.

"The director is ready to see you now." Scordato's assistant ushered him in.

A man behind a massive glass desk stood and approached. His silk blue suit rustled as he moved. Alex's hackles rose as they shook hands. Scordato's smile was about as sincere as a snake-oil salesman. Scordato waved him to a chair in front of his desk and returned to his own perch on the other side of the glass divide.

Wasting no time, Alex got straight to the reason for his visit. "Max Jaeger hired me. I'm investigating the disappearance of a painting his uncle may have taken from the Uffizi Gallery during the evacuation of Florence in 1944."

"As you know, Mr. Caine, I'm well apprised of this so-called missing masterpiece," he said with a flick of his manicured hand. "I, too, was hired to research the painting and find it. However, as I told Max a few weeks ago, I concluded this story of a missing da Vinci is a fairy tale."

"Really? How did you come to change your mind?" Alex frowned, leaning forward, his elbows on his knees. "From what I understand, you spent the entire summer at the Four Seasons in Florence while extolling to Jaeger, via telephone from your lavish suite, the importance of your investigative methods."

Scordato stiffened at the implied insult. "My investigation at the Uffizi produced no records of such a holding. I don't believe the painting ever existed."

"What about Gerhard's letters to his mother discussing the painting in detail?"

"Simply the rantings of a man who wanted to impress his mother." He shrugged. "He was planning desertion and had fallen in love with some Italian woman. I believe the whole da Vinci story was a hoax, a distraction. Most likely, he probably stole some inferior artist's work hoping to raise cash to set up his mistress."

"Max believes the letters are real and that Gerhard made a stunning discovery and only wanted to protect the painting."

"Max just wants to clear the smear on his family's name by finding this so-called da Vinci and returning it to the Uffizi. The man believes his uncle was a hero."

Alex narrowed his eyes, leaning back in his chair. "A newly discovered da Vinci in today's market could be worth hundreds of millions of dollars at auction. Quite the fortune, for just one man."

"I'm the director of one of the most respected institutions in the world." Scordato's back straightened and he thrust out his chin. "Your insinuations are beneath my dignity."

The man was a liar. "You know Scordato, I've done some research of my own about your so-called dignity as it applies to your lavish lifestyle."

The older man's arm shot up, his index finger pointing at the door. "Get out of my office, Caine, or I'll call security and have you thrown out."

Alex stood. "That won't be necessary. The stench in here is getting to me."

"I warn you, Caine, stay out of my way or you'll live to regret it."

Alex ignored him as he walked out the door. His meeting with Scordato was exactly what he'd expected. The guy was a crook and he was after the da Vinci.

He left the Getty angry at himself, wondering if the rest of his day would get better or worse. He glanced at his watch. He was meeting an art historian for a drink in a few hours. His friend Michael Hoffman had recommended her. A former student. Brilliant mind. Michael had raved about her and Alex needed an expert on the Italian Renaissance to help him solve this case. Alex had reached out to her and told her about the job. He tried to hire her on the phone, but she'd turned down his offer. He hoped, in person, he could get her to reconsider.

I'll offer her more money and convince her that solving this case will bring her international acclaim. After all, isn't leaving their imprint on history what all these art historians want? To make the next great discovery?

CHAPTER 2

Los Angeles, California
Present day
August 3

Home. Relief washed over.

Angela locked the door to the guesthouse and tossed her bag on the couch. She'd been renting the tiny one-bedroom since her arrival in L.A. A friend of Professor Hoffman's had come through. Luckily the rent was cheap. Especially for a Midwest gal who'd waited tables throughout her undergraduate degree while working her butt off for a scholarship.

But now, all of her hopes and dreams had gone south. She dreaded going into work. What used to bring her immense pleasure, immersing herself in the art of the Renaissance, had become a burden. Scordato had ruined that for her. Her days were filled with anxiety, unable to concentrate, hoping that she wouldn't get called into his office. She felt like she was being watched—stalked even. Between Scordato's leering looks and her lack of sleep, she was walking a razor's edge. She couldn't take much more. She yawned. Tired. She was always tired these days. Sleep had become her enemy, or rather the lack of it.

It was early and she wasn't meeting the detective until 7:30 p.m. A nap would be a dream come true. She kicked off her shoes and lay down on her bed. The guesthouse was so quiet she could hear the creaking in the walls and floors. Scordato's escalating behavior coupled with her heavy workload and lack of sleep had taken its toll on her body and mind. She closed her eyes and gave herself up to exhaustion…

Florence, Italy
August 3, 1475

Fioretta, it's time…

"Thank you, Fioretta, for accompanying me." Leonardo fingered his beard nervously. "Lorenzo insisted I attend this celebration. He's the greatest patron of the arts in Florence and to turn him down would have been suicide."

Fioretta looked up at the tall, thin man beside her. A beautiful man dressed in a rich brocade tunic and leggings. He held her arm and escorted her up the steps of a fortress-like structure. The sun was setting and the palace was surrounded by hundreds of flaming torches.

"It is I who must thank you, Leonardo. I'm thrilled to see the Medici palazzo and to meet the venerable Lorenzo. I applaud the man who's clever enough to court your genius. I hope he likes me."

"He will adore you, I'm sure." The bright, blue eyes twinkled at her. "He is enthralled with any woman who can match his wit, and you, dear girl, are more than up to the task."

As they strolled into the main hall, Fioretta was overwhelmed by the treasures that surrounded her and the extravagance the Medici put forth. Long tables were laden with excesses of food and drink. The richly adorned citizenry glittered as brightly as the torches that lit the chamber. Open arches led to patios where Fioretta could see guests strolling through the gardens and standing amidst the sculptures. She longed to go outside and find a quiet spot to observe the interactions of Florence's elite.

Leonardo handed her a goblet of wine and whispered, "Be prepared, Lorenzo is on his way to us."

Across the room, Fioretta spied a statuesque woman, hair of burnished gold, sparkling eyes, and glowing visage. "Leonardo is that Simonetta Vespucci?" she whispered. "She is breathtaking."

"Yes, Simonetta is a classic beauty, but you are a rare exotic jewel," he told her.

Fioretta was petite, but Leonardo insisted that she was every bit as beautiful as the lauded Simonetta. But then again, her best friend was prejudiced. Leonardo adored her and respected her.

Her thoughts were interrupted as their host stood before her. She straightened her spine to her full diminutive height, hoping to make a good impression.

"Lorenzo may I introduce you to my dear friend, Fioretta Gorini."

She looked into the blackest eyes she'd ever seen. She curtsied and bowed her head in respect. He took her hand and raised her up, his eyes dancing with amusement.

"The pleasure is mine, signorina." He turned to Leonardo and asked, "How is it that an artist has come to know the most beautiful woman in Florence?"

Fioretta blushed. "Signore, please there is no need to rain compliments on me."

"To not speak the truth would be an insult to the greatness of God and his creations."

"I would prefer to be appreciated for my learning and intelligence than the ephemeral gift of beauty."

Lorenzo turned back to Leonardo, laughter gleaming in his eyes. "Now I *am* intrigued. Your Fioretta's philosophical truth is as startling as her beauty. We will have to continue this conversation at another time as I have many guests to greet. I must know where you found this gem." He bowed and gracefully moved through the crowd.

Fioretta sipped her wine considering her interaction with Lorenzo. *The man is an interesting balance between power and intellectual acumen, not to mention an abundance of charm.*

"Leonardo, would you mind if I took some air? You know how I dislike crowds."

"Go, my dear, I'll join you shortly."

Turning toward the doors leading to the garden, she found herself the focus of one man's gaze. There was nothing sinister in his look, on the contrary, it was simply inquiring. She noted the resemblance to Lorenzo, but the younger man's features were decidedly composed in a far more pleasing countenance. His stare was impertinent, but she refused to tear her gaze away. *Surely, he'll realize how embarrassing it is for a gentleman to behave in such a manner.*

It was a standoff, both of them refusing to look away. She felt heat creep up her neck. *Dear Lord, please don't let me faint. The way he looks at me thrills me.*

The young man's eyes burned into her, yet he made no move to approach. The spell was broken when a beautiful young woman grabbed the man's arm and drew his gaze. Taking the opportunity to escape, Fioretta hurried outside and found a bench near a gurgling fountain to sit and regain her composure. Her heartbeat drowned out the world around her. *Who is he*, she wondered?

"There you are, *cara*." Leonardo's voice jolted her back to reality. "Soon we will sup and afterwards we can make our departure. These events are tedious to me."

She took his hand in hers, patting it. "Yes, but it is important for you to mingle with patrons. One day they will be flocking to you, falling over each other to possess the creations of your genius." Her delicate brows lifted. "Poor me, you probably won't have time for your little friend."

"Time for you? A muse who plays me like a fiddle." He tweaked her chin. "Most definitely not."

"Humph." She drew her hand from his and folded her arms over her chest. She was always playfully indignant when Leonardo failed to rise to her teasing.

A Medici bodyguard approached them. "Signor Lorenzo has requested that you and your companion dine at his table, Maestro."

Leonardo rose, extending his hand to her. "We would be delighted."

They followed the man to a private dining room where an elaborately dressed table glittered with Murano crystal and china. They were seated not far from Lorenzo.

Fioretta glanced around the table and found herself once more looking into the eyes of the man she'd fled from. The beautiful lady, who'd interrupted before, chatted beside him, completely unaware of his focus. Fioretta blushed, looking away. To encourage him would be madness. She would ignore him this time. Her attention turned to their host who called to her. In minutes she was engaged in a lively philosophical conversation between herself, Lorenzo, and Leonardo about whether art lacking religious depiction was inferior. All the while, she felt the young man's eyes on her...

Angela come back...

Angela awoke with a start. Her heart pounded and she had trouble catching her breath. She longed to return to the dream and the young man. Why?

Fioretta Gorini was the mistress of Lorenzo's brother Giuliano. Her body trembled. Giuliano and Fioretta's son became Pope Clement VII.

She turned to her bedside table and opened the drawer, pulling out a plain, black leather journal. The journal was almost full. Pages and pages of notes about her dreams. Strange and mysterious dreams from the past several weeks. Dreams about Fioretta Gorini, her life, and her friendship with Leonardo da Vinci. Now she added Giuliano Medici as well.

Glancing at her bedside clock, she realized an hour had passed. She needed to shower and change. She'd text the detective and let him know she was going to be late.

CHAPTER 3

Los Angeles, California
Present day
August 3

It's her.

Alex almost choked on his martini when he saw the young woman's reflection in the mirror. He swiveled on his barstool, his heart pounding in his chest and stared, unable to believe his own eyes. *Angela Renatus and the girl in front of the painting who kissed me are one and the same.*

Alex had managed to grab two seats at the bar of *Bistro Prossima Volta*—one of the hottest spots in LA. The place was packed. The hipsters who flocked there during the dinner rush, crowded around the ornate mahogany bar, drinking and sampling a vast array of Italian antipasti.

Setting his briefcase on the second stool, he'd ignored the angry glances and ordered a dry martini. He sipped while keeping his eyes locked on the Italian mirror stretching along the wall across from him. He could see the reflection of the restaurant's entrance and everyone who walked in. Angela had texted him that she was running late. She hadn't given him a description and he'd neglected to ask. Odd. Alex never forgot to ask. His entire career involved just those kinds of details. And then *she* walked in. And he knew. He knew it was her.

Her dark hair, secured in an elegant bun, enhanced those movie-star cheekbones. Her brown velvet eyes, framed by the black-rimmed glasses, were a striking contrast to her lush, ruby-red lips. Wearing a crisp, white blouse and a gray, pencil skirt, she paused as she scanned the restaurant, unaware of every male head swiveling to get an eyeful. Damn! He wasn't the only guy attracted by the hot librarian look. He recalled the temptress who'd kissed him with wild abandon and shifted on his stool. He couldn't reconcile her disparate behavior. It was as if she were two different women.

When their eyes locked in the mirror, he was surprised to see no reaction or recognition. His pulse quickened. *How can she not know me?*

She glanced down at her watch.

This wasn't at all what he'd expected. Embarrassment, yes. Confusion and accusations, likely. Not this total obliviousness of the erotic passion that had consumed them.

He stood and called out to her. "Angela, Alex Caine."

She maneuvered through the crowd. "How did you know it was me? I think I forgot to give you a description."

"Just a guess."

"Do you prefer Alex or Alexander?

"Everyone calls me Alex," he said with a grin, offering her his hand.

Angela smiled and took it. "It's good to meet you."

Double damn! Gorgeous smile, with a sexy dimple in her left cheek. The touch of her hand sent a jolt through him. Her eyes widened slightly, her hand trembled in his.

"That's weird," she whispered, as though to herself.

"What's weird?" he asked, feigning ignorance. *Does she feel it too?*

She shook her head, a laugh escaping her. "Sorry, it's been a long day. It'll be good to relax. I'm glad you called. Professor Hoffman is one of my dearest friends and my mentor."

Alex lifted the briefcase and stowed it at his feet, gesturing her to sit. "I've known Michael for years. He's been very supportive of my work."

She nodded and sat. "Michael is a vault of knowledge and always willing to help."

Her gaze was direct, but without any recognition that they'd made out a few hours earlier in front of the Botticelli painting. *How the hell do you kiss someone like that and not remember?*

Her brows knitted as she continued to look at him.

He laughed. "Is there something on my face?"

"Forgive me." A rosy hue colored her cheeks. "It's your eyes. They're so unusual."

He sat back and scratched his cheek. "Yeah, I get that a lot." His left eye was pale blue, the right was hazel. "You can blame my parents for the odd combo. Although, no one else in my family has two different-colored eyes."

The bartender approached them. "Angela, the usual?"

Her eyes remained locked on his. And she failed to reply to the bartender. Something flickered in her gaze. Not recognition. But something deep. Intense. He suddenly wished they were back at the Getty, sitting in front of the painting, not in a noisy, packed restaurant.

"Hey, Angela," the bartender repeated. "Do you want the usual?"

Her expression cleared and she glanced up at the bartender. "Sorry, Tim. Yes, please, that would be great. Oh, and some of those yummy meatballs."

"I'll have the meatballs, too. And put it on my tab."

"Got it, man."

"I can't let you do that," she protested.

"Don't be ridiculous. I called *you*." He grinned. "Besides, I'm the one with an expense account."

She shook her head and chuckled. "I definitely don't have one of those."

Alex took a sip of his martini. He couldn't get past her lack of recognition. He needed to test her, to see whether this act of hers was for real. "Besides trying to convince you to work on this case with me, I'm here on business. In fact, I had a meeting with the director of the Getty today."

Her eyes widened. "You knew I worked at the Getty, why didn't you tell me you were planning on being there? We could have grabbed a coffee."

"I didn't want to bother you at work. Seeing the Getty was a pleasure, but a brief cup of coffee wouldn't be enough time for me to get to know you or learn much about your expertise." Alex had spent years studying body language and facial expressions. He knew when someone was telling the truth or evading it. She genuinely seemed surprised. Which made this mystery all the more strange.

The bartender placed a white sangria in front of her. "Cheers." She clinked her glass to his and took a sip. "How did your meeting with the director go?"

"Don't take any offense, but let's just say I'm not a fan of the guy."

She nodded, her eyes glancing down at her drink.

"Correct me if I'm wrong, but you don't seem thrilled with him either."

She took another sip. "I'm having some issues with him."

He didn't press her on the director issues. His focus was still on their unforgettable kiss at the museum. "You know, I have this strange feeling that I saw you today."

She lifted her elegant eyebrows. "You did?"

"Yeah, at the Getty."

"No, that's unlikely. I rarely leave my desk at the research center." She shook her head and a strand of hair came loose. He began to lift his hand, wanting to tuck her hair behind her ear, but caught himself just in time and reached for his drink instead. He needed to unravel the mystery of why Angela had no recollection of what had happened earlier in the day. *This woman is either a really good liar, or she's sleepwalking.*

"So, what exactly does an art detective do?"

"I recover stolen and lost art. Primarily for private individuals and insurance companies."

"Are you here for an investigation?"

"I am."

"Can you tell me about it, or is that top secret stuff?"

"I'm searching for an unattributed Leonardo da Vinci painting that disappeared in 1944."

"Oh, now I understand. My expertise is the Renaissance, and particularly the Maestro."

"That's why Michael recommended you. He thought we might be of help to each other. Join forces. Maybe we were fated to meet," he said, using a phrase similar to the one she used at the Getty. *We are in this together. You must help me. It is our destiny.*

"I don't believe in fate. Unfortunately, I don't know how much help I would be. I haven't come across anything in my research that points to any missing da Vinci, although it's possible I suppose. In my field, it's more likely that existing paintings have been misattributed to another artist. In order to change the attribution of a work of art it usually entails both historical and technical analysis. A lot of experts have to come to an agreement and few of them are inclined to do so."

"The idea of a never before discovered masterpiece in a dusty attic somewhere doesn't spark your interest?"

"I know it happens all the time on TV shows like *Antiques Roadshow*. Somebody's great-great-grandmother had a peculiar painting in her parlor, or someone bought an innocuous sculpture at a yard sale and it turns out to be a famous artist's work." Angela shook her head, her cheek dimpling in a beguiling half-smile. "But a da Vinci? That's a tough one. He was so sporadic in his output and most of his work was commissioned by wealthy patrons. It seems impossible that somebody's grandmother somehow got her hands on a missing *Mona Lisa*."

"I agree. But my client has some letters written by an uncle during World War II. The man was a German art historian serving under the German command when they occupied Florence. He wrote to his mother that he uncovered a particular painting, a wedding portrait. The painting was attributed to a student of da Vinci, but this historian believed it was created by the master's hand."

Angela knit her fine brows. "That's an incredible story, almost too incredible. Do you have any idea how valuable an undiscovered da Vinci would be?"

He laughed. "Yeah, I share your suspicions. I find it a bit far-fetched, but I'm sure you know about the recently found da Vinci sold at auction. It went for more than four-hundred million, so it's definitely worth investigating."

She nodded. "So, what happened to Gerhard? And the painting?"

The hair on Alex's arms stood up. "You said Gerhard. I never told you his name."

Her eyes clouded in confusion. "Of course, you did. I heard you say Gerhard was the uncle and the author of the letters."

"No, Angela, I didn't. I simply said my client's uncle."

She looked incredulous. "I could have sworn... I don't understand... Are you sure?" She shivered.

He reached for her hand. Her palm was damp. "It's okay. Maybe you read my mind," he joked.

She stared at her hand in his but didn't pull away. He felt a spark—the same feeling that came over him at the Getty. Maybe she *had* read his mind. He knew he should let go of her hand, but he couldn't. What he wanted to do was pull her into his arms and kiss her.

"Where do you live when you're not chasing stolen art?" she asked, pulling her hand away she reached for her drink.

"I live in Florence." The oddest of sensations, rippled through him when she pulled away—a yearning, as though holding her hand connected him to something precious.

"You're kidding. It's my dream to go to Florence. I haven't been yet, which is pretty crazy for someone whose whole professional life revolves around the Renaissance," she quipped. "Why do you live there?"

"Because most of my work is based in Western Europe, and Florence is one of my favorite cities, so it was an easy choice to make. This trip out here to California is out of the ordinary for me. I'm surprised you haven't done an internship there. It's usually par for the course in art history." He grinned. "Just think, if you come work for me you'll be living in the eternally beautiful Firenze."

"My professor mentioned that you and I have a lot in common." She smiled. "I'd hoped my internship with the Getty would include study in Florence, but things haven't been going well for me there."

"Do you want to talk about it?"

"I'd rather not right now. I don't want to spoil my appetite."

"Good idea because here come the meatballs."

The waiter set two steaming bowls in front of them and they dug in.

"Hmm, these are fantastic," Alex said. "How about I order us a pizza, too? This is barely going to scratch the surface for me." He laughed.

"Go for it, I'm game." She returned his smile. "I'm usually watching my pennies, but since it's your treat I may as well indulge."

"Good." He picked up the menu. "Let's see what other tasty morsels we can dive into. I've been living in Italy so long that, like most Italians, food has become a major obsession."

"You won't get any argument from me. Italian cuisine is my favorite."

"I love a woman who isn't afraid to eat." He wriggled his brows. "However, we need to expand your horizons beyond meatballs."

Alex ordered them a sampling of dishes and a bottle of Barolo. When they couldn't take another bite, he had the bartender box up and bag the leftovers for her. He offered to drive her home and she accepted. When they pulled to the curb in front of a sprawling mansion, he let out a low whistle. "Pretty fancy. I thought you were counting your pennies?"

"It's beautiful, isn't it? I got lucky. A friend of Michael's allowed me to rent the guesthouse in the back for a song. Would you like a cup of tea or coffee before you go back to your hotel?"

"A cup of coffee would be great."

Angela led the way to a side gate. She'd only just met Alex, but she felt comfortable with him. Safe. Like she'd known him forever. True, she trusted Michael Hoffman's opinion of Alex. But there was something more. When he reached for her hand at dinner, she'd felt a current of energy course through her. A connection like she'd never felt before. Was that why she didn't want the night to end invited him in for coffee?

The garden path led past bordered flower beds to the tiny cottage. Angela loved its ginger-bread house look. As they got closer she realized something was wrong. The door to her guest house was ajar.

"Did you leave the door open?" Alex asked.

"What... no... I would never—"

26

Alex pulled a gun from a shoulder harness under his sports coat. "Get behind me."

"What? You have a gun?"

"Yes, now get behind me, and stay close," he whispered. "Don't talk, okay?"

She nodded and followed him. Chips of wood from the doorframe were scattered on the ground. She couldn't imagine what they must have used. *Maybe a screwdriver and hammer?* Speaking of hammers, she could feel her heart hammering in her chest.

It was pitch black inside, but Alex seemed to have eyes like a cat as he moved efficiently and surefooted through the rooms. Her eyes adjusted to the moonlight filtering in through the window. It looked as if a tornado had cut a path through the living room. The cushions and pillows from the sofa had been tossed aside. Drawers had been opened and dumped on the floor. It was a small place, but Alex checked every closet, under the beds, and anywhere someone might be hiding. The place had been completely ransacked, but whoever had done it was long gone.

He turned to her. "We're good."

As she followed Alex through her formerly safe haven, the upheaval was more than she could handle. Tears streamed down her face. She shivered and wrapped her arms around herself. It wasn't cold, but she couldn't stop shaking. "Who would do this?"

He holstered his gun, put his arm around her shoulders and led her to the sofa. Picking up the cushions, he slipped them back in place and sat her down. "It looks like a burglary, but why you when there's a mansion chock full of goodies? I think we should notify your landlord."

"They're out of town." Her eyes swept the room.

"Don't they have the entire place on an alarm system?"

"They do at the main house, but not here." She crossed her arms. "I'll certainly ask them to install one when I let them know what happened."

"Do you have any idea who might have done this?"

"No, I... I can't imagine."

"Do you want to call the cops?"

"I don't know what to do?" She brushed away the tears with her hand. "I have nothing here that's of any value."

"Well, it's obvious someone thinks you do." He glanced around taking in the mess. "Do you have any gloves?"

"Hang on." She scooted into the kitchen and came back out with kitchen gloves.

"Those will do. Put them on and take a look around to see if anything is missing. With gloves you won't contaminate the crime scene. If anything important is missing, I can call a detective friend of mine to come and open a case file. But my guess is this was a professional job and they won't find a thing."

"Okay. I'll do whatever you think is best."

He pulled his cell phone from his pocket. "While you look, I'm going to find a twenty-four-hour locksmith and get that door fixed. And then you and I can tidy up."

"Thanks, Alex. I don't know what I would have done if you weren't here."

He smiled. "Get busy."

She slipped on the gloves and headed for the bedroom. Everything on her nightstand had been swept onto the floor. Getting down on her hands and knees, she searched the floor and under the bed. She found her clock, her reading glasses, her pen, hair pins, the book she was reading, and some loose change, but her journal was nowhere to be seen. *Why would anyone take my journal?* She searched everywhere in the bedroom, closet, and bathroom, tidying things up as she searched, but there was no sign of it.

"Alex!" She felt foolish when he came running in. *He's going to think you're a nutcase.*

"Are you all right?"

"Yes, I'm fine, it's just that there *is* something missing."

"What?"

"My journal."

"Someone stole your diary?" His look of amusement made her bristle.

"It's not my diary. It's a record of my dreams, sleep patterns."

He cocked his head questioningly. "Why don't we make some coffee and talk. I think you need to level with me about what's been going on."

"I barely know you—"

He lifted his brows at her comment and she bit her tongue, realizing how ungrateful she must sound. She sighed, regretting her hasty comment. Alex was a friend of Michael's, of course she could trust him. Between Scordato's harassment and now the break-in her nerves were on edge. "I'm sorry, that was rude of me. Thank you for helping me. I do need a friend right now."

Seeing him smile made her smile.

"I'll straighten things up here, while you make us a cup of coffee."

She nodded and stepped into the kitchen. *At least the thief didn't steal the Keurig.* She shook her head at the irony. Her Keurig machine had been a gift from her dad when she went off to university. The daughter of a welder from Lake Bluff, Illinois, Angela wasn't used to extravagance, and the stylish kitchen appliance was important to her because it came from her dad.

A few minutes later she felt better with a cup of chamomile tea in her hands, sitting beside Alex on the couch. "I haven't been sleeping well."

"And why is that?" he said, blowing on his black coffee.

"I started having nightmares and suffering from insomnia when I began my internship at the Getty." She paused to take a sip of her tea. "So, I did some research and found out that writing down your dreams can help discover what's really going on. Hence, my dream journal."

"Has it helped?"

"No."

"Care to share what the dreams are about?"

"I took a nap before we met tonight—I know it sounds odd for someone my age, but as I said, I haven't been sleeping well—I dreamt of a young woman who was friends with Leonardo da Vinci and they went to a party at Lorenzo Medici's palace. Crazy, huh?"

"Are your dreams always the same?" He wasn't laughing at her, which made her feel less like a loony bird.

"No, they're different, but they seem to be time capsules of events that took place."

"Perhaps my initial phone call with you about my investigation, along with your stress at work, may have triggered your dreams."

"No, these dreams started well before I spoke to you." She took another sip. "But there's something else…" She hesitated, worried about what he might think of her.

"Trust me, there's nothing you could say that I haven't come across before."

She cleared her throat. "Sometimes, I'll find myself at my desk at work and I don't know how I got there. I mean, it feels like I've missed a chunk of time and I can't figure out if I just blacked out in front of my computer, or if I went off somewhere."

"Did you note that in your journal as well?"

She nodded. "I want it back, Alex. It's important to me."

"I totally get that." He set his cup down on the coffee table. "You mentioned that your internship at the Getty has been stressful."

She nodded.

"I take it your stress has something to do with Alberto Scordato?"

"H-he's harassing me. Inappropriate touching, innuendoes, and he keeps insisting on having dinner together to supposedly discuss work." She didn't realize how tightly she was gripping her cup until Alex took hold of it and placed it on the table. He held her hands in his, his touch calming, but his eyes flashed with anger.

"Scordato's a scumbag. Have you reported him?"

She shook her head. "He's very powerful in the art world. I'm afraid he'll blacklist me. I worked so hard to get this internship and now my whole career is in jeopardy."

She'd been staring at her hands in his, but when she looked up she found his striking, different-colored eyes gazing at her. The concern written there soothed her, a safe harbor in a storm.

"I have to wonder if Scordato is behind your break-in."

"Why?" Reluctantly, she pulled her hands away.

"Because he's the one responsible for you being miserable at the Getty. And he's connected to the missing da Vinci."

"How is he connected?"

"He was the consultant for Max Jaeger, my client. Scordato quit after spending the entire summer in Florence. Now he's declaring the painting doesn't exist."

She leaned forward. "But I never told him about the journal."

"Did you tell anyone about it?"

She sat up, her eyes wide. "I told Kathryn, his assistant."

"Well, I guess we solved the case of the missing dream journal."

His phone pinged and he took it out of his pocket and swiped for the message. "The locksmith is on his way over. Look, the last thing you need to be worrying about is that asshole. It's getting late and I'm not leaving you alone tonight."

"What do you mean?"

"What I mean is you're going to bed and I'm going to sleep on the couch. Tomorrow we're going to straighten this place up and I'll drive you to work. Stay away from Scordato, I'll deal with him—"

"What are you going to do?"

"I can't tell you now, but suffice it to say, you won't have to worry about him ever again."

"I hope you're right."

He reached for her hand and squeezed. "I'm going to do everything in my power to make sure that predator gets what's coming to him."

"He's really powerful, Alex."

"He may be powerful, but he's fallible. I have an important lunch meeting, but I'll pick you up after work. I think we should have dinner and talk about your future plans."

They both stood. "Thank you for listening to my sob story." She smoothed her hair back. "Does the job offer still stand even after all of this?" She gestured to the topsy-turvy room.

"It stands, Angela. I think we'd make a great team. I know we've just met, and it's really none of my business, but I want to help you." He smiled. "Now get some sleep. We'll talk more in the morning."

She went to the linen closet, grabbed a blanket, towels, and a toothbrush, and set them on the couch while he was on the phone with the locksmith. Waving goodnight, she slipped into her room and closed the door.

Twenty minutes later, after grabbing a hot shower, Angela lay in bed and stared at the ceiling. The hoot of an owl echoed outside her window. She tossed and turned, unable to sleep. She dreaded returning to work tomorrow and having to fend off the director's advances. Alex told her to stay away from him. She would certainly try.

The more she thought about Alex the more she wanted to accept his job offer. It wouldn't be the gold star on her resume she'd hoped for, but there was the bonus of living in Florence. Besides, it might be exactly what she needed to get her life back on track.

The problem was her attraction to Alex. What woman wouldn't be? He was caring, intelligent, successful, and hot. But this was tricky territory. She'd have to be careful, not to get emotionally involved. She already had enough problems fending off the unwanted attention from Scordato, worried that he might blacklist her. But this was different. It was hard to fight off your own feelings for a knight in shining armor. She sighed, letting go of her tumultuous thoughts. She needed sleep.

She grabbed an extra pillow and slipped it under her knees. Using a deep breathing technique she'd read about, she blew out a big breath, then breathed in deeply through her nose, holding it for a few seconds then let it out slowly through her mouth. Repeating it several times, her eyelids grew heavy, her body sinking into the softness of the bed… Her mind began to drift as a breeze fluttered around her, tucking under her legs and shoulders, lifting her up. Lighter than air, she opened her eyes to complete darkness. Hearing a voice, she turned her head and glimpsed a bright light in the distance, as though at the end of a tunnel. Whether she floated or walked, she had no idea, but she wasn't afraid as the wind picked up, swirling around her, propelling her forward. Closer and closer, until she could see a young woman standing in a pool of light.

Reaching out, she touched the woman's shoulder.

Fioretta...

CHAPTER 4

Florence, Italy
Leonardo da Vinci's Studio
September 1, 1475

"*Amico mio*, you have been working on this sketch of me for hours. I'm exhausted. I must stretch." She stood up from the platform where she'd been reclining, her body draped in only a sheet.

Fioretta yawned, forgetting to cover her mouth. She shivered, feeling a tingle on her shoulder. Her aunt had warned her that the Devil himself could catch you unawares and enter your body when you yawned. She shook off the foolish notion but crossed herself just in case. Her aunt was always trying to scare her. Admonishing her for going out, even to the market. And especially for her friendship with da Vinci. If her aunt knew that Fioretta was posing for Leonardo she would have an apoplectic fit. Unfortunately, secrets were necessary if she was to have any enjoyment in life.

"If you must, Fioretta. But I'm close to getting what I've been looking for. I would like to continue once you've had time to rest."

"Leonardo, you must practice patience." She walked around the artist to view the drawing. "Is this what I look like?"

Leonardo regarded his drawing and frowned.

"I think you need to work a little more on this one—"

A knock at the door brought an end to her words. Leonardo opened the door and bowed.

Fioretta grabbed her clothes and tried to flee to the back of the studio, but she stumbled on the sheet, tripping to the floor. When she looked up, she stared into brown eyes so dark they seemed black. A young man dressed in royal garb stared back at her.

33

"Giuliano Medici, meet my model and friend Fioretta Gorini."

O Dio, it's the impertinent young lord from the Medici Palazzo. Seeing her like this he must think her a fool or a wanton woman. Who else posed for artists? She was certain her blush was discernible from the roots of her hair to her toes. She struggled to arrange the sheet adequately so she could stand without revealing any of her body.

He smiled and bent to help her up. "At your service, signorina."

"You will excuse me if I don't curtsy."

Leonardo had retrieved her clothing and stood there with a grin on his face. She grabbed her clothing, still holding tight to the sheet, and with as much dignity as she could muster left the room to change.

She could hear the two men speaking in hushed whispers and then breaking out in laughter. She was determined to behave with dignity and bring Giuliano Medici down from his high horse. As for Leonardo, she'd give him a piece of her mind later.

When she returned to the studio she was perfectly attired. She'd loosened her hair and because she had no comb to tame it with, it fell wild about her shoulders. She heard Giuliano suck in his breath when he looked at her. He bowed again. "I apologize, Fioretta, for my unbecoming behavior. Please forgive me."

"In truth, you owe me two apologies." Her deep curtsy emphasized her dignity.

"Two?"

"Please excuse me for a few minutes." Leonardo gathered up his drawings. "I need to make some notes on our sitting, Fioretta. I'm sure you can entertain our guest accordingly."

Frowning at Leonardo, she watched him retreat to the back of the house, then she turned to Giuliano. "Yes, two." She held up two fingers, fixing her gaze on him. "The second is for the discomfort you caused me at your palazzo."

"I beg your forgiveness. I'm afraid I was swept away by your beauty and unable to find anything that compared to you with favor. I've been inquiring about you ever since."

"A poet you are not, sir. Just because you found me in compromising attire, do not think you can seduce me with such declarations."

Giuliano's countenance sank. "Please indulge me, Fioretta. I do not wish to insult, deceive, or seduce you. I'm simply speaking from my heart."

"You would do well to teach your heart to be respectful of this woman."

Giuliano dropped to his knee and took her hand, pressing it to his lips. "I am your servant. I only wish to know you better, Fioretta. Please allow me a chance to prove myself to you."

His lips on her hand heated her blood. She didn't understand what was happening to her. Her anger had dissipated, replaced by a longing to share his company. Never had a man knelt before her. It made her giddy, her face flushed.

Giuliano rose, still holding her hand in his. "Do you think we might start over? I feel destiny at work here. I believe God has brought us together."

Her eyes dropped to her hand in his. "Perhaps we can get past the awkwardness of those first moments. But let us leave God out of this."

"I'd like that very much."

She smiled, meeting his gaze. "Can I get you a glass of wine?"

"Yes, if you will share one with me."

She returned with two glasses. "Shall we sit in the garden? The weather is lovely."

"Yes, wherever you wish. I am your servant."

She led him outside and they sat on a bench near the fountain. The sound of water trickling and bees buzzing provided an accompaniment to their conversation.

"Fioretta, might I be so bold to ask how you came to know Leonardo, and why, in a city as small as Florence, I have never laid eyes on you before I saw you at the palazzo? You're not betrothed, are you?"

"I'm not from Florence but rather Siena." She smiled. "I'm not betrothed, and I don't mind telling you how I came to be posing for the Maestro."

"Please tell. This is a story of the greatest interest to me."

"Very well." She told him about her meeting in the marketplace with Leonardo and his desire to paint her. She had Giuliano laughing uproariously about her first meeting with the artist and how they bickered over an eggplant at the mercato, each trying to dissuade the other from purchasing it. She also shared the sad story of the death of her parents and being forced to live with her aunt, a woman with no compassion for her. Giuliano touched her hand, his eyes radiating warmth and understanding. The minutes flew to an hour. Giuliano seemed to have nowhere on earth he'd rather be. And then, as if it was the most natural thing in the world to do, he leaned in and kissed her.

Her eyes closed and she pressed her lips more fully against his. It was the first time she'd ever been kissed. When they broke the kiss, they were both breathless.

She opened her eyes and found him gazing at her. She leaned in closer. "Again, please."

A breeze tickled the back of her neck and the garden began to spin around her. Caught up in a whirlwind, she flew through a dark tunnel, away from the light. The force of the wind overwhelmed her. She fought to breathe, but her lungs refused to fill.

"Giuliano help me…"

Strong arms wrapped around her, anchoring her.

She awoke with a start, gulping air as if hours had passed since she'd taken her last breath. Her body was coated in sweat and her eyes brimmed with tears. She pressed her fingers to her lips, still feeling the burning imprint of a kiss.

She opened her eyes and realized Alex was holding her, comforting her. It didn't make sense. "Alex…" She shook her head, trying to focus on the here and now. "Why are you holding me?"

"I heard you calling me."

"I was calling you?"

"You must have had one of those dreams."

"No, not a dream…" This was different. Somehow, she'd projected into the past by her own volition. Her head throbbed. "Please, I need a glass of water."

While Alex went to get the water, she stared at the ceiling, wondering what significance was to be found in her dream or vision. She didn't even know what to call it. What did it all mean? Was her vision connected to the missing da Vinci that Alex was searching for? Were her previous dreams somehow part of the puzzle? And if so, had she and Alex been fated to meet? Her mind twisted and turned from all of the unanswered questions plaguing her.

Alex handed her a glass and she gulped down the cool liquid. It revived her.

"Do you want more?"

"No, I'm better, but I don't feel like talking about the dream."

"Okay, I'm not going to press you, but I can't help you, if you don't trust me."

"I know, Alex." She gave him a wobbly smile. "I just need to get some sleep and get through tomorrow. Thank you for everything you're doing for me." She reached for his hand and felt an immediate jolt of warmth surge through her.

He felt it, too. She could see it in his eyes.

He could see it in her eyes, that attraction between them. Every time they touched his world tilted. He wanted to comfort her, but he also just plain wanted her. He needed her to trust him. It wasn't just because of Scordato and the investigation—it was something more. Something deep in his gut.

"Angela, I have a confession to make to you."

"What kind of confession?"

"We met before—well not actually met but we interacted." *Shit*, he was already blowing the explanation. "Let me start at the beginning. Yesterday, when I went to the Getty to see Scordato, I had some time to kill before the meeting, so I wandered around the museum. I saw a woman sitting in front of Botticelli's portrait of Giuliano Medici." He paused, searching her eyes for some recollection, but there was none.

"I don't understand. If we'd met I would have remembered, Alex. What are you talking about?"

"The woman was speaking Italian, which I'm fluent in, and I was irresistibly drawn to her."

"Okay."

"Let me make this perfectly clear—I know what I saw and heard, and I don't experience visions, at least not that kind. Angela, the painting and the woman spoke to each other, and I saw and heard them."

"That's pretty weird."

"Trust me, it only gets weirder. The woman turned to me and said, *I will love you forever. You are the only man I will ever love.* She also said, *We are in this together. You must help me. It is our destiny.* Then she kissed me."

"Okaaaaay… So, what does this have to do with me?"

"Everything. You're the woman."

Angela drew back as if he were a snake coiled to attack. "I don't remember any of this. How could you not have told me? At the restaurant, you acted like it was our first meeting."

"I didn't know the woman in the trance at the Getty was you, until you walked through the door at the bistro. I was completely blown away that you didn't recognize me, let alone that you had no memory of that kiss."

"Why didn't you tell me when we got here?"

"Are you kidding? Your house was broken into. Your safety was all I could think about. I guess it slipped my mind. I apologize."

"You said I spoke Italian?"

"Yes."

"And I told you that we were destined to be together?"

"Yes."

"I don't understand any of this or what it means."

"Believe me, neither do I." He scrubbed his hands through his hair. "But I have a feeling my encounter with you at the Getty is connected to your dreams."

"It's all so strange. We need to figure this out."

"We will. We'll talk about it more tomorrow." He glanced at his watch; it was 3 a.m. "But in the meantime, I think we both need sleep."

She nodded but seemed to hesitate. "Can I ask you something else?"

"Sure."

"Did you enjoy it?"

"What?"

"The kiss."

"You're damn right I enjoyed it."

Her lips quirked in a smile. "I'm glad, at least one of us remembers it."

"Remember it? I'll never forget it."

Her smile turned into a grin. "Thanks."

"You're welcome. Now get some sleep."

CHAPTER 5

Los Angeles, California
Present day
August 4

The aroma of freshly brewed coffee greeted her.

Slipping on her robe Angela scooted from the bathroom to the bedroom, a smile on her face at Alex's thoughtful gesture. A few minutes later she emerged, securing the belt of her wraparound, floral-print dress. Noting the changes to the living room on her way to the kitchen, she shook her head in wonder. Had she imagined the break-in last night? How had Alex accomplished putting everything back without making any noise?

In the kitchen, she found him standing at the Keurig, unshaven, still wearing his clothes from the night before, and looking sexy as hell. Seeing a man in her kitchen was so out of the ordinary, but with him it felt natural.

"Good morning, Alex. Did you get any sleep last night?"

"Morning Angel." His lips quirked as he set two steaming cups of coffee on the table. "Military service has its plusses. Functioning on less sleep is one of them."

She tilted her head at the unfamiliar nickname. "You called me Angel."

"So I did. Does that bother you?" His brows shot up in question.

Heat suffused her face. "No, of course not. It's—no one's ever called me Angel. My dad calls me Angie, but everyone else uses my full name. I guess I never inspired a nickname in anyone other than my dad…"

"I'm a nickname kind of guy." He winked.

"Really?" She couldn't help but smile at his cheeky expression. "What's your nickname?"

"Stud."

She threw her head back and laughed.

"I'm serious. The guys in my unit named me Stud."

"Hmm, why doesn't that surprise me?" She crossed her arms over her chest, an exaggerated smirk on her face.

"Hey, it's not what you think." His hands went up in mock entreaty. "I love to cook and that got me a lot of attention."

"Ah, I see. You woo women with your flair for food."

"Among other things."

"Well Stud, you'll have to cook for me—" Catching herself at her forward remark, her face flushed at his slow smile. "Um, thanks for making coffee and cleaning up the living room. I didn't hear a thing. Not a chair being moved, or a drawer being opened. I didn't hear you shower either."

"Another plus of military service, stealth."

She stepped forward to get to the fridge at the same time as he moved to sit down. Bumping into each other they both laughed. Alex reached out and steadied her shoulders.

"Oops, bad timing," she quipped.

"I think, *good* timing." He smiled, his hands warm on her shoulders. His extraordinary eyes held a roguish gleam as though he were contemplating teasing her with sexy banter. But he completely surprised her by stepping back, extending his arm with a knightly flourish and executing a courtly bow.

"After you m'lady."

"Why thank you, m'lord." She curtsied. *Damn, he's way too attractive.*

"How'd you sleep?" He pulled out a chair at the bistro table and sat.

Taking a carton of milk out of the fridge, she turned back to the table. "Not bad, after that dream or vision or whatever it was. I guess your presence kept the boogeyman away."

"Happy to serve. Do you have time to stop for pancakes? We don't have any IHOPS in Florence and I have a hankering."

She couldn't keep herself from grinning. "IHOP? I'm having visions of Renaissance Florence and Leonardo da Vinci and you're having visions of pancakes?"

"I told you food plays a big role in my happiness. And breakfast tops my list."

"Blueberry pancakes sound like heaven. You certainly know the way to a girl's heart. Let's do it."

I like him, hell I like him a lot.

Alex dropped her at the Getty after their IHOP pancake extravaganza. She couldn't remember having so much fun with anyone while doing what amounted to nothing.

Opening her laptop, she fell into a groove and immersed herself in research and analysis. She was so focused on her work that she didn't notice her phone light up or hear the low buzz of the conference line. She picked up and got an earful from Scordato.

"I want you in my office now."

Before she could even answer he hung up.

So much for avoiding him. She squared her shoulders for yet another confrontation.

"Angela, my dear." He came around his desk, his teeth bared in a grin. "It's time we had a heart-to-heart talk." His hand landed on her shoulder, pressing into the tendons of her collarbone.

Her back stiffened and she shrugged off his hand.

His eyes narrowed, his smile shifted into a frown.

He's Jekyll and Hyde in an Armani suit. I can't do this anymore.

He moved forward trapping her against the desk. "You're aware hundreds of applicants vied for this internship." His index finger traced a line down her cheek. "And you were hand-picked by me for this important position. But that bright future you envisioned for yourself can only be achieved if you work *with* me, not against me. Through hard work, commitment, and dedication." His finger moved to the opening of her blouse. "And most of all, passion."

"I beg your pardon? I—" Before she could pull away, his hand grabbed her around her throat and he pushed her against his desk. The pressure of his hand forcing her mouth open and vulnerable to the invasion of his tongue.

Gagging, she struggled to push him away as he ground his pelvis against her and, with his other hand, yanked up her dress.

Gasping for air, she struggled against his iron grip. "Stop! No!"

His lips traveled down her neck and bit hard into the sensitive skin of her shoulder. She managed to free her arm and reaching down, squeezed his balls as hard as she could while smashing down on his foot with the heel of her shoe.

He released her with a howl. "You bitch."

Run. Run. Run. She stumbled out the door, moving as fast as she could.

"Alex, you're telling me that, besides this proof of Scordato's self-dealing and kickbacks, he also made unwanted advances to one of the interns?"

Alex sat in a plush suite of offices, in a high-rise in Beverly Hills, across from Carl Fellows, the chair of the Getty board of directors.

"He's a menace to the well-being and reputation of your organization." Alex leaned forward. "I'm certain if you speak with female employees as well as past female interns, you'll find a pattern of despicable behavior."

Fellows nodded as he made notes on his tablet. A real-estate mogul and an avid art collector, Fellows had been elected chair of the board last year. He also happened to be an old friend of Alex's mother. Six months ago, he'd reached out to Alex and privately hired him to look into Scordato. There had been too many rumors circulating over the years and Fellows wanted to get to the bottom of it. When Jaeger contacted Alex about the da Vinci painting, Alex had to wonder why Scordato had resigned from the side-gig as Jaeger's consultant, considering Jaeger had basically given him carte blanche when it came to payment as well as a lavish expense account. It didn't fit into Scordato's MO. Alex was certain the bastard wanted the painting for himself and was trying to dissuade Jaeger from continuing his own investigation.

"You've given me everything I need to present to the board," Fellows said, placing the file in his briefcase.

"I hope you'll agree that Scordato needs to be fired at the very least. If you want my advice, you should consider legal action against him."

Carl plucked at his well-groomed goatee. "You're absolutely correct, the board won't condone any scandals. I've heard rumors about Scordato's predatory behavior, but never had any proof."

"Why the hell didn't you investigate sooner, if you had an inkling?" Alex's stomach turned. "Who knows how many other women have been subjected to this prick's vile tactics?"

"Do you think this young woman is going to bring charges?"

"I don't know, but my advice to her would be to do it."

"Alex, for God's sake." Fellows held up his hand. "I promise you, I'll handle Scordato and he won't be in any position to wield any power over anyone ever again."

"You make sure of that, Carl." Alex stood.

"Alex, I want you to know I'm grateful for your role in finding concrete evidence against him. In fact, I'm going to call your mother as soon as we conclude this meeting and tell her that the Getty is indebted to you."

"Thanks for the vote of confidence, Carl. Just make sure you get that bastard."

Alex drove back to the Getty, determined to convince Angela to work for him. All during his meeting with Carl, his thoughts were on her. How, in such a short time, had she become so integral to his life?

He parked the car and went looking for her. He didn't find her at her desk. When he asked the receptionist about Angela, he was alarmed to learn that she'd packed up her things and stormed out of there without a word. *Shit! Scordato.*

He was tempted to storm into the asshole's office and beat the shit out of him right then and there, but he needed to find Angela. He was worried about her. He'd asked her to wait at the Getty for him. If she quit, she might have gone home. He texted her but there was no reply. Then in a flash it hit him, he knew where she was.

Like yesterday, she sat in front of the portrait in the red room, in a somnambulistic state. He sat beside her and waited. Would she acknowledge his presence?

Her eyes were riveted on the painting. He might as well have been invisible. The light in the gallery shifted. Everything happened exactly the same as the day before. The portrait grew luminescent. The youth's eyes opened. But instead of looking at Angela, the young man directed his gaze at him.

"We have not kept our promise," the youth addressed him. "Don't you see? Our beloved Fioretta is in grave danger."

Alex didn't answer. He shook his head, hoping he was hallucinating and not losing his mind.

"The murderers will kill again," the young man continued. "They are driven to possess the painting. The answers lie in Florence. You must return with Fioretta... Beware... Wherever she goes, so go those two *diavoli*, Pazzi and Baroncelli."

"Wait!" Alex couldn't believe he was talking to a centuries-old painting. "How do I find these men?"

"You know who they are... Don't fail her again. Or you will doom us for eternity..."

Alex stood and moved closer to the painting, but the young man had turned his gaze toward Angela. Tears were streaming down her face.

"Angelo mio," he whispered. "Do not weep for me. Follow your heart and claim your *destino.* Time has shifted… What was before will be once more. Find the painting. Find it and know the truth."

"Amore mio, don't leave me." Angela reached out toward the painting.

Crying openly now, each wrenching sob flayed Alex's skin. Her sorrow was his sorrow, her pain was his pain. Every beat of her heart echoed within his own chest. Every fiber in his body strained to touch her. He couldn't stop himself even if he tried. He pulled her into his arms.

Brown eyes turned forest-green gazed into his. Invisible forces drew him to her. Her lips, inches from his whispered, "You promised we would be together forever. You swore a vow before God." Her hands moved over his chest and caressed the planes of his face, each touch branding him, possessing him. Not a cell in his body was capable of resisting her.

He'd spent his entire life being in control. He was a man of logic, a man who managed situations, sought answers, solved mysteries. When her lips locked on his it was like white lightning surging through his veins. He wanted to lay her down in the middle of that public gallery and fill her with his body, heart, and soul.

"Giuliano," she whispered. *"Mio caro sposo."*

Regaining his sanity, he pulled from her embrace. He answered her in Italian. "I am not Giuliano. I'm Alex Caine. I'm not your husband." But hadn't Giuliano implied that they were one and the same?

In the blink of an eye, the spell was broken.

Confusion clouded Angela's eyes. Spellbound, he watched her moss-green eyes transfigure back to brown and then she fainted in his arms.

Lifting his hand, he cupped her beautiful face, waiting for her to wake up. *Come back to him.*

He glanced back at the painting. It was Giuliano Medici who had spoken to him. Now, it was just a painting. *Just a painting.* He bit back a bark of laughter. He tried to analyze what had happened. Was he to believe that Angela and he had lived before, had been lovers before, had married before? The whole concept was out of this world.

He needed to do some research on Giuliano Medici. He needed to understand the rules of how reincarnation worked. *Rules? I'm thinking about rules?* He shook his head at his wild thoughts. He didn't put much stock in religion. He'd seen too much destruction in the world in the name of religion. Reincarnation was another form of quackery that kept people ignorant and led them to do foolish, dangerous things.

And yet, what he saw was no dream. He was awake, in full possession of his faculties. The young man in the painting had come to life and implored him to act. To protect her. Telling him who he really was.

Jesus, is it possible that I was this man? And Angela was Fioretta?

Can this be a mystery that has been lying in wait for us for five-hundred years?

Everything about their finding each other seemed plotted, as if an invisible hand was directing the action.

So many questions unanswered. *But even if our distant lives are resurfacing, what does Max's uncle, a German soldier, and the evacuation of Florence have to do with us?*

Those answers eluded him, but he knew they resided within Angela. She was the key to the mystery. He suspected the director of the Getty, Alberto Scordato, knew that, too.

"Angel, wake-up."

Her eyes fluttered open and she stared at him in a daze before her vision cleared and she flung her arms around his neck. "Alex, I'm so happy you're here. How did you know where to find me?"

"Remember I told you this is where I first saw you. Let's get out of here, Angela. We have a lot to talk about and I don't want to do it here." He was tempted to kiss her again, but that, too, would have to wait until he got to the bottom of what had happened to her that morning. It occurred to him that every inch of the Getty had video cams for security. They were fish in a fishbowl and there was a shark circling the bowl.

Alberto took a swig of whiskey. Carl Fellows, the head of the Getty board, had called him for a meeting. *That bitch Angela must have squealed.* But she had no proof, just her word against his. He said/she said. He wasn't worried. Even if those fools on the board dumped him none of it would matter once he got his hands on the da Vinci. His lips twisted into a sneer as he watched the day's video from the red room flicker across his TV screen. He rewound it for the third time and watched it again.

He'd nearly fired Charles when he'd learned there'd been a malfunction with the cameras and there wasn't any video footage from the day before. Luckily, he'd gotten today's footage.

It was bizarre, to say the least. His intern, Angela, had returned to the red room and sat before the Botticelli in some kind of a trance. What he found interesting was seeing Alex Caine join her on the bench. What he couldn't understand was what instigated Alex to ask, "Wait! How do I find these men?" What men was he talking about? And why did he approach and address the painting?

Alberto ran his fingers through his silver hair. There was no one else in the room, so who the hell was Alex talking to and why did Angela suddenly cry "*Amore mio*, don't leave me." Not to mention her weeping and Alex taking her into his arms and kissing her. It didn't make any sense.

As he watched Angela and Alex kiss, it occurred to him that the detective and the intern getting together might work to his benefit. If the girl was the key to finding the painting, the detective might be the tool needed to actually unravel the mystery. All Scordato had to do was keep them in his sights and make his move when the time was right. Take the painting and rid himself of the dynamic duo.

He could think of numerous possibilities for how to dispose of the two. Perhaps a lovers' quarrel that resulted in a murder and suicide.

He couldn't do this alone, he needed an accomplice. Someone he could trust. He needed his cousin Enrico Fortuna. Enrico's ties to the Mafia would come in handy. He picked up his cell phone and punched in a number.

"*Cugino, come stai*? I have an offer to make to you." He laughed. "An offer you can't refuse."

"I'm listening," said the gravelly voice on the other end.

"No, not on the phone. Why don't I come to Tuscany for a visit and we can discuss everything?"

"*Bene.* We can get some hunting in. I believe you owe me a chance to even up the score," Enrico said with a raspy chuckle.

"When I tell you what I have in mind, believe me, you won't be keeping score. You'll be celebrating."

"In that case, when are you coming?" Enrico asked?

"I'll get back to you tomorrow."

"*Arrivederci.*"

"*Ciao.*"

CHAPTER 6

Los Angeles, California
Present day
August 4

"I'm going to kill him." Alex gripped the wheel as he drove them back to Angela's place.

"I'm just glad to be free of him." Angela hugged herself, rubbing her hands up and down her arms.

"Are you sure you're okay?" Concern laced his eyes.

"I'll feel better once we get on the plane." Angela filled Alex in on the drive home about Scordato's latest escapade and how she'd gotten away from him. The trouble was, she didn't know what happened after she fled Scordato's office up to the moment she found herself in Alex's arms, on the bench in front of the painting of Giuliano Medici. Alex told her she must have had another blackout. "God, I have to get ahead of this." She rubbed her forehead. "What if I black out when I'm driving or crossing a busy street?"

"Don't worry, I'll be with you from here on in. I won't let anything happen to you," he said. "By the way, you're hired." He grinned.

She blew out a breath. "I hope I can be of value to you. I don't want you to think I'm doing this as a way of escaping."

"Are you kidding? I'm lucky to have you working with me on this investigation. Besides, there are so many strange coincidences here, I think it's fate that we met."

She glanced at him. "Do you really?"

He turned into the driveway. "There's a reason why this is happening, and it's somehow connected to your dreams. The only way for us to figure it out is by finding that painting."

She nodded, her eyes tearing up. If he hadn't been with her last night and today, she didn't know what she would have done.

Alex parked the car and escorted her to the door. When she took out her new house keys to unlock it, he stayed her hand.

"Here, hold my briefcase. I'll go in first."

"Do you think that's necessary?"

"I'm not putting anything past that jerk." Alex pulled out his gun and went inside. A few moments later he came back out and opened the door for her, taking the briefcase from her hands.

Kicking off her shoes and tossing her bag on the couch, she sighed with pleasure as her tired, bare feet hit the cool tiled floor in the kitchen. Pouring ice tea into two glasses, she strolled back to the living room, handed Alex a glass and curled up on the couch beside him.

"What about your journal?" Alex polished his tea off in mere moments and set the empty glass on the coffee table beside his briefcase and iPad. "I could break into Scordato's place and steal it back."

Alarm shot through her. "What if you get hurt?"

He laid his hand over hers. "I promise I won't get hurt. I can't promise I won't hurt *him* though."

She shook her head. "It's okay. He's probably using it for his sick and twisted fantasies." She shuddered and made a face.

"Now I really want to beat the shit out of him."

"Do you really think the board of directors will fire him?"

"They have him dead to rights."

"Thanks to you."

He gave her a crooked smile and scratched the five-o'clock shadow on his face. She took a sip of her tea, trying not to think about how sexy he was. She was tempted to throw caution to the wind and kiss him again. *Twice we've kissed and I can't remember a thing. I wish to heck I could though.*

Alex glanced at his watch. "It's still early for dinner. I've got some phone calls to make that'll take a while. Why don't I do that here and you can have a lie-down and grab a shower?"

"Are you sure you don't mind hanging out here for a while?"

"Are you kidding? I wouldn't be a very good knight in shining armor if I didn't." He stood and gave her a courtly bow, making her giggle. "Besides, I have my office right here." He held up his iPhone and iPad. "And, I stopped at the hotel before my meeting this morning. I've got everything I need."

Angela told him to help himself to anything he wanted in the kitchen. A cool shower was just what she needed to scrub away Scordato's scummy handprints from her skin. A few refreshing minutes later, Angela slipped on one of her favorite outfits, a scooped-neck, pink-cashmere, twin-sweater set with a pair of white, skinny jeans. It felt girly and sexy and was casually elegant enough to go anywhere. A pair of gold high-heeled sandals gave it enough evening sparkle for their dinner date. She turned in front of her full-length mirror, her eye catching the flutter of the window curtain. *Fioretta. What are you trying to tell me... ?*

Comforted that Alex was in the next room, she kicked off her shoes and stretched out on her bed. Could she make herself have another vision? Taking slow, deep breaths, she allowed her mind to drift as her body sank into the softness of the bed. Once again, a gentle breeze tickled her skin, lifting her up. She opened her eyes and found herself in a dark tunnel once more. The wind picked up, swirling around her, propelling her toward a white light, and the figure of a woman...

Florence, Italy
January 10, 1478

Fioretta Gorini shivered as a breeze tickled her skin. She glanced behind her, but a heavy curtain covered the window. She'd heard of wise women who had the second sight and could foretell the future... She crossed herself and pushed her dark thoughts away. This was a joyous day for her. The happiest day of her life. She fondled the necklace that rested just above the swell of her breasts. Set in gold and embedded with rare gems, it was a gift from Giuliano. Her lady's maid, Katerina, tied the white silk ribbon through her dark curls.

"My lady, you are radiant."

"Thank you, Katerina." Fioretta embraced her maid, happiness shining from her eyes.

"Signor Giuliano will surely be speechless."

Fioretta blushed and smiled at the petite blonde woman who'd been her lady's maid for as long as she could remember.

"I agree with Katerina," a male voice declared. "You are glowing in your beauty."

Fioretta turned and beamed at her dear friend. Leonardo had just stepped into the parlor.

"I will assist the cook on the final touches for the meal and make certain all is in order." Katerina left the room.

"Maestro, are you sure that I'm perfect?" Fioretta pirouetted, her white velvet gown swirling around her. "I want Giuliano to be pleased when he sees me."

Leonardo smiled. "Fioretta, *sei bellissima*. You are certainly an angel sent from heaven to steal the hearts of mortal men. I can assure you, Giuliano will be more than pleased. He is head over heels for you."

She ran to Leonardo and embraced him. Standing on tiptoe, she gazed into the blue eyes of her friend. "Will he think I'm as beautiful as Simonetta or my likeness in the wedding portrait?"

"Fioretta, while I am an artist, I'm unequal to the task of capturing your true beauty. Only God himself is capable of creating such perfection. Simonetta was a renowned beauty, but contrary to all accounts, it's you and not she who captured Giuliano's heart." He kissed her forehead.

She took his hand. "Leonardo, before everyone arrives, I want to thank you."

"For what, *bella*?"

"Had we not met in the marketplace I don't know how I would have survived the loneliness of living in Florence. You opened your heart to an unfortunate orphan and gave me the rarest of gifts, your friendship."

"That day was most fortunate for me. I found a friend, as well." The fine lines around his eyes crinkled with his smile. "As I recall, we argued over a *melanzane*. We both reached for the same eggplant, and you, clever girl, tried your best to dissuade me from said eggplant, insisting that this specimen was a most unfortunate vegetable, and I should choose another. If my memory serves me well, you claimed that the eggplant, which neither of us let go of, was bitter and tasteless, and I countered that it was of sublime flavor. You were a very cunning girl to use such feminine wiles on me and think you could trick me."

"You refused to give in, no matter how many times I fluttered my lashes at you."

"Ah, yes, but it led me to register your extraordinary eye color. The scientist calculated the odds of such a color, but the artist dreamed of painting those eyes the color of green forest moss."

She shook her finger at him. "You must admit I was brave, risking my aunt's wrath to visit your studio without a proper chaperone. Had she found out, I would have been locked in my room for eternity."

"Your aunt is an old crow, who hasn't an ounce of foresight to see what a rare gem you are."

Fioretta sighed, not wanting to think about the uncaring woman who became her guardian after her parents died. "My aunt does not believe a woman needs an education. She considers it unsuitable for women to discourse on the topics of men."

"She's a fool, Fioretta. I'd match your ability to reason as well as a man's. God granted you not only beauty, but a sharp mind."

"Speaking of my beauty, Maestro," she began, with a cheeky grin. "Please, may I see the portrait before they arrive?"

Before he could respond, there was a knock at the front door. Leonardo brushed his hand gently over Fioretta's cheek. "It seems the groom is already here, signorina."

Leonardo opened the door, and the cold January wind blew flurries of snow into the studio. His bright blue shirt and leather doublet contrasted starkly with the dull winter's light. His deep voice was effusive with warmth and conviviality as Giuliano Medici entered with a male companion. "My lord, welcome to my humble home, and a warm welcome to your dear friend, the poet," Leonard said in greeting. "Paolo," he called over his shoulder to a curly-haired assistant who came running. "Come take our guests' cloaks and bring wine."

Giuliano turned to his companion with a smile. "Angelo Poliziano, poet, humanist and dear friend, I want you to meet Leonardo da Vinci, the most brilliant artist in all of Florence."

Leonardo laughed. "If not the greatest artist, certainly the most distracted." Leonardo shook Angelo's hand. "Alas, I take up one project and find myself drawn to another, which is frustrating to those who employ me."

"Your many endeavors are merely a sign of a brilliant mind. Such praise from a Medici is not easily won. I am very pleased to make your acquaintance," Angelo said.

"The pleasure is mine. I have been looking forward to this meeting. I am well-versed in your poetry. My favorite, of course, is your *Stanza for the Magnificent Giuliano de' Medici*."

Giuliano grumbled. "Angelo, that poem of yours has only furthered the misconception of mine and Simonetta's love affair. No one believes when I tell them what we shared was a poetic, courtly love not found in the bedroom but in the mind."

"We all loved her, did we not?" Angelo said. "Her loss, at such a young age, was a tragedy. To not immortalize her would have been unjust. I stand behind my work, whether it is misinterpreted or not. Only you and Simonetta know the truth, and she is with God."

Giuliano shrugged. "Let the world think what it likes, the truth of who I love will soon be revealed."

"Giuliano, I implore you to explain…" Fioretta had been watching the men's exchange. She and Simonetta had become friends soon after Giuliano began courting her and the reminder of Simonetta's death on her wedding day saddened her. She stepped forward and Giuliano's gaze locked on her. He raised his hand, silencing Angelo.

Fioretta curtsied to the men and walked to Giuliano. He bowed with deference to her. "Every moment apart from you I have missed, *cara*. I am alive only when I'm in your presence."

I love this man. Standing on tiptoe, she touched her lips to his in a welcoming kiss. "My lord."

"Fioretta…"

"Giuliano, *amore mio*, did you speak to your brother? Has he agreed?"

A cloud of misery passed over Giuliano's face. "He has forbidden it."

"Oh…" She sagged in disappointment.

Giuliano lifted her chin. "It doesn't matter, *dolcezza mia*. I am here, am I not? Our marriage will go forward tonight as I promised. I would defy God himself to wed you and make our child legitimate."

She wrapped her arms around his neck and delivered a dozen kisses to his face. "You are too good to me, my love."

Giuliano cleared his throat and she stepped back, dropping her gaze. "Now, *angelo mio*, let me introduce you to my dear friend."

She'd been so intent on Giuliano that she'd paid little mind to the other men. She felt the color rise in her cheeks. "Forgive me, Giuliano, I must learn to behave more discreetly."

"Never, *amore mio*. Soon I will shout my love for you from Giotto's campanile so that all the world will know." He gestured to the older man standing beside him. "This is Angelo Poliziano, whom I have told you so much about. He will be a witness to our marriage, Fioretta."

She curtsied. "Great poet, you do us honor. I was moved by your stanza glorifying Simonetta. Whomever you honor with a verse will be immortal. I believe your poems will outlast our brief hours."

Angelo bowed, "I see you are not just the personification of beauty but are charitable in your praise and wisdom."

Giuliano beamed. "Leonardo, I believe a toast is in order."

Fioretta clapped her hands. "Maestro, first, please show Giuliano and Angelo the portrait. I cannot bear to wait any longer."

"I am yours to command, fair lady. I only hope I've done your beauty justice. I pray you think I've immortalized you and Giuliano the way Angelo's poetry immortalized Simonetta and Giuliano." Leonardo pulled the sheet off an easel, revealing his work of art.

The extraordinary painting depicted the young couple standing opposite each other, their hands extended as though about to touch. Giuliano, dressed in Florentine red velvet, gazed with love at the face of his intended. Fioretta wore the same white gown of velvet she had on now, but she faced outward as if holding the gaze of the viewer. Her smile was a work in motion, not quite realized, as though she held a secret known only to herself.

The two lovers seemed to float above the city of Florence with the magnificence of the Duomo behind them. A banner heralding the Medici coat of arms bore five red balls. The five *palle* were adorned on a yellow banner to the left of them. The painting was masterful, rendered in exquisite detail. The beauty of the two lovers mesmerizing.

Angelo whispered, "Leonardo you've captured the freshness of youth and love, while at the same time elevating its power above church and state. The painting is both powerful and transcendent."

"The artist can only paint what he sees and feels."

"My friend, I am humbled before your talent and greatness," Giuliano said. He raised Fioretta's hand to his lips and kissed it. "*Amore mio*, the Maestro has given you immortality."

Fioretta smiled and caressed her stomach. "Every painting by the Maestro will live forever. My immortality rests here with our child. I pray our families will accept, love, and embrace this child."

"It will happen, *tesoro mio*. I promise you." He bent to kiss her, his eyes brimming with love.

Leonardo raised his glass. "To your future, Salute!"

After the marriage was formalized by a priest, who'd been sworn to secrecy, the celebrants sat down to a simple but delicious meal.

Fioretta excused herself from the table. On her return, she was about to pull back the drapes separating the hall from the main studio when she heard Giuliano and Angelo whispering. "Giuliano, this plan of yours worries me. A marriage not sanctioned by Lorenzo is bound to bring disaster. I'm worried for you, my friend, and for Fioretta. You are contracted in marriage to another, or have you forgotten?"

"I implored Lorenzo to sanction this marriage, but he refused. I reminded him that, while he married to further the power of the Medici, I would not. I warned him I would marry for love and nothing less. He will not deprive me of my happiness."

Fioretta held her breath and peeked around the drapery. The two men stood near a work table where dozens of Leonardo's silver pencil drawings of horses and strange mechanical devices were displayed. Angelo picked up a drawing and studied it.

"Where is Fioretta living? Certainly not here with Leonardo."

"She was living with her aunt, but that situation is no longer tolerable. I've purchased a villa for her, not far from the Via Larga. I adore her so much, there is nothing I wouldn't do for her."

"And if Lorenzo figures out, before the child is born, that you haven't obeyed his wishes?"

"Lorenzo is not only my brother, he's my teacher, mentor, and best friend. We are like the bread and wine of the Eucharist, one without the other is unthinkable. Don't fret, Angelo, after the baby is born, I'll announce my marriage to Lorenzo. I will give him the opportunity to stand up and recognize the child and Fioretta. He will argue, he will challenge, but he will never sever the ties of blood. In the end, he will accept."

"I pray you are right, my friend."

Giuliano squeezed Angelo's shoulder. "Come, let us return to the party. This is a time for celebration."

Fioretta released the breath she'd been holding and covered her belly protectively with her hands. As much as she loved Giuliano, she knew he was impulsive. Until the baby's birth and Lorenzo's blessing gained, she would not rest easy.

She returned to the table. Caressing Giuliano's cheek, she asked, "Is there something you need, husband?"

"Only to hear you call me *husband* every day of my life."

"A simple request that I will fulfill joyfully." She pressed her lips to his, eliciting a resounding applause from Angelo, Leonardo, Giuliano's bodyguards and Katerina, who'd joined them.

The wine flowed long into the evening, and toasts to the newlyweds were made by all, but none were more heartfelt than those spoken by Giuliano to his beloved. "I promise you, *amore mio*, that this life will never divide us. I will love you today, tomorrow, and into eternity. Our wedding portrait will speak of our love long after you and I have passed from this earth."

Fioretta lay her hand against her beloved's face, pouring all of her love into her gaze. Feeling another breeze tickling the back of her neck, the room began to spin around her.

The swirling wind lifted her up, pulling her into a dark tunnel. Spiraling backward, she closed her eyes…

She opened her eyes. Her hands smoothed the softness of the quilt on the bed. Her closet door stood open, just as she'd left it. The alarm clock on her nightstand read 6:30 p.m. Everything was the same and yet everything had changed.

It wasn't a dream.

I was Fioretta Gorini.

The love of my life was Giuliano Medici.

My dearest friend was Leonardo da Vinci.

She sat up, swinging her legs over the bed. Her heart pounded in her chest.

Alex.

He's the only one who can help me understand what's happening.

CHAPTER 7

Los Angeles, California
Present day
August 4

The restaurant was located nearby in West Hollywood. The French Door was everything Angela hoped it would be, intimate and candle lit. Alex ordered a bottle of Puligny-Montrachet. He swished the wine in the glass, inhaled the fragrance, and took a sip. Satisfied, he nodded to the waiter to pour.

"To moving forward."

She touched her glass to his, and they both sipped.

"You seemed preoccupied on the drive here. Did you get a chance to rest before we left?"

"Yes and no." She set her glass down. "I had another dream. But it wasn't a dream. I'm positive now that what I've been experiencing are past-life visions."

Alex laid his hand over hers. "Tell me."

"I saw my wedding—Fioretta and Giuliano's wedding."

"But they never married."

"How do you know that?"

"I've been doing my research on the Medici family."

"The historical record is wrong. Fioretta and Giuliano were secretly married."

His brow furrowed. "So, for five hundred years the truth has been hidden? That's one hell of a secret."

She nodded. "There's more…"

"More?"

She bit her lip in indecision and searched his eyes. She wanted to unburden herself. She decided to test the waters. "Fioretta Gorini and Giuliano

Medici were married in Leonardo da Vinci's studio in Florence. His gift to them was a bridal portrait, a stunning painting of Fioretta and Giuliano."

"Damn." He shook his head. "Was this the first time you had a vision of their marriage and the painting?"

"Yes, why?"

"Because of the journal. It's in Scordato's slimy hands."

She thought back to the entries in her journal, much of it included snatches of her dreams, but lacking in the awareness she had now. "Despite how creeped out I feel that Scordato has my journal, there's nothing in it about the painting or the secret marriage."

"I'm certain his days are numbered." Alex refilled their glasses. "Unfortunately, it's possible the board will simply fire him and agree not to prosecute."

A flash of anger bolted through her. "Why would they do that?"

"A long drawn-out lawsuit isn't to their benefit. Better to minimize the scandal and hold Scordato to a confidentiality agreement where neither party discusses what happened."

"And why would Scordato agree to that?"

"They have enough exculpatory evidence to destroy him." He took her hand in his. "Have you thought about pressing charges?"

"No." She shook her head. "I never want to see him again."

"My offer is still open, you know."

"What offer?"

"To beat the shit out of him."

She quirked a smile. "I'll let you know if I change my mind."

Despite Angela's worry about Scordato, or perhaps because of it, Alex entertained her with stories from his travels. When the waiter arrived, Angela decided on the pistachio-crusted goat cheese with roasted baby beets, and the Mediterranean Sea bass. It looked too good to pass up. Alex ordered the spinach-and-cheese-stuffed ravioli, and duck breast and leg confit with blood orange marmalade sauce.

"And my beautiful friend and I will share the cannoli, but don't rush the courses; we're in no hurry." Alex winked at her.

Everything Alex did, including that wink, attracted her. Her instincts told her to trust him. In a short time, he'd become a lifeline for her. Despite what she'd been through the past few months, Angela was looking forward to working with Alex. "I'm so excited about our trip. I can hardly believe I'm going to Florence with you."

"I'm excited, too. I know we'll be working, but showing you around Florence and seeing it through your eyes… will be a reminder of why I love living there."

"Don't worry if it doesn't work out. You can always fire me."

"That ain't gonna happen." He grinned. "If anything, I'm sure once we wrap up the case, you'll get a slew of offers from museums and universities all over the world."

"I've actually already had offers from several universities to teach."

"Did you now?"

"Why are you smiling?" She was having trouble keeping her heart from doing backflips. "Is it so hard to believe that I could be offered a teaching position?"

"I just pictured you walking into a first-year art history class with that gorgeous hair and those killer legs; the administration trying to figure out the sudden upsurge in male enrollment in art history. Yours would be the most popular course on campus." He wiggled his brows. "Hmmm, makes me want to go back to school."

She burst out laughing. He was a charmer, that was for sure. She'd have to keep on her toes if she didn't want to fall head over heels for him.

And what if you did?

The dinner was perfect. Their conversation, like the wine, flowed easily.

Alex leaned forward, the intensity of his gaze made her feel like she was the only person in the world that mattered. "I know about your love of art and your work, but tell me about your childhood?"

She smiled and took a sip of her wine. "I'm a small-town girl from the Midwest. I grew up outside of Chicago, in Lake Bluff, a little town on the shore of Lake Michigan, near the Lake Bluff Naval Base. That's where my father worked. My mother died giving birth to me. My world revolved around books. My best friends resided between the pages of history, art, and literary novels. I couldn't wait to escape and write my own life," she said with a self-deprecating smile and a shrug. "Now it's your turn to bare your soul, detective."

"Have you got a few hours to kill?"

Angela loved the way he scratched his stubbled jaw as he was thinking.

"My father was in the diplomatic corps and my mother was an expert at packing and unpacking. Our lives were in constant flux. We moved a lot, so I don't have much in the way of roots. When I went off to college, my mother finally threw up her hands and said, 'Enough!' They divorced, mother's remarried, father's sworn to the single life. My mother lives in San Francisco and my father calls London home. I see them once a year, taking turns between Thanksgiving and Christmas. I guess you could say that early nomadic life made me something of a loner.

"After college, I rebelled, enlisted in the Marines, trained as a SEAL and was deployed to Afghanistan. When I got out I wanted nothing to do with the real world, so I got my master's degree in art history. Art seemed a great escape. I tried teaching but didn't have the patience. A friend turned out to be my first client—a stolen Dali. I retrieved it and the rest is history."

"Are you saying academia isn't the real world?" She crossed her arms. "Because I can assure you it can be just as cutthroat as any other career path."

He shook his head. "No, that's not what I meant. I just needed to immerse myself in something that didn't include bombs and war."

"It must have been a terrible struggle, returning home and readjusting to civilian life."

A cloud passed over his face, his eyes darkening. "It's hard for me to think about those years. I was really close to the guys in my unit... they didn't all make it. A part of you dies out there, too. With them." He blew out a breath. "Sorry, I've never told anyone that before."

Her face rested in her hands as she listened to him. Their backgrounds were as different as night and day, his childhood was privileged, hers was not, and his military service left her in awe. She'd never let herself become vulnerable with any man, never wanted to let go of that part of herself that she kept tucked away. But since meeting Alex, she felt an overpowering pull. For the first time in her life, she wanted to take a risk...

Angela stood outside the restaurant while Alex went to pay the valet and retrieve his car. The night was warm, the jasmine that climbed the trellis at the entrance perfumed the air. A feeling of contentment flowed through her; she closed her eyes and breathed in the fresh, floral scent.

Caught off guard, a heavy force knocked her off her feet. Completely winded, it took her a moment to recover enough to make sense of what was going on around her. A man had barreled into her, followed by another man who rushed out swinging his fists. A young woman was close behind, screaming at them to stop. The two men were shouting, grappling on the ground inches from where she still lay.

Angela stood on shaky legs, reaching for the trellis to steady her. Apparently, they were fighting over the woman. One of them had cheated with the other man's wife. Everyone outside was so busy filming the ensuing drama with their cell phones that no one had even noticed or bothered to help her. Exchanging bruising punches, the two men were a bloody mess as the sound of approaching sirens grew louder. Waves of dizziness rolled over her and, like a fade out in a movie, everything went dark.

Florence, Italy
Duomo Cathedral
Easter, April 26, 1478

Fioretta moved slowly through the crowd of pious Christians. The weight of her pregnancy encumbered her progress down the aisle. At his behest, a cadre of Giuliano's friends had escorted her to the cathedral. They surrounded her protectively. Fortunately, her fellow Florentines made way for her, parting so that she could reach the front of the nave.

She stood before the altar and looked up to admire the soaring ceiling of the *Cattedrale De Santa Maria Del Fiore*. Easter was her favorite time of year. The celebration of the resurrection of Christ combined with Easter's pagan roots and celebrating the spring equinox was a festivity of the rebirth of the land and life after winter's slumber. This Easter was especially poignant as she was due to give birth next month.

Filled with joy to be having her first child with Giuliano, Fioretta hoped that his brother Lorenzo would finally sanction the marriage and announce it publicly.

We need to begin our real lives together. No more hiding behind closed doors.

She prayed Lorenzo would embrace their child and give his blessing. It seemed impossible that he wouldn't. She knew how much the brothers loved one another. How could Lorenzo not wish Giuliano to be happy? When she'd met Lorenzo at the celebration at the Via Larga he seemed, although a very intense man, charming and reasonable. She remembered his compliments, not only to her person, but her mind. Giuliano had assured her that Lorenzo would be impressed by her wit and dazzled by her inner beauty as much as her outer looks.

Most nights Giuliano spent at their villa, but last night because of an infection to his eye, he'd slept at the Medici palazzo. Her husband took every precaution to protect the life of the child that grew within her. Sometimes her happiness seemed a dream. Even during their one night apart, she'd missed him terribly and couldn't wait to see his handsome face.

The voices of the choir rose to the heavenly dome, sounding like a chorus of angels. The nave was filled with worshipers and it seemed forever before Giuliano arrived. He stood several feet from her. As always, in public, they kept their distance.

I cannot wait until next month when the baby is born. All of this foolishness will end at last.

Their gazes met and his eyes said more than his words could ever convey. Joy filled her and she nearly spoke aloud what was in her heart. His smile and sly wink told her that he had read her thoughts.

Thank you, God, for blessing our love.

Giuliano scanned the crowd, in all likelihood looking for Lorenzo. She, too, had looked for his brother, but couldn't find him among the throngs of worshipers.

The bell chimed the Elevation of the Host and the crowd grew still. All eyes were focused on the priests at the altar. It was the holiest of moments when the priests intoned the scripture *accepit panem in sanctas ac venerabiles manus suas,* "… he took bread into his holy hands—"

A flicker of light caught her eye and she turned, glimpsing the flash of steel. "Oh, dear God, stop him!" She screamed in agony as a man plunged his sword into Giuliano's chest.

His eyes grew wide and he stumbled backward. "Here traitor!" the assassin shouted as another man joined him, stabbing a second blade into her beloved. Her blood-curdling screams rose above the crowd, echoing through the church. "Giuliano! Giuliano! Giuliano!"

It was like watching a scene in a play. Fioretta could do nothing as her husband fell to the ground in a pool of blood. She tried to reach him, but his friends grabbed her and pulled her away from the madness, toward the exits. "Let me go!" she cried, but it was of no use.

The crowd, like a stampede of cattle, trampled everything in its path. She tried her best to protect her abdomen and her child, but the throngs of panicked worshipers elbowed and shoved trying to escape.

Fioretta fought the bile that rose in her throat. Her escort half dragged her, half carried her outside the cathedral. She sobbed and swooned. Strong arms kept her from crumpling to the ground. Somehow, they procured a carriage and hustled her inside. She sank into the seat sobbing. "*Ti hanno amazzato! O dio! Amore mio.*" Dear God, they've murdered you.

When they reached the villa, the servants took possession of her and thanked Giuliano's men for delivering their mistress safely home. As they led her away, she heard the men recounting the horrible events that had taken place. Giuliano's murder played over and over in her mind. She wept inconsolably. "They left him on the floor of the church alone." In a state of delirium, she pleaded, "Someone needs to help him."

Everything became a feverish blur after that. She woke several hours later, the afternoon sunlight stealing across her bed. She could hear the seven bells in Giotto's campanile echoing the disaster that had befallen the republic. The bells signaled that the city was threatened. It was a call to arms that every Florentine would answer. Armed and ready to defend their city, they would rally in the Piazza della Signora to protect the seat of government.

She drifted in and out of sleep until she heard a commotion downstairs, her servants arguing with someone. The door to her room burst open and Leonardo blew in like a storm. With his long blond hair, wild and disheveled, he looked like a madman. "Leonardo, my friend." She opened her arms and he rushed to her.

"Fioretta, I'm so sorry. I came as soon as I could, but those foolish servants of yours tried to turn me away."

"I'm glad you were persistent." Tears streamed from her eyes, hitting the coverlet. "Have you brought me news?"

He sat on the edge of her bed and held her hand. "The city is in chaos. The Medici palazzo is an armed fortress. The people are rallying to their cause and the streets teem with men chanting *Palle! Palle!* The conspirators are being hunted down one by one and given judgment of immediate death. The mob is hungry for blood and vengeance. The city has become a place of madness and is preparing for an assault."

"Who did this, Leonardo? Who took my Giuliano from me?"

"Speculation is rampant that it is Pazzi and the Pope's nephew who are responsible."

"The Pope knew of this evil plot?"

"Believe me, the blame will never reach him. He will go unpunished, at least in this life. Afterwards, he'll find his reward in Hell. Thank God, you were not harmed, and the baby is safe."

"Yes, my poor orphaned child is fine. But I am a rudderless boat adrift at sea. All my dreams have been laid to waste. There is no future, only the past and its ephemeral glory." Her voice broke. "My love is dead. I have no wish to live."

Leonardo's eyes flashed with anger. "I will not listen to such foolishness. You have a child to think of, a Medici child. You must pull yourself together. God has dealt you a tragic hand, but you must overcome it for the sake of the baby."

"I know you mean well, my friend, but you weren't there. You didn't see what they did to him. I will never be able to erase it from my mind." Her eyes alit on the wedding portrait across from her bed and she covered her face with her hands and wept.

He wrapped his arms around her. "You have a friend, Fioretta. I will never abandon you."

Alex held a sobbing Angela in his arms. She was inconsolable since he'd found her unconscious on the sidewalk at the restaurant. The police had wanted a statement from her, but Alex had told them it was impossible. He'd lied, explaining that Angela was an epileptic who'd had a seizure and needed to be taken home immediately. Using his detective status, he informed the officer that she'd have no memory of what had occurred and would be of no help to their investigation. The officer, who had plenty of other witnesses, let them leave.

He was crazed with worry for her and knew she was in no condition to go home. He did the sensible thing and drove her back to his hotel. She was so dazed, she collapsed again when he unlocked the hotel room door. He carried her to the bed and laid her down. Running a washcloth under cold water, he pressed it to her forehead.

She stirred, opening her eyes. "Where am I?"

"You're in my hotel room."

The blush that filled her cheeks made him smile. From the moment they'd met, every time he touched her, he felt a rush of attraction and something deeper, a yearning that took his breath away.

"You were completely out of it and the hotel was closer than your place."

She grasped his arms, her eyes wide with fear. "I saw him—*my* husband murdered in a church..." she whispered. "I was there. I could hear the choir, see the inside of the domed ceiling... It was Easter mass. I screamed. I could feel all of it like it was my own memory..."

"I wish I'd been there to help you through it," he said softly. "How was it triggered?"

"I don't know exactly... I was knocked down by those two guys fighting and then I fainted, I guess. But I remembered the vision." Tears filled her eyes. "It was horrible, Alex, seeing Giuliano murdered."

"I'm sorry." He caressed her cheek, wanting to tell her about his own supernatural chat with the painting of Giuliano, but then he'd have to explain why he hadn't told her about it already. He didn't want to upset her more, especially after everything she'd been through with Scordato and her own visions.

"I should probably get home." She moved to get up.

"You're not going anywhere, Angela. You're sleeping here in this bed. I'll sleep on the sofa in the other room."

"But..."

"No buts. I'll call downstairs and have a toiletry kit sent up. Tomorrow we'll go to your place and pack your things."

When she wrapped her arms around him and buried her face in his shoulder, he asked, "Are you okay?"

She leaned back and met his gaze. "No. I'm worried and scared."

He brushed away a tear that slipped down her cheek with the back of his knuckles. "It's going to be all right. I promise you, nothing bad is going to happen to you. I know what I'm doing."

She smiled, sniffling back her tears. "My bodyguard, huh? You'll keep me safe from the big bad wolf."

The way she looked at him made his blood heat.

"Alex, I..."

Before she could finish the sentence, he pulled her into his arms, his lips locking on hers. Every part of him touching her, needing her, wanting her. She kissed him back, her arms wrapping tightly around his neck, her breasts pressing into his chest. Aching for her, he groaned, "Angel..." His lips slid up her neck, inhaling her, kissing her, tasting her.

All he wanted was to make love to her, but he couldn't. *Not yet. Not here. Not when she's this vulnerable. I won't take advantage of her, even though, dear God, I want her.* He rested his forehead against hers, fighting for equilibrium, willing his body to obey him.

Her eyes were closed, her own struggle to gain control of herself was etched on her delicate features.

"I'm going to make that call now. Get you a toothbrush..." His throat closed and his words came out like a shoe scraping gravel.

"Okay." She was breathless and it pleased him more than he could admit. "That kiss..."

"I apologize, I shouldn't have…"

"Don't apologize. I wanted it, too."

He smiled and tucked her tumbled down hair over her shoulders. Desire flared in her eyes. It matched his. But he wouldn't take advantage of her. Not in the vulnerable state she was in.

It was going to be a hell of a long night.

CHAPTER 8

Florence took her breath away.

Angela gazed out the window of the car, whisking them along the Lungarno Amerigo Vespucci roadway, awestruck by the sunset. The dusky sky laced with clouds reflected purple, pink, and yellow off the Arno River.

Pinch me, I must be dreaming.

She gasped when the elevator doors opened to Alex's apartment. The entry boasted a frescoed wall painted with an early Etruscan agrarian scene. The color palette of seafoam green and ivory inspired relaxation, tranquility, and contemplation.

Like a deluxe spa from the pages of In Style Magazine.

Beautiful wide-planked, wood floors led to a sunken living room, bordered with floor-to-ceiling windows, opening to a wraparound terrace.

Angela soaked up the view of the ancient city. The skyline dominated by the spectacular five-hundred-and-fifty-year-old Duomo di Firenze, Filippo Brunelleschi's floating dome.

Alex's home was in the heart of the city, a two-story penthouse in the Palazzo Rucellai, an historic building dating from 1446. The neighborhood was designated pedestrian only and harkened back to a time before auto horns and combustion engines became the ambient music of city life. A pain in the neck in inclement weather, but it made the Via della Vigna Nuova a quiet street.

"Your home is incredible. The art recovery business must be very lucrative."

His lips lifted in a smile. "It pays the bills. I rent it out in the summer for a couple of months and it carries itself."

"Where do you go? I can't imagine anywhere better than being here."

"I have a small villa and vineyard near Montefioralle."

The hairs on the back of her neck stood up. "Montefioralle? Where have I heard that name before?"

"It's a tiny, ancient village in the hills of Chianti. It's a pretty well-known tourist destination."

"No, it's something else. When you said, Montefioralle, I felt like I knew it. I could visualize it in my mind." Her eyes widened in excitement. "What if there's a connection somehow?"

"There's only one way to find out." He grinned and pulled her in for a hug. "I promise to take you there."

"Thank you." She hugged him back, her eyes fluttering closed. She breathed in his woodsy-citrus scent. Absorbed the heat from his sinewy frame. All angles, planes, and muscles. *I could get used to this.*

"We need to do some investigating here, in Florence, first," he said as they broke apart. "but we could drive up on a weekend."

"I think just being here is helping already." She almost leaned back into his embrace. Almost. Caught herself just in time. It would be so easy to lose herself with him and then what? She trusted him instinctively, down to her core. But feeling physically safe wasn't the same as feeling emotionally safe. His globe-trotting lifestyle told her "player" and yet he'd been nothing but caring and sweet, practically goofy, with his exaggerated winks and eyebrow wiggling. *Goofy or not, he's probably got girlfriends in every major city he travels to. You're here to work, to solve this mystery. That's it.* Slipping her hands in her pockets, she pasted a smile on her face.

"Good, I'm happy to hear it." He hefted her bags and she followed him up a spiral staircase to the second floor.

She skimmed her hand down the bannister, "This staircase is a La Corbusier, isn't it?"

He threw her a smile over his shoulder. "It sure is. I bought it at auction. I love its openness, how it showcases the view."

"It's amazing."

"I'm glad you like it."

He opened the door to a bedroom that featured a sitting area with a wall-to-wall bookshelf, a big picture window, and a feature wall painted with a trompe l'oeil illusionistic fresco depicting a scene from Pompeii. An antique Italian baroque desk and chair sat in the corner of the room. The bed was set back from the sitting room behind a sheer curtain, in its own nook. Soft gray and dove white walls were adorned with photos of the Italian countryside filtered through a glaze of fog that echoed the soft muted colors of the bedroom suite.

She turned in a circle, taking it all in. "It's the most beautiful bedroom I've ever been in."

"Wait till you see the master suite." He winked. "I'll show you around the entire apartment after you get settled."

"I can just imagine." The heat in her face made her wish it was dark. *Don't even think about it Angela.*

"Are you hungry? Want something to eat?"

"Famished."

"Let's do something about that." He grinned. "Why don't you unpack, freshen up, and meet me downstairs when you're ready? Just follow your nose to the kitchen."

The shower relaxed her, which she needed. Being in Florence was exciting, but she wouldn't rest until they found the painting. Ricocheting back and forth between the past and the present scared her, and her last journey back had been emotionally agonizing. Witnessing Giuliano's horrifying death had overwhelmed her. The pain. The agony of it all. She shook off the tragic memories. She was still having a hard time processing everything, especially the notion that she was recalling her past life as Fioretta.

Stop it! Whatever had happened in her past life was in the past. There was a reason why she was getting these visions, but she had her own life to live. Pulling on a pair of black leggings and a cream silk, ruffled blouse with a black cinch belt, she followed the aroma of a garlic and tomato sauce to a sparkling white-tiled kitchen with shiny, stainless-steel appliances.

Alex stood at the stove, an apron tied around his waist. Leaning against the wall she smiled as he pinched several leaves from a basil plant on the window sill, rolled the leaves together and chiffonade them before tossing them into the thick, bubbling sauce. He stirred and took a taste. "Much better."

"You like to cook, don't you, Stud?"

He threw back his head and laughed. "Told ya. I'm irresistible, I'm charming, and I make a mean Marinara."

"Don't forget humble."

He laughed as he sliced open a pack of linguine and slid it into the boiling water. "This isn't cooking, this is just reheating, but I do love to cook. Good therapy. Especially chopping. You wouldn't believe the things that come to mind when I'm chopping."

Why does everything he says and does have such an effect on me? She was fighting to maintain her distance and keep their relationship on a professional level. Intimacy would only confuse things, especially because they were here to investigate a missing masterpiece, not on a honeymoon or a lovers' getaway. But no amount of self-talk could stop the crazy feelings that flowed through her when she was near him.

Alex's voice interrupted her musing.

"Why don't you go find the library? The wine is poured, and mixed green salads are on the table. I'll just finish up in here and bring the pasta?"

"We're eating in the library?"

"My library serves double duty as my more formal dining room. Either we eat there or in the kitchen. I thought you'd like the library."

"Wise choice for the bookworm." She laughed. "Do you need me to bring anything to the table?"

"The bread's in the oven warming, madam librarian. Can you take it in?"

"Now that's a job I'm fit for because I'm useless in the kitchen." She leaned back, placing her palms behind her on the edge of the counter. "When I was growing up, my dad didn't have time to cook and usually picked up takeout on his way home."

"If you want to learn, I'll teach you. You can start as my sous chef. Cooking isn't such a big mystery. It's a joy. And something that most Italians, both men and women, love to do."

"Then I look forward to my first culinary lesson."

Is this what being in a relationship is? The simple comfort of just being in the kitchen together? She wasn't much of a cook, but the idea of learning from Alex seemed the most desirable thing on Earth.

She couldn't stop smiling as she hugged the bread basket to her chest and walked down a long hallway in the direction of the library. Opening the double-wood doors, she drew in a breath. The wall opposite the door featured another picture window, offering a spectacular view of the Duomo. The walls on either side contained floor to ceiling shelves, bursting with books. In the center of the spacious room was a massive carved-wood table with red-velvet upholstered dining chairs. Two, four-branch candelabras hung from the ceiling. In each corner was an art Deco torchiere, providing a warm ambient glow.

On the table were two place settings of fine china, sterling silver, and crystal wine goblets filled with dark burgundy. She set down the basket of bread and wandered to the bookshelves.

Alex entered the library carrying a lidded casserole dish and placed it on the table. "Come on, let's eat this pasta while it's hot. You can decide if my library meets your high expectations later."

"I already found at least a dozen books I'm anxious to crack open. This is an impressive collection."

"Even though I have a master's in art and work in the art world, sometimes I feel like I'm all brawn and no brain. Collecting art books is a hobby that comes in handy in my work." He uncovered the pasta and the fragrance of simmering tomatoes and basil filled the air. Angela leaned forward and inhaled. "Wow, that smells delicious."

"It is." With practiced ease, he served them both. He raised his glass. "Now wine is something I do know about. This is a 1985 Tignanello, a very fine wine." Holding the goblet delicately by its stem, he swirled the burgundy-colored vintage and inhaled. "Perfect." He touched his glass to hers. "To finding the painting and sorting this reincarnation stuff out so that we can get on with the joys of living. Like cooking, eating, and getting to know each other better."

"I'll drink to that." She sipped. "Hmm, I could definitely get used to this wine. The prospect of getting to know him filled her with pleasure and loosened her inhibitions.

He began to grate a large hunk of Parmesan over her plate. "Say when."

She smiled, said nothing, and continued to sip her wine.

He grated and grated and grated, throwing her a questioning glance when she remained silent. "Are you having a little pasta with your parmesan?"

"No, I just love watching you grate."

"Well, in that case…" He grinned and flexed his forearms as he gave a final grate. "

She burst out laughing. *I love flirting with him…*

The meal was delicious. Her heart did a somersault when he broke off a chunk of crusty bread and used it to swirl the pasta around his fork. His passion for food, art, and books matched her own. She wished she could remember kissing him in front of the Medici portrait. Twice. Last night's kiss had left her breathless. "So, what's on the agenda for tomorrow? Where do we start, detective?"

"I thought we'd check out the Uffizi. It's closed on Mondays to the public. However, the director is a friend, and I'm sure she'll be delighted to escort us on a private tour. I texted her and should hear back soon. I'm curious to see your reaction when you see the art in person."

"Why, what do you think is going to happen when I see it?"

"I don't know, but it seems like a good place to start. It's the Medici collection—been at the Uffizi since 1769. It's likely the wedding portrait was there during World War II."

"You're probably right. It would make sense."

"Exactly. That's why I think seeing the art in person might trigger some memories."

She nodded. "A private tour of the Uffizi? You *do* have pull. And then what?"

"Then the Church of San Lorenzo, where both Giuliano and Lorenzo are buried."

"Ah, Michelangelo's masterpiece he never finished. He was called away to Rome for a small project called the Sistine Chapel."

"You call the Sistine Chapel a small project?" He laughed. "What else do you know about the tomb?"

"Maybe I'll surprise you when we're inside it." She speared a few crunchy leaves of the salad with her fork and popped it into her mouth, savoring the blend of tart lemon juice and smooth, full-bodied extra virgin olive oil. "You are planning on working me hard, detective."

"I am, but I'd be a terrible Tuscan host if I didn't wine and dine you properly. All that art is sure to spur your appetite. I thought we'd go to one of my favorite restaurants. At least I know we have one thing in common, we both like to eat." The mischievous smile that played across his lips made her heart flutter. Oh God, there he goes again. *Damn, don't go there Angela. Hold on to your composure or we'll never get to the bottom of this mystery.*

She whispered, "Into what dangers would you lead me, Cassius, that you would have me seek into myself for that which is not in me?"

"Okay, smarty pants, what's that about?"

"Shakespeare, *Julius Caesar, Act II.*"

"And what, may I ask, are you referring to?"

"I'm not sure. The words just came to me." Shaking her head, she tried to clear it.

"Am I wrong or is that passage inferring that I'm a mirror reflecting things inside of you which you cannot see?" There was a fire in his eyes.

"I don't know. I'm confused as to why it came to me." She turned her fork in a circle, twirling a strand of spaghetti around it. She needed to distract him and herself.

"I think it's relevant. Maybe something is buried in your subconscious. It's like what we felt when we kissed. I'm having as much trouble as you trying to figure this out. I'm also fighting an urge to kiss you again."

"Really?" she squeaked out. The intensity in his striking, different-colored eyes took her breath away. She shook her head as though trying to convince herself she wasn't attracted to him. *Yeah, good luck.* "I don't think I can handle any more confusion right now." She didn't want to say anything about how much she wanted him to try. Instead, she popped the swirl of pasta in her mouth.

Alex reached out and took her left hand in his. She felt instant sparks as she stared into his eyes.

"I won't do anything until you want it, Angela. I promise you, it will be your move first."

"Thank you. I appreciate your ability to resist me."

"Let's just solve this case and get to know each other better in the process. As for resisting you, I'm failing miserably."

She loved spending time with Alex and swapping stories from each other's childhoods, but by nine-thirty she could barely keep her eyes open. He marched her straight to the guest room and gave her a light peck on the forehead, before heading to his own suite, which was lucky because one more minute and she would have made the first move. And that would have been a disaster. She was exhausted, emotionally and otherwise from everything that had happened the past few days, let alone the six months working for Scordato. The cool, silky linens welcomed her and in a matter of moments, she fell into a deep, sleep.

Florence, Italy
May 26, 1478

The pains stole Fioretta Gorini's breath. It was as if her insides were being torn from her. The contractions were so intense she bit right through her lip and droplets of blood stained the bedding. "God, take me now," she screamed between gasps for air. "Fetch the physician, Katerina, something is wrong. And have Alphonso bring Leonardo."

Wave after wave of pain wracked her body. The wait for the doctor was interminable. Katerina rushed into the room. "He's here, Mistress."

The doctor looked as if he'd come from his bed. Scraggly beard, stained cloak, and noxious breath made her gag. Another pain hit and she fought to catch her breath.

"How long has she been like this? Have you summoned the midwives?"

"I'm not dead yet," Fioretta hissed. "Of course they've been summoned. Do something." Another pain hit. "Can't you see something is wrong? What good are you to me if you can't help me?" Seized with another contraction she moaned, "Get it out. Please, take this child from me."

The doctor's gaze darted around the room. "I'm sorry, Signorina Gorini, there is not much I can do. Your labor is hard, and the baby is fighting his entry into the world. I will leave a potion for the midwives who are familiar with its dosage and use. It will ease your pain somewhat."

Fioretta gritted her teeth as another wave of pain shot through her. She clawed the sheets, scrunching them beneath her fingers. "Leave me," she shouted at him. Bowing, he made a quick departure. "Dear, God, that man is useless."

The midwives arrived and raised Fioretta's head to administer the foul concoction the doctor left. She retched. "This is vile, I'd rather die than drink it."

"You must heed the doctor's instructions, signorina." Fausta, one of the midwives, poured the liquid down her throat.

Fioretta gulped, squeezing her eyes shut. "Why has God cursed women with the torture of childbirth?"

"We have been cursed since Adam and Eve in the Garden of Eden," Gabriella, the other midwife, said. "Now you must walk; it will place the baby in the right position for birth." Together with Katerina's help, the midwives eased Fioretta out of bed.

"I can't walk. Where is Leonardo?"

"He awaits downstairs. Don't worry about him. Alphonso will see to his needs."

"But I need him," she growled.

"It would be unseemly and difficult for him. He is a man after all. He will come when the child is born."

Katerina and the midwives supported Fioretta as they circled the room. Each step was a nightmare of pain. She cried like a wounded animal and cursed the three women as if they were the source of her agony. She clutched her stomach as she stumbled forward, their hands digging into her armpits. "Witches, that's what you are. Go back to hell where you came from." *All I want to do is sink to the floor and die.*

The torture went on for hours, the midwives and Katerina took turns dragging her pain-wracked body past the wedding portrait. "You did this and then abandoned me." She sucked in her breath bearing down before doubling over. "You are a traitor and a scoundrel for causing me such agony. I want to claw your face. AHHHHH!" She dug her nails into the women's skin as she addressed the portrait on yet another agonizing walk around the room. "When I see you again, I will kill you," she wheezed.

"Breathe, Mistress, focus on the child," Katerina soothed.

"No more! I will not walk another step. Please, I must rest."

Mercifully, the women helped her to the bed. The birthing chair was removed from the room. The fresh bedsheets were soon soaked with sweat and blood—Fioretta heard the midwives whispering, "She will be gone by morning, poor dear. Her strength and life recede with every passing minute. It is now in the hands of God." The three women crossed themselves.

The fools think I cannot hear them. I know I'm going to die. I want to die. All that is left for me is to be delivered of this child and join my beloved Giuliano.

"Katerina," she whispered.

Katerina took Fioretta's hand, misery stamped on her face. "Yes, Signora, what can I do for you?"

Another pain ripped through her and she squeezed the petite woman's hand in a death grip, digging her nails into her servant's skin. Her piercing scream brought the midwives to her bed. With what was left of her strength she bore down. "Please, God!" She felt her body empty, the blood gush from her, the numbing relief of giving birth. Gabriella held him, his cry pierced the air, replacing hers.

Katerina lifted Fioretta's head and forced a few drops of water down her parched throat. Gabriella quickly washed and swaddled the boy, placing him in her arms.

Her life was draining from her, the blood seeping into the sheets. Fausta, working feverishly, cleaned and packed her as best she could, her dark eyes reflected what Fioretta already knew.

She was dying.

"My son. We shall name you Giulio." She kissed his head, the dark hair soft and downy. She whispered, "Soon you will meet your grandmother and your family. I won't be with you, but *amore mio*, your father and I will watch over you from heaven if God allows."

Fioretta glanced up at her loyal servant and friend. "Katerina, bring Leonardo to me. And I need you to go to the Medici palazzo and summon Lucrezia Tornabuoni, Giuliano's mother, and bring her here. Hurry."

"What should I say, Mistress?"

"Tell her it is a matter of life and death that concerns the Medici.

Leonardo sat on the edge of the bed, holding Fioretta's hand. "What can I do for you, my muse, my dearest friend?"

"I don't have much time left, Leonardo." She gazed into his bright blue eyes, so dear to her. "I've summoned Lucrezia to entrust my son to her care. But I couldn't leave this world without saying farewell to you, my dear friend."

"No." His tears fell as he pressed his lips to her hand. "You will leave me, but I know Giuliano waits for you."

"Don't weep, it's what I pray for. What he promised." Her gaze shifted to her wedding portrait. "You have given me friendship and my immortality."

"I will miss you, Fioretta. The painting never did you justice."

"You are wrong. The painting is a masterpiece. You will be known as the greatest artist of all time."

He shook his head.

"Know the truth, as I know it."

He lifted her hand and kissed it once more. "Leonardo, my strength is dwindling and I have one more task left to me on this earth."

He bent to kiss her brow. "Farewell, my friend."

Minutes later, Giuliano's mother arrived. She was tall, stately, and dressed in mourning black. A sheer white veil hid her hair, but even the anguish of losing her son could not steal her beauty. Her eyes swept the room. Her back to Fioretta, she faced the wedding portrait. After a moment she turned to Fioretta, her gaze resting on the child. "What can I do for you, Signorina?"

Fioretta took a breath and used what little strength she had to tell Lucrezia the story of Giuliano's and her love.

"*Mia cara madre*, I beg your kindness and forgiveness. Your son, Giuliano, was the love of my life and this child, who I have named Giulio, is the proof of our love. We were married in the studio of Leonardo da Vinci and Angelo Poliziano was our witness."

"Fioretta, you and Giuliano brokered this union without approval. This marriage was not sanctioned by Lorenzo, the head of our house. Giuliano was promised to another."

"Yes, I know, but Giuliano swore that God himself could not keep us apart. You, of all people, know how strong-willed Giuliano was. His intention was to announce our marriage after our child was born and beg Lorenzo for his blessing." Fioretta's eyes swam with tears. "Now that will never be."

"What are you asking of me, Fioretta?"

"I am asking for your kindness and forgiveness, Signora. I will not live out the hour. I would plead with you to take your grandchild and raise him as your own. Let him take his rightful place as a Medici."

Lucrezia didn't answer. Her eyes roamed the room, resting, again, on Leonardo's portrait. She moved closer to examine the painting. "Is this your wedding portrait?"

"Yes. Giuliano commissioned it from the Maestro, Leonardo da Vinci." Fioretta wiped the tears that blinded her. "He said it was our immortality."

"May I have it?"

"Will you care for my son and raise him as a Medici?"

Lucrezia gazed in the direction of the portrait. "My son loved you well."

"Your son is waiting for me. He promised we would be together for eternity. Ours was a love out of time. Eternal."

"Your marriage must be kept secret. It will not be recognized, and the child will grow up believing he's a bastard. There are alliances to consider."

"That doesn't matter to me. He's still a Medici. In God's eyes, we were married. What matters is Giulio Medici, *mio figlio*. What matters is that Giuliano's son grows to be a man of consequence within the arms of his family."

Lucrezia sat on the edge of Fioretta's bed and caressed the infant's face. "I loved my son. Perhaps your child will heal our family's heart. He looks just like Giuliano." She smiled.

Fioretta pressed her lips to Giulio's head, kissing him. "*Addio cuore mio.*" Tears blinded her as she gazed at her baby for the last time. "Take my son and go. Come for the painting when I'm gone. I wish it to be the last thing I gaze upon. Thank you, Signora."

Lucrezia lifted the sleeping infant. "Go in peace, Fioretta. May God be with you."

"It is not God who will be with me. It is Giuliano."

There would be no sleep for him tonight. Alex's senses were on alert, knowing that Angela was in the next room. Since the moment he laid eyes on her, he felt driven to protect her. Finding out he was the reincarnation of Giuliano Medici only magnified his determination to keep her safe, hell it was more than that. It was a need right down to his core. Slipping out of bed, he padded on bare feet to the balcony and gazed out at the flickering lights of the city he called home. Clad only in his boxers, the night breeze tickled his skin. Florence had been good to him. He hoped it would continue to be so.

A mournful cry down the hall made him bolt inside. Rushing into Angela's room, he gathered her thrashing form in his arms and held her tight.

She wept in her sleep. He didn't know whether to wake her or just hold her until she stopped. Her eyes fluttered open and her words sent a chill down his spine. "Giuliano, *amore mio*, you waited for me. I told your mother that you would."

She was trembling against him and it was driving his imagination to places he shouldn't go. He tried to put a few inches between them, but Angela pressed deeper into his embrace. It took every ounce of his strength not to kiss her. "Angela, you had a nightmare. I'm Alex Caine, you're in Florence at my apartment. Do you remember?"

Her eyes cleared, but she was still gripping his arms. "Alex, I'm sorry." She released him and lay back on the bed. "I guess it was another nightmare."

"Do you remember anything?"

"I gave birth to my son and then I died."

She began to shake again, tears flowing anew. He held her in his arms as she told him everything from her dream. *My God, first she experiences the murder of her husband and then the agonizing birth of her son, only to bleed to death.* He couldn't keep his own knowledge from her any longer. He needed to tell her about his experience at the Getty and his extraordinary conversation with Giuliano.

He was already half in love with her... *Fuck, who are you trying to fool?* He loved her. He never believed in love at first sight, but this was different—he knew her—it was inexplicable. He'd always known her in his soul. Tomorrow. He would tell her tomorrow after their visit to the Uffizi. She was exhausted, he wouldn't add to her burden.

He held her through the night. Eventually, she fell asleep and he soon joined her in slumber, his arms still wrapped around her.

CHAPTER 9

Florence, Italy
Uffizi Gallery
Present day
August 7

"First, we'll have a tour and then we'll enjoy a nice espresso."

Celestine Marchesi was dressed in a beige suit, elegant but understated. Her thick dark hair was swept up into a French roll. She'd welcomed Alex and Angela with exuberant kisses on both cheeks. Leading them through the Lorraine Atrium, where marble busts of members of the Medici family greeted them, they proceeded down the hallway to the Eastern Corridor where the museum rooms dedicated to art periods and specific artists were found.

"I know you are mainly interested in those artists who painted during the lifetime of Giuliano and Lorenzo Medici, so I will, if you don't mind, dedicate our time to them." Celestine exuded an attractive mix of Italian charm and smooth confidence.

"Excellent, that is exactly what I had in mind," Alex said.

Outside Botticelli's gallery, Angela froze. Placing her hand on the wall, she smoothed it down the flat panel. "There's a door here that leads to Vasari's Corridor."

"How do you know that?" Celestine's voice switched from warmth to suspicion.

"I don't know." She flushed. "Maybe I read it somewhere?"

"You know I recall a BBC documentary about it some time ago," Alex piped up, attempting to diffuse the tension.

"I don't recall this entrance ever being filmed, but it's possible... There have been many film crews here over the years. It is difficult to keep track of everything." Celestine shrugged and continued down the hall.

"Crisis averted," he whispered in Angela's ear as they followed behind. She blew out a breath. "Thanks for that."

"I got your back baby." He winked. "And a very fine back it is."

She shook her head and wagged her finger at him as they continued down the hall.

"Above us is the original wood beam ceiling of the Medicean theater. Rooms ten through fourteen hold the collections I think you will be most interested in."

They stood before Botticelli's *Birth of Venus* and *The Primavera*.

At her gasp, Alex slipped his arm around her waist. "Angel, are you all right?"

She looked up at him and he saw forest-green eyes filled with sadness—Fioretta's eyes.

Sorrowfully, she whispered in Italian. "*La mia amica, Simonetta. O Dio, Sandro l'adorava, la sua morte lo ha distrutto.*"

Celestine's eyes grew wide. "Am I hearing correctly? Did she just say my beautiful friend Simonetta? How could she know that Sandro Botticelli adored Simonetta and was crushed by her death? That's just romantic speculation."

"Angela has been studying the painting in great detail for months, as part of her research," Alex said smoothly, wrapping an arm around Angela's shoulders and drawing her close so that Celestine couldn't see her eyes. I'm sure it's just exhaustion and jet lag," Alex lied. "Can you give us a few minutes of privacy?"

"Of course. I'll wait for you in the da Vinci gallery." Celestine walked ahead. He hoped she wouldn't grill him on his flimsy explanation of Angela's behavior. The fewer people who knew about her past lives regression, the better.

Angela sank into his arms and wept against his chest. When she finally looked up at him, her face inches from his, her expressive eyes kindled his desire. All thoughts of trying to calm her were swept away and, unable to stop himself, he claimed her mouth, his tongue delving deep inside her parted lips. The room spun around him as if they were on a merry-go-round. Reality and the present were lost in a passion that roared through him like a summer brush fire. Fighting to regain control, he broke the kiss and was relieved to see the beguiling, brown eyes of Angela once more.

A deep red blush colored her cheeks. "Alex, why are you kissing me in the middle of the museum? Where's Celestine?"

He scrubbed a hand up and down his face. "I'll explain later. Right now, we have to meet her in room fifteen, Da Vinci's room."

He held her elbow. "After we see the da Vinci paintings, I'm going to ask Celestine to show us some paintings by Leonardo's assistants, particularly Salai and Boltraffio. The wedding portrait was most likely attributed to one of them. Maybe when you look at their work up close, you might be able to determine if the painting we're hunting is a da Vinci or one of theirs."

"Boltraffio was the better artist of the two, but I'm certain now that the portrait is a Leonardo da Vinci."

Alex nodded. "It's possible Lorenzo Medici himself created the cover-up. If he didn't want the world to know about Giuliano and Fioretta's marriage, what better way to make sure than attributing the portrait to an unknown artist. It would guarantee that the painting would remain in the shadows of history."

"I've been thinking the same thing," she said. "It kind of makes for a very challenging search. Not only the painting but revealing the hidden historical truth. It makes you wonder how many other things we consider true about the past are shadowed in misconceptions and cover-ups."

"Room fifteen contains da Vinci's Annunciation and his unfinished Adoration of the Magi. It also contains Verrocchio's *Baptism of Christ*," Alex said.

Angela's eyes lit up. "Leonardo helped paint the Baptism of Christ. He was one of Verrocchio's assistants at his atelier."

They joined Celestine, who, thankfully, didn't mention what had occurred in Botticelli's rooms.

Eyeing the painting, Celestine asked, "Angela, what do you think? Most historians believe this angel was painted by da Vinci's hand, which is distinct from his master's. It is said that it resembles Leonardo as a boy."

Angela nodded. "It does look like him. Leonardo told me he often painted his own image in his work. He considered it his signature."

Celestine gaped at her. Alex cleared his throat.

"I mean, from the descriptions I've read… apparently, Leonardo was very handsome as a youth. Many of those who knew him have written of his physical beauty. I see his hand in the sweetness and empathy of the face, and in the luminescent curls on the angel. Leonardo was obsessed with hair and was meticulous in reproducing it. He probably worked on a lot of the background, too, because the brushwork bears his signature style."

Celestine smiled. "You have a discerning eye, Angela. Shall we continue, and then have our coffee?"

The rest of the morning was spent admiring the sculptures in the connecting hallway with its *grottoesque* ceiling painted with bizarre arabesques of animals and plants. They spent time viewing Raphael, Titian, and Parmigianino's *Madonna of the Long Neck*.

Celestine and Angela continued their discussion of Leonardo's meager, but extraordinary output. Alex enjoyed hearing Angela expound on her expertise of the period. Not only was he magnetically attracted to her, but he was also impressed with her mind. Her insights into da Vinci's battle between his scientific and artistic endeavors were perceptive and exemplified her depth of knowledge of the genius.

After their gallery tour was completed, Celestine served them rich, dark espresso in her spacious office. She shared some insights about the Medici Chapels and the Church of San Lorenzo, which they planned on visiting after lunch.

Angela excused herself to go to the restroom. She didn't want to alarm Alex, but her head was throbbing, and there was a whirring sound in her ears. One breakdown in front of the director of the Uffizi was enough. She followed Celestine's instructions down the hallway, pausing once to brace herself against the wall across from a closed door. She'd been hearing voices all throughout the tour. Sometimes loud, sometimes faint, like a radio tuner. It had been all she could do to remain calm and alert.

Voices floated out to her from the other side of the door. She tried to make her feet move away but she couldn't help herself, couldn't stop herself. *I recognize those voices…* Raising her hand to knock, the door swung open and a gust of wind pushed her inside.

It took a minute for her eyes to adjust to the darkness. The blinds were drawn and there was very little light. A man was arguing with a woman. They spoke Italian. Angela could read Italian, but speaking it was another matter. The couple ignored her as if she were invisible. Her heart was beating so loudly it sounded like cymbals crashing in her ears. The room spun around her. The door shut behind her and she shuddered, sensing the past was once again supplanting the present.

Focusing her attention, she realized that the man wore a German army officer's uniform from World War II and the woman had on a dress with padded shoulders and a narrow waist. They were young and very attractive, he fair and blond, she dark and doe-eyed.

Her instincts on high alert, Angela sensed that the Italian woman was her in a past life. Just as Fioretta was. But why was she being shown this woman and this man? All she could do was stand and watch...

The man paused, his polished, high boots reflecting the sunshine streaming through the blinds, which somehow were now open.

"Sophia, the allies are advancing, and we will be evacuating Florence in the next few days. I will not leave the painting here in Florence. I'll keep it safe and return it after this madness ends."

Sophia frowned, her arms stiffly folded above her waist. "Gerhard, you can't just take something that isn't yours. That's stealing, it's too dangerous. It's bad enough that if we're caught by the Germans, it will be death by firing squad, but if we're caught by the partisans we'll fare no better. We'll be accused of stealing Italian patrimony and God only knows what they'll do to us."

"We won't be caught. These fools don't know what they have. The first time I laid eyes on this portrait, I knew it was a Leonardo da Vinci. This painting haunts my dreams and I will not leave it in the path of war. It isn't safe here. What if someone takes a liking to it and steals it? What if a bomb falls and accidentally hits the Uffizi? If I could, I'd take them all. Anything to keep these priceless treasures safe and out of harm's way."

"Gerhard, Florence will not be razed. The priceless works of art will be safe."

"Not from thieves, Sophia. This is a seemingly worthless, unattributed painting that could easily be taken and sold on the black-market. I will not let that happen."

The man wrapped his hands around the woman's waist and pulled her toward him. She didn't fight but ran her fingers through his blond hair. "Come with me, Sophia. We belong together. It's summer; we'll make our way to the Apennines and find a small village where we can wait out this war. We'll hide the painting and retrieve it when there's peace. We can return it, if you like, or, if we're smart we'll keep it. It's worthless in their eyes, just some inferior student's work. They won't miss it."

"And, what if I say no?"

He laughed. "You always say *no*." He brushed his mouth over hers, his tongue flicking against her lips. "And then you say *yes*." He kissed her, ferociously, passionately, and she returned his kiss with feverish abandon.

"My little minx, you know you can't live without me." His hands roved her body, his fingers pressing her skin as if he were a sculptor and she a mound of clay. "I need you—I have, since the first time I laid eyes on you."

Angela watched, mesmerized, unable to move. Her heart hammered and adrenaline pumped through her veins. The temperature in the room climbed from the heat of Sophia and Gerhard's kissing, and Angela felt a bead of sweat trickle down between her breasts. She was embarrassed and aroused at the same time. She didn't want to watch, but she was incapable of stopping. This wasn't anything like travelling through time and astral-projecting inside another person's body. This was like watching a movie.

Gerhard's hand cupped Sophia's breast, his thumb circling her nipple and she moaned, whispering, "*Caro*, I want you. Here. Now. There's no one here, just us."

Gerhard groaned, and his hand swept everything off the desk. Pushing her against the desk, he lifted her skirt and began touching her in ways that elicited soft moans of pleasure.

Angela's feet were anchored to the floor. Her cheeks burned as if a fever were consuming her. Taking a deep breath, she pressed her legs together, trying to stop the throbbing.

Sophia's fingers loosened Gerhard's belt and unzipped his fly, yanking his pants to the ground. She wantonly begged. "I want you inside me. I need you. Now!"

It was all the encouragement Gerhard needed. He shoved Sophia down on the desk. "Spread your legs," he commanded.

She didn't move. A whisper of a smile played upon her lips.

"Sophia, do as I say. You want this and I want it, too. Spread your legs."

"I do want it, *amore mio*. But I love when you take control."

He grabbed hold of her legs and wrenched them apart. Leaning over her, he grabbed a fist of hair and pulled her head back. He licked her neck, and like a soldier who'd found his enemy's weakness, he drove himself into her with thrusts that made her cry out. "Are you happy now, *cara*? Is this the way you like it?"

"Yes… yes… yes… don't stop."

Dizzy and weak, Angela sank to her knees.

Gerhard quickened his rhythm, plunging deeper and faster until Sophia stiffened, digging her nails into his back, and cried out his name. With a burst of hyper thrusts, he stiffened and roared, "*Dio mio*, I love you." Collapsing on top of her, his lips found hers.

She threaded her fingers through his hair as he kissed her. She struggled to gather her breath. "I think this is the only room in the museum we haven't made love in. Another notch on your belt my love."

"I love you, Sophia. You will come with me, yes?"

Her fingers caressed his face. "I love you, too, Gerhard. Yes, God protect us, I'll come. But I have a better idea. We'll go to my family home. My brothers will not turn us away."

The young couple kissed once more. When they pulled apart Gerhard looked up and it was as though he were looking directly at Angela. That's when she saw his eyes—one pale blue and the other hazel. Her world started to swirl and spin and then everything went dark…

"Shit!" Alex's knees almost buckled when he rushed into the office and saw Angela lying on the floor, unconscious. He checked her breathing, and grabbing her purse sifted through it, pulled out a bottle of hand sanitizer, opened it, and waved it under her nose. When her eyelids fluttered open, he sighed in relief.

"It's you…" she breathed.

He held her, caressing her hair and back. "What happened?"

"They were here, in this room… a man and a woman."

He looked around the room. "What man? What woman?"

"Gerhard and Sophia."

"The same couple we're investigating?"

"Yes! H-he wore a German officer's uniform, she was dressed like a movie star from an old movie. So beautiful." Angela grabbed hold of his shirt; her eyes looked dazed. "They were arguing about the da Vinci painting. About taking it with them. H-he couldn't bring himself to leave it here. He wanted to hide it. It was crazy, I could see everything, but they couldn't see me. I-I know now…" Her breathing quickened like she was running a race. Alex was worried she would start hyperventilating.

"What do you know, Angel?" He caressed her flushed face.

"I-I'm her. I'm Sophia." She was shaking now. "And I saw Gerhard's eyes. He was looking at me." She cupped his face in her hands. "He had different-colored eyes. Your eyes. Am I going crazy, Alex?"

"Hush, calm down, honey." He pulled her back into his arms, the hammering pulse in her neck worried him. "It's going to be all right. I promise."

His own heart began pounding in his chest. Angela knew she was Fioretta and now she'd also discovered she was Sophia. Both women had a connection to the painting. Alex knew he was Giuliano in a past life, and from what Angela had told him about Gerhard's eyes, he'd been Gerhard in a past life as well. A Nazi officer, no less. *Shit.* This was getting way too twisted. "What else do you remember?"

She pulled away, her cheeks red with embarrassment. "Th-there was nothing else. That was it."

He searched her eyes. She was hiding something from him. He'd get to the bottom of it later. *You're hiding something too, buddy.* Guilt churned in his gut. Angela was going through this ordeal, thinking she was alone but she wasn't. He had to tell her what he knew and soon, or he might lose her. "Let's call it a day. We can go back home and rest, eat something, and talk."

"Okay, I'm not much good for anything else today, I feel like I've just run a marathon."

"Angel, you need to remember these people are no longer alive." He helped her up from the floor, steadying her when she wobbled on her feet. "They exert no real hold over your life. Okay?"

"Yes, I know," she replied with a frown. "It's not like I went looking for this. I can't stop it from happening. When I was on my way to the bathroom, I heard the voices and it was like some sort of supernatural force pushed me inside." She began to tremble again. "I'm scared that I'll keep getting pulled in deeper and deeper. What if I end up in this dream state and I can't come back?"

"I won't let that happen to you. I promise," he said fiercely. He wrapped his arm around her shoulders and gave her a sideways hug as they made their way from the Uffizi. He refused to think that he could lose her to this strange, creeping possession. The whole thing was like some bizarre, paranormal novel. At this rate, he wouldn't be surprised if a vampire showed up on his doorstep.

Their past lives, for some reason, were intruding, but he would not allow them to steal her present life or her future. But no matter what came next, he vowed to protect her. No matter the risk.

Beyond the windows of Alex's apartment, Florence glittered like a jewel. Alex had cancelled their dinner reservations and instead ordered a pizza and a salad from a local bistro, the remains of which were still on the table in the library.

"I know you're upset, but can we talk about what happened?" He laid his hand over hers.

"I'm not upset, I promise." She sighed. "I'm sorry I'm so quiet. I'm just trying to remember who I was before this whole thing started."

He scratched his stubble and decided to jump in. "There's something I have to tell you."

She raised an elegant eyebrow. "I can tell, you're anxious because you're scratching the side of your face."

"Ah, so you're getting to know my quirks, are you?"

"Yes, but I like you anyway."

He lifted her hand and kissed her palm. "Good, because I like you too."

She blushed and it was all he could do not to pull her into his arms and kiss her breathless, but he had to tell her before they could move forward. "Just as you know that you were Fioretta and Sophia…" He blew out a breath. "I know that in past lives, I was Giuliano and from what you told me about Gerhard's eyes, I must have been him too."

"Of course." She gripped his hand. "If you were Giuliano, it stands to reason that you were also Gerhard."

"Not exactly thrilled about being a Nazi in a past life." He scratched the back of his neck with his free hand.

"Gerhard wasn't evil," she said softly. "You know that, don't you?"

He shrugged. "Well, we can't pick our past lives, I guess. But I made up for it in this one. This time I was on the right side." He quirked a half-smile.

"You're a good man—a courageous man." She cupped his face with her hands. "I can't even fathom what you went through in Afghanistan. I hope one day you can share it with me."

I want to. God, how I want to. He gazed into her velvety eyes, shimmering with a luminous beauty. He'd never talked about it with anyone, except for his therapist and other vets. Never wanted to until he met Angela. They may have been together in past lives, but he yearned to know her in this one.

He had to come clean about what he knew. "The painting you sat in front of at the Getty. The one by Botticelli—"

"Yes?"

"Your last day at the Getty, you had the run-in with that asshole Scordato and you ended up sitting on the bench facing the Botticelli. I woke you up from a trance state remember?"

She nodded.

"What I didn't tell you was that the painting spoke to me. Giuliano told me he failed to protect Fioretta, and it was my duty to protect you at all costs because the past was doomed to repeat itself."

Angela gasped, pulling away, she stood and began to pace. "The painting spoke to you? Why didn't you tell me this sooner?"

"At first I didn't know what to think. I had to process everything in my own mind. And you were so distraught about Scordato and then you collapsed outside the restaurant and had another vision. You were going through so much baby, I couldn't dump that on you too."

"But that's precisely why you should have told me." She crossed her arms over her chest. "I was going through so much—I felt all alone."

"You're not alone." He stood and laid his hands on her shoulders. "My priority was keeping you safe and getting you away from Scordato. I was going to tell you after we got to Florence and now I'm telling you. Forgive me."

"Do you really think all of this is fate?" Her lips trembled and her eyes filled with tears.

"We kissed twice in front of that painting. Your eyes changed color from brown to green. You spoke in Italian. You told me you loved me. That we were destined to be together."

"I was in a trance."

"Yes, but you knew it was me. On some level, you knew I was Giuliano," he said softly.

Tears were streaming down her face now. He pulled her into his arms, holding her tight.

"No more secrets," she whispered thickly. "Please, we have to be honest with each other. Promise me."

"I promise… Speaking of which, I get the feeling that a lot more happened in your vision this afternoon than what you shared with me." He leaned back and saw her ruby-red blush.

"Yes, but I was kind of embarrassed by what I'd seen…"

"What did you see?" He smiled at her flustered expression.

"Sophia and Gerhard made mad passionate love on the desk. It was the most erotic thing." Her eyes were wide and if it were possible, she blushed even more.

He grinned. "Shit, that must have been hot."

"But that wasn't the weirdest part."

"Go on…" He wiggled his eyebrows at her, making her laugh.

"They spoke in Italian and I understood every word they said…"

"Is that all?" He was having fun teasing her.

Angela leaned in closer and whispered, "Every time he touched her I felt it like a sensory memory, and I…" Her cheeks turned a darker shade of crimson. "I enjoyed it." She looked down, clearly embarrassed.

Damn! Her words had awakened his own sleeping giant. He wanted to carry her upstairs to his room and spend the next few days in bed, loving every inch of her luscious body. But he couldn't. Not now, not when she needed his strength to lean on. "Well, that's a hell of a lot better than some of your other past visions."

"It's not funny, Alex."

"Sorry, humor is a coping mechanism," he admitted. "For a while I considered stand-up comedy then I realized I was terrible at it."

She arched her brow. "I think that was a wise decision."

"Ouch." They both laughed at that and then he said in all seriousness, "Your past selves are reaching out to you for a reason and it has something to do with the missing da Vinci."

"Maybe… there's more. Maybe they want to help me stop whatever cycle keeps repeating itself. And it's getting stronger, more demanding. It's as if these lives are merging into mine. Taking over my life." She pressed her fingers to her temples.

He removed her hands and gently massaged her temples.

She sighed from his ministrations, a soft moan escaping her lips.

"We'll figure it out. Together. I promise you, I'm not going to let anything happen to you."

"I'm not sure you can stop it. I seem to be the conduit and they're not about to let go of me. If Giuliano in the painting told you to protect me because of history repeating itself, then that means danger is ahead. But what?"

Her frustration was as great as his. He didn't have any answers for her, at least not yet. "I wish I knew the answer to the mystery, but together we'll figure it out. I keep thinking there's a score to settle, some cosmic vendetta that must be satisfied."

"I seem to be the bait."

"Not on my watch." He caressed her face. "I'd like to take you to the Church of San Lorenzo where both Lorenzo and Giuliano are buried. Tomorrow, if you're up to it."

She nodded.

"Then in a couple of days, we can head out to my vineyard in Montefioralle. It will give us some respite from everything. Besides which, you had a strong feeling that Montefioralle factors into this mystery. Even if it doesn't, it will give us a chance to just chill out and breathe some fresh country air. Read, hike, whatever you want. I need to check in with my manager anyway to see how the grape harvest is coming along."

"That would be wonderful." She sighed. "Whatever happens, we're going to be honest with each other from now on?" she asked.

"I promise." He kissed the side of her cheek and drew her back into his embrace. No matter what danger lay ahead, he would protect her with his very life. That didn't mean he wasn't worried. Little by little, with each episode, the dreams and visions were becoming more visceral and debilitating.

How the hell can I stop this from hurting her?

CHAPTER 10

It was magnificent.

Angela was awestruck when she entered the Church of San Lorenzo to see, in person, the pinnacle of Renaissance architecture designed by Brunelleschi and Michelangelo. She walked through the nave in reverent silence. Renaissance means rebirth and San Lorenzo was one of its masterworks. A rebuttal to the Medieval dark ages that had preceded it. Here, great artists, thanks to the Medici family, had been given a chance to build a monument that embraced humanist achievements in learning and wisdom.

"So, professor, do I get an art history lesson, or are you going to keep the story to yourself?"

"Actually, this place ties in rather strongly to our mystery. After Giuliano and Lorenzo's deaths, Michelangelo was hired by his childhood playmate Cardinal Giulio de Medici to design and build the New Sacristy here. I don't know if you know it, but Michelangelo was like a son to Lorenzo and he grew up at the Medici Palazzo."

"Giulio de Medici?"

"Giulio was Fioretta and Giuliano's son. He later became Pope Clement VII."

Alex whistled. "Our son the Pope, now there's a feather in our cap."

Angela smiled. "We did good, didn't we?"

"We sure did, baby." He glanced around. "Knowing that we were here before is beyond anything I could ever have imagined. Tell me about the New Sacristy, where I'm buried."

"Michelangelo's design for the New Sacristy was a space symbolically embodying 'Human Life.' After death, the soul would be freed to pursue the pleasures of an active sporting life and the contemplative philosophical life. His design aligned with his own spiritual quest and belief in the hereafter."

"Michelangelo believed in reincarnation?"

"No. There's no proof of that. I think his belief was more influenced by his devout Catholicism. More a belief in the spiritual hereafter."

Alex and Angela exited the church and walked around its perimeter to the back where the entrance to the Chapel of the Princes was found. The chapel was built to display the grandeur and wealth of the Medici Grand Dukes. The soaring walls of the mausoleum were inlaid with marble, granite, jasper, alabaster, lapis lazuli, coral, and mother of pearl. The elaborate Baroque tomb and its soaring frescoed cupola were a lavish display of excess, but this was not Alex and Angela's destination. The reason for their visit was downstairs.

Only a few people at a time were given entry to the New Sacristy. Finally, Angela stood at the front of the line with Alex behind her. When the group before them exited they would be let in. Just as the tourists filed out, Angela stepped in first. Glancing over her shoulder, she noticed Alex had paused to look at something. Before she knew what was happening, the door slammed shut locking her inside.

"Alex!" She pounded on the door but could hear nothing on the other side. A whoosh of wind whispered in her ear and she turned, pressing her back against the door. Frightened and confused, her gaze swept the claustrophobic space where priests would dress before conducting the Mass. The funerary chapel was square and dense. Soaring in heights that exceeded its width and length. The second story, designed with faux windows of solid marble, enhanced the oppressiveness and made Angela shudder. She recalled one art historian's comparison of the chapel to purgatory. She understood that feeling of entrapment. At this moment she wasn't sure if she'd ever get out.

Only at the top, where the dome floated, were the possibilities of heaven and freedom given expression. From a surround of windows thin streams of light filtered down. She lifted her face to the light, hoping to conquer the fear that had formed a knot in the pit of her stomach.

The art historian in her brushed her fears aside and stepped toward Michelangelo's monumental sculptures of Night and Day that bookended the carved statue of Giuliano, who posed relaxed and breast plated. He appeared to be a Roman warrior at ease. On the opposing wall were Dawn and Dusk, which flanked the sculpture of Lorenzo, a decidedly more intro-spective figure that appeared to be contemplating life, death, and eternity. Both statues were supposed to represent Giuliano's and Lorenzo's name-sake cousins, but Angela had always sensed that they were really Giuliano and Lorenzo whose effigies Michelangelo had planned, but never begun.

Giuliano's sculpture was an idealized symbol of man's physical perfec-tion and beauty. It was her favorite of Michelangelo's sculptures. Now, as she gazed at the statue, her eyes filled with tears. The beauty of Michelangelo's genius made her cry. She might have remained in a state of contemplation if a whispering voice hadn't filled her ears. "Fioretta, *amore mio.*"

She whirled around, but there was no one there. Invisible fingers brushed through her hair and she whirled again, her heart stampeding in her chest. Goosebumps rose on her arms as she felt a cold breath on her neck that whispered, "Fioretta, *ho aspettato un eternità per essere riunito a voi.*" She repeated the words in a whisper, "My darling wife. I've waited so long to be reunited with you." Hadn't she just told Alex that she didn't think the ghosts of the past could intervene in the present? Yet, she was being caressed by Giuliano, a man dead for over five-hundred years.

The light in the chapel dimmed, casting shadows over the monumental statues. She turned in a circle, the chapel spinning around her, trying to find the source of the ghostly voice that continued its recitation of words of love. "What do you want from me? Why are you haunting me?"

She sank to the floor, closed her eyes and pressed her hands over her ears. She tried to block out the voice that invaded her mind. "I'm not Fioretta. I'm Angela," she repeated over and over.

Silence answered her and it grew colder in the chapel. She opened her eyes and she was frozen by fear. Walking toward her, no not walking, floating, was a man, a man she knew in an instant. It was a youthful Giuliano Medici, his dark hair lifted as if he walked outside and a breeze blew through it. Eyes dark as night held her gaze. Taking her hands, he pulled her up from the floor, embracing her. He caressed her back and pressed his lips to her ear, sending shivers up and down her spine.

"Please," Angela begged, "what do you want from me?"

Lips pressed on hers until she was sure she would faint dead on the floor. Her blood pulsed loudly in her ears, sounding like the roar of the ocean when you hold a seashell against your ear. Her heart jackhammered against her breast as if trying to break free of her chest cavity. All she wanted was Alex to come crashing through the door to save her.

The voice that spoke to her wasn't audible, it filled her head, drowning out every other thought. *Angela, you are the only one who knows the destiny of the painting, our painting, but others are searching for it. Evil men who will stop at nothing to get the painting, even murder. You must destroy them—their evil must end here. In this life.*

To release your memory, you must become one with Alex. When two become one, you will be guided to our wedding portrait. Twice we've been torn apart, only as one can the evil be broken. Alex is as much a prisoner of the past as you are. Freedom is within your grasp. The lines of time will be erased, and evil will be eradicated. Love will once more enrich your life. This time it will not be taken from you. You hold the power to free all of us.

Marsilio Ficino, my teacher said, 'The soul exists partly in eternity and partly in time.' He wrote that for us, Fioretta. Remember these words; you must free us all. It is time for this to end... to end... to end... Giuliano's voice echoed, fading away.

The ghostly figure that held her was gone before she inhaled her next breath. Somewhere the pounding of fists on wood matched the pounding of blood in her temples. She slipped to the floor.

Alex was frantic. He and several security guards tried without success to breach the door to the sacristy.

"I don't understand, *Signore*, this door is never locked. There is no explanation for why we can't open it. We may have to call the *vigili del fuoco*."

"Damn it, the fire department isn't going to bust down these doors and risk any damage. Isn't there another way in?"

"No. The entrance to the church was permanently sealed off years ago. This is the only way in or out."

"Help me. Let's both put our shoulders to the door."

With a concerted effort, they rammed their shoulders into the door. Without the least bit of resistance, the door flew open and they stumbled in, both falling over in their momentum. In the claustrophobic space, Angela's motionless figure was immediately discernible. Alex rushed to her. Kneeling, he lifted her wrist and felt for her pulse. "Her pulse is steady, thank God. Can you get me some water?"

"*Si*, I'll be right back."

Alex lifted Angela in his arms. "Angel, come back to me." He took a quick look around the mausoleum. It seemed as if the marble statues were staring at him; the eeriness made him shiver. The guard returned with a water bottle. Alex opened it and pouring some water into his hands he bathed her face. Her eyes fluttered open and he held the bottle to her lips. She took a tiny sip and gazed at him. There was a dreaminess in her eyes, a faraway look, but he was happy to see her eye color was brown and not forest green.

"Alex, it happened again."

"I know, Angel. I saw something, too."

"You did. What?"

"I can't be certain, but from the corner of my eye, I swear I saw Giuliano walk by. It was a blur, but enough to get my attention. That's why I paused, and then the door shut. I've been going crazy trying to get in here, to you."

She lifted her hand to cup his face. "It's okay. He's trying to protect us."

"Three times I've seen Giuliano. What does it all mean? I thought you were the one with the second sight?" He covered her hand with his.

Her brows knitted. "Each time you saw him, you were with me…"

His eyes widened. "Son of a bitch. *You* were the catalyst and the conduit. He was able to communicate with me through you. I've got to hand it to him. He's clever."

"And so are you."

He kissed her palm. "Let's get out of here and you can tell me everything when we're home. Okay?"

Her gaze was soft, trusting, and it nearly gutted him. In combat, he understood the rules of engagement, who the enemy was, how to take down a target. In his investigative work, he knew how to track down thieves and bring them to justice. But this? How was he going to protect Angela from centuries-old ghosts? And after this latest stunt by Giuliano, he was beginning to wonder if these spirits were helping or hindering him? Past life or not, Giuliano was becoming a supernatural pain in the arse.

Scordato sipped an espresso from his hotel balcony in Florence, sighing with pleasure. For two days his cousin Enrico had followed Angela and Alex. A long-time "soldier" for the mafia, Enrico was an expert at tailing and avoiding detection. But he had some help from a very unique contact, a former Russian spy who now made a lucrative living as a contract hacker. And a woman, no less. Working for the mafia and various terrorist organizations, the hacker, known only as "Madam X" cost a fortune but was worth every penny.

Their private visit to the Uffizi and now the Chapel of the Princes was all the proof he needed to know that the painting by Leonardo had everything to do with the Medici and most likely Giuliano Medici. Piece by piece, the puzzle as to who or what was in the painting was taking shape.

Excitement coursed through his veins. Soon he'd make his move. The more he thought about Caine, the more he looked forward to doing away with him. It was obvious that Mr. Hero was responsible for his firing. The Getty board, presenting him with evidence, did not want a scandal and asked him to resign, citing personal reasons. They also denied him his severance package. He laughed in their faces and signed the ludicrous letter they'd drafted. Those idiots had no idea what he was capable of. What a brilliant mind they'd lost. Besides, he would soon be richer than Croesus. Not to mention the fame that would come with finding the missing da Vinci. He would be lauded from all corners of the globe, and every major museum and gallery would be clamoring for his notice.

Once Caine was out of the way, Scordato would drug Angela and use her mind to get to the painting, then he'd use her body for his pleasure.

He shifted in his chair, his cock stiffening at the anticipation of taking her by force. She'd whetted his appetite. He couldn't stop thinking about their last encounter and how she'd managed to physically overcome him and get away. She liked it rough? He'd make certain she would get exactly what she wanted. He might even keep her around a bit, or maybe he'd just give her to Enrico and let him have his pleasure with her before killing her.

He finished his espresso and phoned his cousin to make certain everything was in order.

"Did you pay our errand boys?"

"Yes."

"Give them their orders."

"Consider it done."

Beyond the windows of Alex's apartment, Florence glittered like a sea of diamonds. Angela couldn't help but wonder at what the Medici would have thought of their city today. Lost in her own thoughts, she sipped her glass of wine. Since they'd returned from the Basilica, she'd been trying to make sense of Giuliano's words.

She turned from the window and glanced at Alex seated on the sofa. His eyes were downcast, gazing into his wine glass. He looked up, his face twisted in anguish.

"Angel, I know you're upset and I know I failed you, but I swear it won't happen again."

"I'm not upset with you, I promise… I'm just trying to remember who I was before this whole thing started."

He set his glass down on the coffee table and went to stand before her. "I promise you you're not alone." He lifted her hand to his lips. "I don't understand why, but every instinct I possess tells me we'll get through this together. I won't stop until you're free and we find that painting."

Searching his eyes, she found only sincerity. She needed him in so many ways that it scared her. If he betrayed her it would be a dagger to her heart. "He kissed me today."

A fire lit in Alex's eyes. "Who kissed you?"

"Giuliano touched me, kissed me. It was eerie, but I didn't feel threatened. He said things… things I'm not sure I understand."

"Like what?"

She could feel her cheeks burn. "He said you and I must become lovers. That the hiding place of the painting won't be revealed until we are. He said there are people who seek the painting and would kill us for it. He said we have to destroy them once and for all, otherwise we'll never be free."

Alex's lips twitched. "My man, Giuliano, is quite the pimp. And here I wanted to deck the guy. What else did he say?"

"I'm not making love with you just because some ghost says I should."

"No, of course not. A lot of what he said to you sounds like what he said to me." He wrapped his arm around her shoulders and drew her to the sofa. "I'm glad we're getting out of Florence. We both need a break from ghosts and visions. Montefioralle should do the trick. The fresh country air, the views. The home-made pizza." He raised his brows suggestively. "You'll feel better as soon as we get there, I guarantee it."

Her eyebrows lifted and she smirked mirroring his exaggerated expression. "You sure know how to get my attention. Fresh air is nice—but seducing me with pizza isn't fair. Really, Alex, you're figuring out all my weaknesses."

"Hey, I'm just following Giuliano's instructions." He grinned. "Besides, I need to check in with my manager and see how the grape harvest is coming along."

"I'm excited to see your vineyard." She smiled. "And to relax. These episodes are so taxing. I need some recovery time. Not only have we discovered that we were Giuliano and Fioretta, but Gerhard and Sophia. It adds another layer to what's happening. I need to put some distance between the past and the present, if only for a short time."

"Agreed." He glanced at his watch. "Where the hell is that food delivery?" He phoned the restaurant and after a brief exchange, he hung up. "The restaurant is backed-up on their deliveries. I'm going to run over there and pick up the order. You'll be fine here by yourself?"

"Sure. I'll set the table."

"Back in a flash."

Alex, immersed in his own thoughts about Angela, paid little attention to the people he passed on the street. A few blocks from the Palazzo Rucellai he ducked into an alleyway that was a shortcut to the restaurant. He realized too late that he was being followed. A giant of a man approached from behind. Instinctively, he reached for his gun and cursed when he realized he'd left it back home.

Glancing ahead, he spied another thug walking toward him from the other end of the alley, blocking off any possible escape. The second assailant was slender, shorter, and farther away. He could tell by his stance and his hesitant approach that he'd be the lesser threat.

Scordato. It has to be him. Who else would be doing this? Alex wasn't working on any other cases. Max had paid him handsomely to be his exclusive client until the painting was found. No, this had Scordato's stench all over it.

Alex had checked in with Fellows yesterday while he was making dinner for Angela—the Getty board member informed him that they'd fired Scordato. Alex was happy about that, but it also meant that the scumbag was completely free to indulge his machinations and plotting...

But there was no time to think about his hated adversary right now. Only his military training would save his ass. He was outnumbered, and he knew he had to strike preemptively. Neither man held a gun, but that didn't mean they weren't packing.

When Green Giant was just behind him, Alex struck like a lightning bolt with a roundhouse kick landing solidly on the guy's genitals. The thug doubled over cursing. But Alex wasn't done with him yet. He followed up with a knuckle punch to the solar plexus, toppling the giant to the ground.

Alex shifted his attention to the second assailant, but he turned too late. Bean Pole clearly moved faster than his buddy, Green Giant, and came running at him with a switchblade. Alex lifted his arm, the blade slashing through his leather jacket and slicing through his skin. Searing pain lanced through him.

Utilizing the rush of adrenaline that roared through his body, he focused on the wiry thug. Bean Pole circled him, warily, blade ready, his eyes darting back and forth from Alex to his partner writhing on the ground. Alex rushed him; with his fists gripped tight into weapons, he punched and made contact with Bean Pole's jaw, sending his head snapping backward. He followed through with a kick to the ribs and the knife went flying.

Behind him, Green Giant was still out of commission on the pavement, except for an occasional groan. Another minute and he'd be recovered enough to reattack. Alex knew he could continue to fight, but he also knew his chances of winning were diminishing. He was bleeding like a stuck pig. Glancing back at the giant who was just beginning to move, he turned and delivered a powerful chop to Bean Pole's neck, striking him precisely at the vagus nerve. With his blood pressure and heart rate disrupted, the man dropped like a stone.

Alex gripped his injured arm to staunch the flow of blood and made a dash for the end of the alley. The bistro sat kitty-cornered, less than a block away.

All told, Alex had been gone less than an hour, but for Angela it felt like forever. She paced restlessly, terrible scenarios playing over and over in her mind. When she heard the key in the door she rushed to the entrance, calling his name. Alex was locking the bolt and security chain when she threw her arms around him. "I was so worried about you."

He gasped, dropping the bag of food. She felt him stiffen and, stepping back, saw the blood. "Oh, my God." Horrified, she stared at his torn and bloody jacket. "What happened?"

His good arm pulled her close. "It's okay, just a scratch. I'll be fine."

"But what happened?"

"Two thugs ambushed me in an alley. My fault—"

"Why?" Her hands cupped his face. "Were you robbed?"

His hesitation told her everything. "Scordato did this."

"Believe me, my arm is nothing compared to what those two goons are feeling right now."

"Alex, this isn't a game. If he's capable of this, who knows how far he'll go?"

"We'll be exercising a little more caution from here on in. He's probably just trying to scare me because he blames me for the board firing him. And we know, he wants the painting. He has no job, and his career is on the line, so he's stepping up his game."

"I'm scared, Alex. You could have been killed."

"Baby, I've been doing this a long time. I can handle a couple of thugs." He caressed her face. "Why don't you take the food to the table while I change my clothes?"

"We'll deal with the food later, I want to see that cut."

"Please, Angela, just do as I ask."

"No."

She slipped her arm around his waist and went upstairs with him. Like an army general, she told him to strip and asked him where the first aid kit was.

Turning back to him, she sucked in her breath at the deep gash in his arm, oozing blood. "You need stitches."

"It's nothing, Angela. There's butterfly tape in the first aid kit."

"It's not nothing." She bit her lip. Willing the tears away, she swabbed the cut and applied antibiotic cream, then bandaged it securely.

"Why didn't you come back here right away?"

"I was hungry. I wanted to pick up the food."

She rolled her eyes. "What are we going to do about Scordato?"

"Don't worry about him. Once we find the painting, he'll crawl back under the rock where he came from, his tail between his legs."

"What if he tries again? Or does something worse?"

"I'll be ready for him." His hand touched her cheek. "Trust me, Angela. I'll protect you."

"It's not me I'm worried about. It's you."

"Don't. I promise everything will be all right."

His hand slid down to her shoulder. A tremor shot through her. She glanced away, focusing on zipping up the medical bag, fighting the burning desire to demand more from him. If she opened that particular Pandora's box, there would be no turning back. The fire that flared between them would consume her, burning down any emotional defenses she had left.

CHAPTER 11

Florence, Italy
Present day
August 9

"My lady, your coach awaits you."

Angela was certain she must be dreaming. "Is this your car?"

Alex held open the door of a gleaming red Testarossa Ferrari. "No, it's just one of my cars." He smiled, closing the passenger side door. "A hobby of mine is buying old cars, fixing them up, and re-selling them. This one's new though, and I can't wait to get it out on the road."

"I've never been in a car that's worth more than a house in my home-town." She ran her hand over the luxurious leather dash.

He cleared his throat, his face flushing as he hefted their bags and stored them in the trunk.

"Private art detective must pay well," she added with a smile, to soften her comment as he got in beside her. From what he'd told her so far about his childhood, he'd certainly grown up in a more affluent setting than she had.

"I get paid well for doing what I do." He shrugged with a half-smile. "I like fine things, but I wouldn't say I'm extravagant." He keyed in the ignition and the beast came to life.

She should have known by his home that Alex Caine settled for only the best, but she couldn't help herself from gaping at the growling tiger of a car. If this wasn't extravagance she didn't know what was.

"I'm sorry," she said. "I didn't mean to suggest you're a rich, playboy type."

He laughed at that. "Well, if spending most of my time in my garage fixing old cars makes me a playboy, then I'll buy that."

"How fast does this car go?"

"Fast. Wanna try?" His eyes lit with his challenge.

"No way! I wouldn't know where to begin."

"It looks like I have one more thing to teach you. Bringing you up to speed on cooking and driving Ferraris could take years."

"Years, huh?"

"The nuances and details might even take a lifetime. Here, allow me." He reached across her for the seat belt strap, and in one smooth move, pulled it and snapped it into place. His proximity and the way he stared at her lips made her catch her breath.

God, I wish he'd just kiss me already. He'd been her husband and lover in two past lives. Would she throw caution to the wind and let fate take its course once again?

"You're feeling fairly cocky and sure of yourself today, aren't you?" She steadied her breath, hoping their banter would calm her nerves.

He grinned. "That's what a car with *coglioni* does to a guy. It makes him brave." He winked and settled back in his seat.

She laughed and shook her head at his antics. He had a silly and fun sense of humor—something that had been sorely lacking from her life. It was refreshing. She enjoyed his teasing.

"I have something for you." He reached behind his seat and grabbed a leather satchel. Pulling out a goldenrod envelope, he handed it to her.

"What's this?"

"Gerhard's letters that I translated. You can read while I drive. It'll keep you busy while I break the sound barrier. There's twenty-five of them, the most relevant are about the painting and Sophia."

"I can tell you from my vision of her, Sophia was aptly named," Angela mused. "She reminded me of her namesake Sophia Loren, sizzling hot and sexy."

Alex backed the Ferrari out of the parking space and zoomed for the exit. "I'm glad I missed that part of your illustrious past life. I wouldn't have enjoyed seeing you make love with another man."

"That other man was you, Alex."

"I suppose you're right, but I have no interest in competing with some past version of myself. Besides, the new one is a vastly improved model." His brows waggled provocatively.

She giggled. One more thing she thought was adorable, his outrageous eyebrow wiggling. "You don't have to worry about any dead men for competition."

"Is that an endorsement for my resume? Are you considering giving me a test run?"

"No smart-ass." She rolled her eyes. "I'm just saying that given the choice of dead or alive, I'll take the living, breathing, warm version with blood flowing through his veins."

He laughed and punched the air. "Score! One for the Alex-meister."

Angela opened the envelope and pulled out the pages within. She was struck by the neat penmanship. *Damn, he's such a perfectionist. I guess that's what boarding schools do for you.*

Alex had been right—by the time they reached the main highway, Strada regionale 222 Chiantigiana—she was so immersed in the letters she didn't even notice when Alex seamlessly shifted gears. The engine purred as the great Testarossa tiger was unleashed and the countryside flew by in a blur.

May 10, 1944
Cara Mama:

I miss you very much, but if there is any place that feels like home to me it is Florence. For me, the occupation is not too bad as my duties are not about conquering my Italian brethren, but more about gaining their trust and cooperation. I am here to protect the art, although, eventually I'm sure the Fuhrer will have other plans for it.

I'm working at the Uffizi Museum, which you remember as the home of many of Florence's greatest art treasures, particularly the Medici collection. I cannot rhapsodize enough about the beauty of the gems that are contained within this palace. Each day for me is filled with wonder. To be able to examine and study these masterpieces of the Renaissance is a dream come true. I only wish that it was under different circumstances.

As an aside, I am working with an art historian here at the Uffizi. She is highly qualified and knowledgeable and seems to hold no malice towards me, which makes our relationship quite pleasant. Her name is Sophia and I will tell you she is a far cry from your average academic. Because of you and your insistence on speaking only Italian when Papa was out of the house I have a leg up on all the other German officers here who require translators.

Sophia and I hold diverse conversations about art and history, which makes our disagreements both exciting and stimulating. Like you, Mama, she is a determined woman who is willing to argue her beliefs. I must admit I like her very much...

Angela glanced up and caught a glimpse of the magnificent Tuscan landscape that flew past her window. She thought about Gerhard, a man with divided loyalties. He must have loved his homeland and been horrified at the rise of the death cult of Nazism.

At any other time, other than a time of war, he would have led a life immersed in academia, writing papers, and teaching at a university. Gerhard was the kind of man who spoke to her sensibilities, they shared a common passion, which made her affinity to him even stronger. She skimmed through the letters that reported little more than his daily routine and his growing fondness for Sophia.

June 10, 1944
Cara Mama:

I am sure that by now you have heard that Rome has fallen to the allies and that Germany is fighting an uphill battle. I've heard there is an allied invasion taking place at Normandy. The end is drawing near. Each day our losses grow, and it is doubtful we will be able to hold Florence for much longer. However, I try to keep my thoughts on the work at hand. I am in constant worry for the art that is so delicate and perishable. I cannot fathom the thought of a bomb dropping on this most beautiful of cities. I would do anything to protect the irreplaceable treasures that abound here. It horrifies me to think that what took over a thousand years to build could be eradicated in an instant.

Speaking of treasures, I have made a discovery that I believe is noteworthy. Sophia and I were scouring the storage rooms and came across a painting that caught my eye. It is a Renaissance wedding portrait unlike any I have ever seen before. Since very few works from the period bear the artist's signature, historians have relied mostly on historical documentation to authenticate a work, or their own expertise of an artist's style, or just their own instinct.

Sophia indulged me and we combed the archives for any documentation on the painting. The portrait, which is sublime, Mama, was a possession of the Medici family. It is attributed to the atelier of Leonardo da Vinci, in other words, to one of his students, although there is no specific student named. Mama, I am certain this painting could only have been done by da Vinci himself.

The brushwork and attention to detail, the braided hair of the young bride encrusted with pearls, and her mesmerizing smile, the way she looks out of the portrait with the same knowing smile of the Mona Lisa. I fell in love with her. The background, if you could see it, is like a snapshot of Florence as if taken from the wings of a bird in flight.

Only the Maestro himself could have created such perfection. Only the Maestro himself could have imagined this perspective. This is the kind of work that is the most endangered. Because it isn't considered a major work it could easily be stolen by soldiers who'd think it wouldn't even be missed. I am determined to not let that happen.

Sophia and I have argued over this endlessly. Although, most times I let my beautiful co-worker get the best of me, on this subject I have no intention of acquiescing.

I think by now, you've become aware that my feelings for Sophia are more than those shared between colleagues. In fact, I am very much in love with her and intend to marry her. I would have married her already if it were not for this impossible war. I know you will love her, Mama. In many ways she is so much like you. Headstrong, determined, and a heart of gold. I have so much more to tell you, but it will have to wait.

Your loving son,
Gerhard

Angela paused, again, in her reading and gazed out the window. Cypresses bordered the road, and beyond that, a patchwork quilt of vineyards lined the hills. An overwhelming feeling of *déjà vu* overcame her. *This isn't the first time I've traveled this road...*" Alex, how long have you owned this vineyard?"

"I bought it two years ago."

"Who owned it before you?"

"It was part of the estate of an old woman. She was the last of her family who chose to live in the countryside and treasured the agrarian life. I don't know her name. It was held in probate for some time before it went to auction. Mine was the lucky bid. Why do you ask?"

"I know I've been here before."

"That's strange. I experienced the same thing when I first came here. I fell in love with the area from the first moment I arrived. I spent a week hunting for property with my realtor. At first, I considered a country villa, a weekend retreat that wouldn't require too much upkeep. I never dreamed of owning a vineyard, but when I saw Casa del Sole it became an obsession. I had to own it."

"I can't wait to see it."

"You're going to love it. The main house is a little rustic, but it's got great bones and I kind of like the shabbiness of it. The only part I've totally modernized is my bedroom and bath. It's a little out of time with the rest of the house, but the mix of old and new suits my taste."

"I wonder where Sophia's family home was? The letters say she was from Chianti. This is Chianti, isn't it?"

"Chianti is the designation for the wine growing region specific to the wine. It encompasses a lot of villages. Montefioralle is definitely in the heart of Chianti."

She stared out the window. "I know I've been here before. There must be a town hall where they keep records, or maybe the church. What do you think?"

"I think it's a great idea. At least we know Sophia's last name, Caro, but I doubt we're going to find anything on a Gerhard Jaeger."

"That's true, but maybe he assumed another name, another identity. At least it's a start."

She continued to stare out the window into the fractured light filtering through the trees. A glint of sunlight flashed, blinding her. She blinked, her hand raised to block the light. From the corner of her eye she saw movement. She squinted, catching sight of a man chasing a woman. The woman was laughing, running, turning occasionally to see how close the man was to her. Her dark tresses danced around her shoulders and hid her face when she turned to look back at him. The tall, blond man was closing in and about to catch her. Angela was mesmerized by the romantic vignette and wondered what would happen when he caught the young woman. The Ferrari swept around a curve and with a sigh of disappointment she lost sight of the couple.

"Did you see them?"

Alex stole a glance at her. "Did I see who?"

"The beautiful couple, running through the trees?"

He gave her a curious smile. "It's just beautiful landscape, honey."

A chill skittered up her spine. It was a vision. A window had opened. Two worlds overlapping each other, one in the here and now, and one that took place seventy years before. "I saw us, them, Sophia and Gerhard, they were running, laughing." A great sadness swept through her. "They were happy, in love. What happened?"

Alex reached for her hand. "I don't know, Angela, but it means they were here, in Montefioralle. Your second sight confirms it."

Tears blurred her vision. "It does, doesn't it? We're on the right track. We're getting closer to the truth."

"I wanted to get you away from all that craziness and stress and all I've done is bring you closer to it."

"I don't think I can avoid it. The mystery will not let go of us until it's solved. We're being led, Alex."

"I suppose you're right." Alex drove up a gravel road and stopped in front of a set of heavy wooden gates. A sign announced *CASA DEL SOLE, UVA E VINO*. *He pressed the buzzer and a female voice answered,* "*Si.*"

"*Ciao Maria, sono Alex.*"

"*Bentornato, Signor Alex.*"

Alex drove slowly up the winding driveway and three barking dogs encircled the car, their tails wagging. "We just put an electric gate in. I need to get a clicker from Maria. Maria and Joseph are the couple who work for me. Joseph runs the vineyard and Maria runs everything else. I'd be lost without them."

"Interesting biblical names, Mary and Joseph."

"Ha, I never thought of that. She is kind of like a universal mother type, though, and Joseph is the strong silent type. A man of few words, but a man of action. I was super lucky to find them, they're from Romania. When I bought the house the couple who'd taken care of everything for the prior owner retired."

"So, Maria and Joseph never knew the prior owner?"

"No, they never met her."

Alex pulled around a fountain that featured a statue of a drunken Bacchus holding a wine glass aloft, he straddled a wine barrel with a spout that flowed a continuous stream of burgundy water into the fountain basin. "Very clever, Alex."

"Wish I could take credit, but it was here when I bought the vineyard. Somebody had a sense of humor."

Alex hopped out of the car and helped Angela out. She was surrounded by three dogs who licked her and vied for her affection. "They're gorgeous. I miss my Dad's Lab, Misty." She bent, allowing them kissing access. "What are they?" She giggled as the dogs jockeyed for head pats. "I've never seen these breeds before."

"*Seduti!*" All three dogs' hinds hit the ground, their eyes locked on Alex. "They're all Italian breeds." He rubbed the head of the sturdy, shaggy-toffee-colored dog. "This is Zabajone, we call her Zaba, and she's a Spinone, an ancient, large breed of hunting dog."

He patted the head of the second dog, short-haired with rusty brown spots and soulful green eyes. "This young lady is Amarena, or just Ama for short. She's a Bracco Italiano, an Italian Pointer. You'll find her to be very girly. She chases birds, squirrels, rabbits, and anything else that moves all day long, but when it comes to taking food from your hand, she's as delicate and mannered as a princess."

He rubbed the short red coat of the third dog. "And last but not least, my compadre, the other lord and master of the house, Tiramisu, whom we call Misu. He's a Segugio Maremmano, an Italian Scenthound. Misu and I stick together; he comes to me with his girl troubles and I confide mine to him."

Angela's laughter brought all three dogs to their feet and they once more resumed licking her hands and turning in circles, begging for attention. "Somehow, I don't imagine you with girl troubles."

"Maybe that's because there are no girls in my life. Or rather, were no girls," he said with a wink. "Look at these traitors, they're all abandoning me for you."

"They just have very good taste. They can spot an easy mark." She continued to scratch and pet as she looked up and took in the stone façade of the house where old vines of bougainvillea climbed stone support columns. Large terracotta pots, overflowing with white roses, flanked the stone steps that led to the front doors. All the woodwork, shutters, window frames, and the arched double-front doors were painted a deep azure blue. Two gnarled old wisteria draped the porch, their yellow blooms contrasting colorfully with the white-stucco exterior and red-tiled roof.

"Alex, this house is beautiful. You mustn't ever change it."

He laughed. "I'm not going to, just a little modern renovation, plumbing, air-conditioning, the boring essentials. I've already redone the kitchen. Maria blesses me regularly for that modernization. But if you like it the way it is, then that's how it will stay."

Heat suffused her cheeks. "I—I didn't mean to tell you what to do with your home. It's not my place…"

Alex placed his finger on her lips, shushing her. "Don't, Angela, please. I want you to feel comfortable here. Besides, I told you I love the worn edges and lived-in quality of the house. I imagine myself living here full-time one day when I'm old and gray."

What would it be like rocking back and forth on the porch swing, holding hands with an older version of Alex? Is that so crazy to think about?

A plump, smiling woman with salt and pepper curls, wearing a crisp white apron over a simple blue knit short-sleeved sweater and a gray A-line skirt, opened the front door and stepped out on the front porch. Effusive in her greeting, she pumped Angela's hand until finally she couldn't contain herself and kissed Angela firmly on both cheeks, hugging her in a bracing bear hug. Angela hugged her back, instantly warming to the motherly woman.

While Alex spoke in Italian with Maria, Angela stole a glance around. As far as the eye could see, vineyards climbed trellised slopes surrounding the property. Silvery leafed olive trees peppered the landscape, providing shade from the bright Tuscan sun. Everywhere Angela looked, a picture-perfect postcard view greeted her.

Alex grabbed their two suitcases from the car and Angela followed him into the expansive entry. Wide, wood-planked floors, polished to a gleaming glow, spanned out to a cozy living room with a massive stone fireplace. The blackened hearth was a reminder of the hundreds of fires that had burned there. Beyond the living room, sliding glass doors opened out to the patio and the gardens beyond.

"I'll take you on a tour later. Our big meal of the day is lunch, and I have a sneaky suspicion Maria's gone all out for you. She's serving al fresco on the patio. Pizza oven is prepped and ready, so we don't have much time. Got to make the pies when the embers are hot."

Making homemade pizza in an outdoor oven in Tuscany? Have I walked onto the cover of *Bon Appetit* magazine? I must be dreaming. First Florence and now the Tuscan countryside.

Alex was fulfilling all those wishes she'd never expected to come true and it scared her. She didn't want her feelings for Alex to be confused with the world he offered, or with their past lives. Her attraction to him wasn't about having a fairytale life. She wanted it to be for all the right reasons. She wanted it to be because kissing him made her knees weak, and looking into his eyes made her skin tingle, and when he touched her, her body lit up like a Christmas tree. But most important, she wanted to be his favorite hello and his toughest goodbye. She knew it was a schoolgirl dream, but it was her dream and she had no intention of settling for less.

She followed him up the stairs, and the feeling washed over her again, raising the hair on her neck and arms, that prickly sensation of having done this before, having been here before. Not only was she repeating what had already happened, but she was repeating all of it with the same man she'd loved in a past life.

Another world and time were barely hidden. She had a feeling that all the memories of her past lives were just out of reach, waiting to be unlocked. She was standing on thin ice, ice that was about to crack. When it gave, would she drown in a river of time without end or would she become strong with the knowledge of it all? Could she right the wrongs of the past?

At the top of the stairs was a hallway. "Here we are." Alex nudged a door open with his shoulder. "My room is just down the hall." He set her suitcase down on the polished wood floor.

Sunshine poured through a vertically paned window, illuminating the yellow-glazed walls. In the center of the room was a heavy wood-framed bed with a rod iron headboard that twisted in a curlicue design. The bed was covered in cream damask linens and multiple pillows of cream and beige velvet, inviting an afternoon nap. A large wardrobe of heavy dark wood rested against one sidewall. On the other side, a door led to what Angela assumed was the bathroom. The room was as tastefully decorated as her room in Alex's Florence apartment. Hanging on the wall were photographs of hillsides with row upon row of vines plush with grapes and olive groves with old-fashioned olive presses. In the photos, the landscape looked much as it would have looked five-hundred years ago and certainly seventy years ago. In the photos of the countryside, time stood still.

She walked to the window and looked out at the terraced hillside, at row upon row of manicured grapevines, which even from this distance, she could see were laden with fruit. "Alex, when is the grape harvest in Chianti?"

"We call it the *vendemmia* and it's usually in September, but it really is at the exact moment when the grapes reach their full ripeness. It can't be more than a few weeks away, a month at the most."

"Sounds amazing. I'd love to see it." Alex stepped up behind her and he took a firm hold of her shoulders. His touch was like a drug and she couldn't stop herself, she relaxed against his chest.

His warm breath sent tingles down her spine. "I have this sneaky suspicion you will."

She felt as if she were melting in his arms. The closeness of his lips to her ear kindled goosebumps and made her knees grow weak. "Really?" Her voice sounded breathless to her ears.

"Really." He turned her, and leaning down, covered her lips with his.

With a will of their own, her arms locked around his neck and she pressed herself fully into his embrace. The heat between them intensified, and she knew when they broke the kiss her cheeks would be as bright as the lights on a Christmas tree. Gasping for breath, their lips parted but their bodies still pressed together.

He kissed the tip of her nose. "We better not keep Maria and Joseph waiting. You did express a passion for pizza."

She was incapable of words and nodded.

"I'll meet you downstairs on the patio in a few minutes." With that he left, closing the door behind him. She wandered to the bed and flung herself backward on it, grinning. *Hell, admit it, you're giddy from that kiss. The truth is, if he'd kept kissing you, he'd be in this bed with you right now. But then we'd miss out on the pizza... and pizza is tantamount to heaven.*

It took all his strength to leave Angela's room. Another second of her body pressed against him and he was sure he wouldn't have been able to stop himself from going further. The kiss, well he was entitled to steal a kiss, no harm done, but he promised to wait for her to make the next move. *Dammit, I'm beginning to regret that promise.* He was so aroused, he jumped into a cold shower before going downstairs.

Later, when they were back downstairs, seated at the table on the patio, he poured two glasses of Prosecco and handed her one. Lifting his glass, he toasted, "To recovering our wedding portrait, solving the Leonardo mystery, and moving beyond the past and into the future."

She clinked her glass to his. "I couldn't agree more." She smiled. Joseph came around the corner carrying a large tray.

Angela's eyes lit up. "The pizzas. I'm starving."

Her childlike enthusiasm tickled him. Alex was glad he'd convinced her to come to the countryside. "Come on." He rose and took her hand pulling her from her chair. "Take your Prosecco." Holding her hand, he led her to the outdoor kitchen. Plumes of smoke rose from the brick pizza oven. Joseph tossed the dough expertly in the air and then laid the flat circle on the floured, smooth-slate counter. "Joseph, *questa è Angela.*"

Joseph, a tall, dark, brawny man, with kindly brown eyes, lifted his hat and bowed his head respectfully. "*Piacere.*"

Angela offered her hand, and Joseph bent to kiss it, leaving a white dusting of flour. She laughed, "I didn't mean for you to kiss my hand, I simply wanted to shake your hand, Joseph."

Alex translated, and they all had a good laugh. Maria joined them, handing Joseph a glass of Prosecco. After another toast, she ladled the sauce on the pizza and smothered it with grated mozzarella. Then with a flourish, she scattered fresh basil leaves and topped it off with a splash of olive oil. Joseph scooped up the pie and popped it in the oven.

"Mmmm… it smells good." Alex turned to her with a grin. "I prefer thin crust over the traditional Neapolitan thick crust. What about you? Do you have a preference?"

"Well, thin is better for my figure," she replied with a roll of her eyes.

Alex eyed her. "I'd say, regardless of thick or thin, your figure looks good to me."

Joseph pulled the slightly charred-edged pizza from the hot oven. Maria sliced it expertly with a wheel and served it with a simple green salad and fresh tomatoes. After they devoured the first course, Joseph returned to the pizza oven with Alex and Angela in tow. He pushed the embers to the center of the oven and placed a grate over the hot coals. On the grate, he cooked a thick Porterhouse steak that Alex explained was a traditional recipe of the region, *Bistecca alla Fiorentina*. The steak was served with spinach sautéed in olive oil with sliced garlic. It was a heavenly meal. For dessert, Maria served a lemon cake, espresso, and an *aperitivo* of Amaro Fernet Branca.

Several glasses of Prosecco had taken effect, and Angela's lids grew heavy. "Alex, would you mind terribly if I took a nap. I can't keep my eyes open."

"That sounds like a great idea. Nothing better than an afternoon siesta." He couldn't contain the fire that lit inside of him at the thought of napping with her. *But, probably not today.*

She stood and, tottering a bit, grabbed the edge of the table. "I think I drank a little too much Prosecco," she giggled.

Alex stood and put his arm around her waist. "Here, let me help you upstairs."

She gave him a silly grin, her adorable dimple denting her cheek. Resisting the urge to cover her lips with his, he led her up the stairs and sat her on the edge of the bed. He pulled the covers back and she fell backward, giggling like a teenager. "I've never gotten this drunk during the day. Her eyes were wide as saucers as she whispered, "It's kind of nice."

He grinned at her adorable expression. *I could seriously get used to this.* Lifting her legs onto the bed, he slipped off her shoes. She wiggled her toes and giggled again. He sighed, wishing he could get into bed with her. Walking to the window, he closed the drapes, blocking the afternoon light from disturbing her while she napped. "Enjoy your rest, Angela." Before he closed the door, he turned on the overhead fan and glanced back at her. Her eyes were closed, and she smiled contentedly.

Back in his room, he lay with his arms behind his head staring up at the revolving fan. Doing absolutely nothing with Angela was better than doing something with any other woman he'd ever known.

The rumble of thunder echoed in the distance, the sound of an afternoon storm moving across the mountains. He wished Angela was lying beside him, wrapped in his arms. It would be so nice to hold her while she slept. He closed his eyes and allowed his imagination to go where his body longed to be.

CHAPTER 12

Montefioralle, Italy
September 30, 1944

The last thing Angela remembered was sinking into the pillows and hearing thunder in the distance. She blew Alex a kiss and ran up a steep hill, knowing he would chase her.

Large drops of rain fell from the black clouds overhead and, within seconds, came the downpour and she was soaked, but she didn't care. Not one bit.

She slipped in the mud and laughed when he caught her. Turning her face toward him, she smiled into the handsome eyes of her beloved. "Gerhard…"

Gerhard touched his finger to her lips. "My darling, Sophia you need to call me Giorgio."

She kissed the tip of his finger. "I'm sorry. Sometimes I forget. Giorgio Bandini, my accountant from Pisa. The man I will marry this weekend in the Church of Santo Stefano."

"The man your protective brothers nearly shot on sight."

"When they heard your accent, what did you expect? If I hadn't gotten down on my knees and pleaded for your life you'd be planted in the vineyard and bearing fruit." Sophia laughed. "Probably you'd have grown into a sweet Riesling."

"Caressing your lips as wine wouldn't have been such an awful fate."

"You're such a romantic, Giorgio. We can thank the Blessed Virgin that she heard my prayers."

After hours of arguing with her brothers, she'd convinced them to let him live. Sophia knew it was the child inside of her that had decided his fate. Neither of her brothers could make their future niece or nephew an orphan. Since then, things had settled into a satisfying routine. She knew her brothers didn't trust him completely, but they'd come to a détente, allowing him the time to prove his loyalty. One misstep and she knew they'd kill him.

First, the marriage legitimizing their child and then Giorgio Bandini, the make-believe accountant from Pisa, would learn the wine business from planting to harvest. There was always need for a strong body to work the vineyard. Sophia was an equal partner with her two bachelor brothers, Stefano and Roberto, and it was accepted that, as her husband, Giorgio would assume his rightful place.

Lifting her face toward the sky, the heavenly rain poured down over her face and body. The warm summer rain soaked her simple, yellow-cotton dress, sculpting it to her full breasts and legs. Gerhard pulled her against him, his lips locking on hers. She knew well the fire in his eyes.

"Sophia, you are a goddess," he murmured. *"Dio, ti voglio.* I want to make love to you on this soft carpet of grass, your body supple and blessed with our child. You are my everything."

She laid her hand on his cheek and caressed his face. "Wait, we're almost to the cave." She took his hand and led him up the hill.

Reaching the top, they were surrounded by mist; heavy clouds floated around them. Her heart pounded from the exertion of the climb and from the anticipation of their lovemaking. To please her brothers, they'd slept apart since their arrival in Montefioralle. Her ever-protective family insisted they demonstrate restraint until their marriage was blessed by the priest in the chapel.

The cave was a refuge, kept secret by generations of Caros. No one knew of its existence except her brothers. In it were large oak barrels, filled with wine. The finest of each year's production, stored in the cool depths to age. Shelves were built into the sides of the cavern and bottles were racked on their sides, some more than fifty years old. The trail up, although steep, was navigable with a cart pulled by a donkey. Several times a year, the Caro family brought down their finest bottles of Chianti to be sold in the marketplace and enjoyed at celebratory events.

Sophia seemed to magically shift a massive boulder to one side. She turned, chuckling at the look of disbelief on Gerhard's face. Someone had devised and executed an engineering feat. No one in the Caro family knew which patriarch had done it, the lore to that riddle had been lost to the generations that followed. But each successive generation had maintained it and kept it secret. Rumors had been passed down through the family that Leonardo da Vinci himself had designed the mechanism. How fitting, if that were true.

Sophia slipped through the narrow opening and Gerhard followed. It was dark, but Sophia knew her way around. The cave had been her secret refuge since childhood. A young girl's sanctuary when her domineering brothers were too much to bear. She struck a match and lit a kerosene lamp; light and shadow crept up the walls, illuminating the interior. As soon as she slid the boulder back into place, the roar of howling wind and pounding rain faded to a whisper.

Gerhard turned in a slow circle, his head raised to the vaulted ceiling his hands smoothing over the white walls that some ingenious Caro had spackled with plaster. It was cool in the cave and Sophia shivered. Gerhard wrapped his arms around her and rubbed her back.

"*Amore mio*, let's get these wet clothes off and lay them out to dry."

When they were nude she led him deeper into the cave to a linen-covered mattress and folded blankets.

"We can wait out the storm here, my love." They lay down, pulling the blankets up around them. She sighed, resting her head on his chest. "I've never brought anyone here. It's an unspoken family rule. You are now privy to the greatest Caro family secret. If my brothers knew, they'd probably cut out your tongue." She giggled. "Or cut off something else."

"I think we can keep this secret between you and me, *cara*. We're going to need that something else. I plan on keeping you barefoot and pregnant." He tilted her chin up, covering her lips with his. His hot breath whispered in her ear. "Let me pleasure you, my love. It's been so long since our bodies have been one." His two-colored eyes twinkled with mischief. "Besides, *cara*, you've already done far too much. Climbing mountains with our child inside. It has to stop."

"Our child will be strong like her father."

"And how do you know it is a she?"

"Does it matter to you?"

"No, of course not. If we made a dozen girls who looked just like you, I'd be more than satisfied."

"A dozen? You are thinking big."

He held her close, his breath caressing her ear. "Yes, but we need more practice. Those brothers of yours are depriving us of what we both crave."

She responded with a sigh and pressed her pelvis firmly against him, eliciting a groan. "After Sunday, we'll never sleep apart again, *amore mio*."

"I could not ask for more, Sophia. You and our child are all I will ever want."

She relished their foreplay, the teasing, the way her resistance melted away when he touched her. He was like a man of the Renaissance, developed in both body and mind. His love made her bold. She fondled him, catching her breath as he hardened against her hand, mesmerized by the desire burning in his eyes.

"As much as I want to pound you into pleasure and hear your screams, *cara*, I will be gentle." Easing into her with slow, penetrating thrusts, he delivered on his promise, bringing them both to satisfaction.

With a deep sigh, she relaxed in the safety of his arms, enjoying the undulations of his body inside of hers. It was moments like these she would cherish when they were both old. She wondered at the strange twist of fate that had brought Gerhard into her life. She tried to remember what life was like before him. *Work and family, but no love or passion.* Gerhard was the lyric to her melody. Together, they made a beautiful song.

She didn't recall falling asleep but woke to Gerhard's kiss. "I'm sure the storm has passed. I think we'd better return before your brothers turn those bloodhounds loose in search of us."

A quick peck on his lips and she was on her feet. Before she pulled her dress over her head, Gerhard knelt before her, caressing and kissing the small bump of pregnancy that protruded from her belly. "I love you, my *piccolina*; I will always keep you safe."

When they emerged from the cave, Gerhard rolled the stone back. It slid easily into place and the opening disappeared as did the secret cave. "Whoever designed this entrance was without a doubt a genius." He took Sophia's hand and they started down the hill.

Sophia breathed in the fresh air. If it wasn't for the war, she couldn't imagine a more perfect life. On Sunday, she would marry the man she loved. Feeling fortunate and blessed, she caressed her stomach where the child of their love grew safely inside of her. She was buoyant, excited for the future, and satiated from their lovemaking.

"Is there anything quite as lovely as the scent of earth and trees after a rainstorm? Except perhaps the perfection of our lovemaking, *amore*. We should walk through the vineyard on our way back. The grape-laden vines will scent the air like perfume. Perhaps the grapes will cover the smell of our sex and my nosy brothers, with their highly developed olfactory skills, won't be able to sniff out our afternoon lovemaking."

Gerhard smiled, squeezing her hand. "Your brothers are just being protective. Our stolen kisses have not gone unnoticed by them. I'd follow you anywhere, but the only perfume I crave is the scent of your body. I can't wait until we marry on Sunday. I want to spend the rest of my life sleeping wrapped around you, *tesoro*."

It was dusk and the light was dwindling. The trail was treacherous, slippery with mud. It wound precipitously down to the vine-covered slopes below. A dogleg turn brought them face to face with a stranger. Gerhard slipped his arm protectively around Sophia's waist, drawing her close to his side.

"Excuse me," said Gerhard. "This is private property. Are you lost?"

Sophia's heart thundered in her chest. The only access to this trail was through the Caro property and there wasn't any reason for anyone outside the family to use it. No trespassing signs were posted at the entrance to the trail and at the front of the property. An alarm went off, a warning that something was wrong. She burrowed deeper into Gerhard's embrace.

The man just stared at Gerhard, grinning. His eyes darted back and forth from Gerhard to her, before settling on her. He pulled a gun from his pocket and pointed it at them. When he spoke, it was not in Italian, but in German. "What a lovely time for an afternoon excursion." He ogled Sophia appreciatively. "And such a sexy, *Fraulein*. It's interesting that your clothes are not wet what with all the rain." He looked up the trail. "Maybe, you snuck away, and those pretty lips sucked *dein schwanz*. Maybe there's a cave up there, somewhere safe out of the rain."

"Get behind me, Sophia," Gerhard whispered. His eyes narrowed and he smiled coldly at the German. When he spoke, it was in the commanding German of a superior. "Your filthy remarks are regrettable. I'd appreciate it if you'd show some respect to my wife. We don't want any trouble. You're obviously a deserter. In my backpack, I have food and some money. Take it and just let us go. This is partisan country and you'd best move on."

"Did you hear that Dietrich? This man is a deserter, too, yet he dares to warn us to move on while he cozies up to some Italian whore."

From behind them came the laughter of another man. "This is no ordinary whore, Franz. This one is a beauty. I don't even care that this asshole already fucked her. I'll take seconds or even thirds."

Gerhard whirled sideways and pushed Sophia behind him. There were two German deserters, one blocking each side of the trail, both men held Lugers aimed at them. "I warn you, not to come any closer."

Sophia shook with fear. From somewhere deep inside of her came an angry voice. "You need to go! My brothers will be worried and come searching for us. Our dogs will hunt you down and my brothers will kill you if you do anything to us."

The man called Franz's eyes blazed. "We will go, but I think not before we've sampled a little taste of what lies beneath your skirt." He moved toward Sophia, menacingly. "It's been a long time since I've fucked anything as beautiful as you. I bet you're a wildcat in the sack." He rubbed his groin. "*Mein schwanz ist schon hart.* I think your boyfriend will enjoy watching you get fucked by two real men."

Gerhard launched himself at the man with a shout of rage that echoed through the mountains. "Don't touch her, *du Schwein!*"

The gun Franz was holding went flying. The two men fell to the ground, punching and kicking. Dietrich shouted, his gun swinging wildly as he tried to shoot Gerhard, but Franz and Gerhard were twisting and rolling in the mud, grunting and growling like lions in a fight to the death. It was impossible for Dietrich to take a clean shot.

Gerhard yelled, "Run Sophia. Don't look back. Just run and scream." But Sophia stood frozen, her eyes searching the ground. "Go!" he shouted.

She turned and started to run, but then she saw it. Stooping, she bent and picked up the gun Franz had dropped. Spinning around, she saw the two men grappling, their faces bruised and bloodied. Suddenly, Franz threw his body sideways freeing himself from the death grip Gerhard had on him. He yelled, "Shoot the bastard, Dietrich. Now!"

Sophia screamed "No!" as a shot rang out. Gerhard lay still. In the growing darkness, she wasn't sure of what she was seeing. She only knew that these monsters were not going to take her without a fight.

With both hands gripping the gun she assumed a shooter's stance and pointed the gun at Dietrich and before he could take aim, she shot him through the head. He fell backward. She turned the gun on Franz, and then she heard dogs barking and men shouting her name. Her brothers were coming. She yelled over her shoulder, "Stefano, Roberto, help me!"

Franz heard them too. He charged, knocking her down, and ran past her calling her a bitch. He'd knocked the wind out of her, and she lay on the ground trying to catch her breath. She ignored the pain gripping her abdomen, all she wanted was to get to Gerhard. She dragged herself to him and placed her ear to his chest. The faintest of heartbeats echoed through her. She touched his body and felt wetness. Raising her fingers, she could see they were red with blood. She sat up and gently raised his head into her lap. "Gerhard, darling, can you hear me?"

His eyes blinked open. She could barely hear him whisper her name. "Sophia, *amore mio*, I'm so proud of you. You are the bravest woman… I've…" He struggled to breathe.

"Gerhard, my love, hold on, please. Help is coming." She could hear the dogs barking, running up the trail.

"It's too late, love, please let me speak. Know that I loved you more than anything in my life. I only wish I could have seen our child… please, forgive me for not being here with you."

"Gerhard no…" She couldn't stop the sobs or the anger that flooded her. The thought of living her life without him was unbearable.

"Keep the painting, Sophia. Please keep it for our daughter. It is the only gift I will ever be able to give her. Promise me?"

"I don't care about the damn painting. I only want you, Gerhard."

"Promise me, Sophia." His eyes closed, and she knew she was losing him.

She bent her forehead to his, her tears falling in rivulets down his face. "I promise, my love. Promise me, you'll wait for me."

His last words were a whisper. "I will wait for you always."

Alex's eyes flew open.

Had he heard a scream? Thunder rolled across the valley, bringing with it the sound of rain slapping against the roof. The drapery billowed, like a sail filling with wind; he jumped up, closing the French doors.

Then he heard it again, a woman crying.

He raced from the room, running down the hallway and threw open Angela's door. He stood a moment in the doorway, adjusting his eyes to the darkness. Angela lay on the bed thrashing and crying. His heart twisted with pain. The rain was coming down in torrents, the drapes blew like ghosts in flight, and he rushed to secure the French doors against the onslaught. He sat on the edge of the bed and gathered her into his arms. "Angel, wake up, it's just a bad dream, honey." He rubbed her back with a soothing hand and caressed her hair, calming her with his whispered reassurances. "It's okay, Angela. You're safe."

She was sobbing, her words muffled in his shoulder. "It was horrible. I killed a man, and someone killed you. I lost you again."

"Honey, no one killed me, I'm here. Alive. It's just a nightmare. You're not losing me."

She pulled away, searching his eyes. "No, Alex, it happened. I saw it, all of it. I don't mean he killed you, he killed Gerhard. On a mountain, somewhere, I'm not sure where. But, this means—twice—it's happened twice. You've been murdered in two of your past lives. And I've had to watch you die. Don't you see? I can't let that happen again."

"See what? What are you talking about?"

"It's me, Alex. Every time you're with me. Don't you see?" Her hands rested on either side of his face. "We're cursed, Alex, wrong for each other. We only bring each other death and destruction. It's going to happen again. I feel it. I need to get away from you, far away. Maybe then it won't happen. Maybe I can stop it. But the thought of leaving you devastates me."

"You're not going anywhere, and we're not cursed," he said placing his hands over hers. "This is ridiculous, you have nothing to do with this, Angel. Just because something happened in another time, another life, doesn't mean it has to happen again. I'm not letting you go."

He wrapped his arm around her and urged her to lie back down. He soothed her with whispered endearments and soft kisses on her forehead and cheeks. He continued to kiss away her tears as her breathing returned to normal. After a while, she sighed, snuggling into his embrace. Their arms and legs, entwined, as they lay together on the bed. The only sounds were their intermingling breaths and the rain lashing against the windows...

He was having trouble controlling his desire for her. Her body against his was getting the best of him. He held her gaze and saw the vulnerability in her eyes. Her lips were so close. She was feeling it, too. He could feel her desire in the way she looked at him. The way she trembled against him. She was fighting the same battle...

He was tired of fighting it. Sick of battling against the tide when all he wanted was to be carried out to sea. To lose himself in her. To feel the waves of passion roll over him. He'd wanted it from the first moment he'd laid eyes on her. Was that less than a week ago? It felt like a lifetime. Hell, it felt like three lifetimes. *I don't care anymore about the promise I made to wait for her to make the first move. Some promises are meant to be broken.*

He leaned down and claimed her mouth. His lips blazed over hers with a hunger that surprised him. It burned through him consuming whatever doubts he had. At first, he felt her hesitancy… Even so, her lips remained locked with his, supple and yielding, finally melting into passion. Her kiss told him she wanted him as much as he wanted her. They broke for air, gasping.

He could have stopped it there, like he had every time before, but he didn't. His lips touched her forehead, brushing her temple, filling her ear with his warm breath, and then his tongue traced a path down her neck, her scent intoxicating him. He'd never felt the need to possess someone so desperately. This time he wouldn't stop until she was completely his. As far as he was concerned, he could remain in this bed with her for the rest of his life.

She sighed, fingers in his hair, arching her back, opening to his hunger. Outside, the storm raged, but it was nothing compared to the passionate storm within him. Angela was wrong, they *were* destined to be together. He was crazy about her.

"Alex… we shouldn't—I'm afraid… your life."

"Like hell we shouldn't. There is no power on earth that can stop us." Her nipples strained against her shirt pressing into his chest, and she moaned, a siren song calling to him. His heart pounded, desire pumping through his veins. He unbuttoned her blouse and with a flick of his thumb and forefinger released her bra clasp. Her breasts spilled from their confinement. Her sighs melted into moans when he filled his hands with the weight of both breasts and ran his tongue around her nipples. "God, you're beautiful, baby."

Lightning struck somewhere in the distance and a pellucid, white light filled the room, but all he could see were her eyes warm with anticipation, her lips rosy from being kissed. Currents of energy reverberated between them, charging the atmosphere.

The crash of thunder that followed seemed to release something inside of her. She wrapped her arms around him, trembling against him. Pulling away, he wrenched his shirt over his head. All he could think about was her body against his. Her eyes swept over him with a look of admiration, supercharging his desire. Then, like a blind person trying to discover the shape and form of something, she ran her hands delicately over his chest causing his muscles to tense. He didn't move. It was so erotic, this slow dance of discovery. Letting her lead, he groaned as her long, slender fingers travelled over his shoulders, down his back, her gaze locked on his.

"I've wanted to touch you for so long." Her whispered words drew him in like a magnet.

He lay back down beside her and skimmed his hand from the delicate hollow of her throat over her breast, and down to her flat abdomen. He swallowed, drinking in her beauty. "I know I promised to wait for you to make the first move," he began in a raspy voice, "but so much has happened in such a short time. I can't stop what I'm feeling for you, Angela."

"I don't want you to stop... I don't think I've ever wanted anything so much. It's as if my body feels alive for the first time. I've been fighting this for so many reasons, but I don't want to fight anymore. I want to know where this takes us. What it feels like to be completely one with you..."

It was such a sweet sentiment, mirroring what was in his heart. His tours of duty had given him strength and toughness beyond his years, his career had given him success and a measure of satisfaction, but from the moment he met Angela, he knew his life had changed forever.

Being with her, meant more to him than anything he'd ever experienced. Lying next to her, holding her, kissing her, loving her was all that mattered. Somehow, he'd get them through this toxic past life syndrome and settle the accounts once and for all. They'd find that damn painting together and solve the mystery. History didn't have to repeat itself, the chain could be broken. Somehow, he'd change the outcome. Then he'd spend the rest of his life with this amazing woman.

"Angel, I want you with me. I have no intention of not making this last." He pulled her in until every part of her touched every part of him.

Her giggle delighted him. "I can feel you throbbing against me."

"I can't control that part of my anatomy around you." His laughter rumbled in his chest.

"I kind of hope you stay that way."

"Be careful what you hope for." He kissed her slow and deep. For the moment, he controlled his desire, savoring the sweet longing building inside of him. Tasting her silky skin with his lips and tongue, stroking her with his hands, he wanted to imprint his touch on every part of her luscious body. Down he went, eliciting whimpers of desire from her as he made his way to the source of her pleasure and felt it swell beneath his tongue. Her moans grew louder as he pressed his face deeper into her. He was more than content to worship her with his mouth until she came. This part of the promise he intended to keep. He wanted her to say it, say she couldn't live another minute without him inside of her.

When he thought nothing could be better than what he was feeling, her back bowed and her body stiffened, trembling beneath his lips. "Alex—I want you."

He lapped at her, completely lost in pleasing her. When her orgasm finally ceased her body relaxed in contentment. She flung her arms above her head, sighing. "My God, Alex… I… I've never felt anything like that."

His lips travelled the length of her, tasting every inch. "Do you want more, baby?"

Her body quivered, shuddering. "Yes… I want you inside me."

He could hear the need in her voice. His own body was taut with desire. Her sighs of pleasure, melodious and sensual, sent his pulse racing. He could barely restrain himself from plunging inside her. The rain drumming on gutters, eaves, and roof, rhythmically echoed the pounding of their hearts.

Bracing his weight, he rolled on top of her. She'd given him the words he'd been waiting for and it meant more than he could have imagined. Pent-up need made him rock hard. He was afraid of hurting her, but when he pushed slowly in her hips rose and enfolded him in their sweet depths, taking him deep, making them both gasp.

"Angel," he groaned. "It shouldn't feel this good, baby, I won't last."

She smiled, undulating beneath him. "I want you to think of this, every time you look at me."

"Trust me, you have nothing to worry about." He rhythmically thrust inside of her, making sure he hit her clit with every penetration. He was so close to coming and, one thing was for sure, he wasn't coming without her.

Their bodies were soaked with sweat when he felt her nails dig into his back and heard her cry out. The precious sound of her tipping over again sent him over the top and he plunged deep, stiffening with his release.

Enfolding her in his arms, he lay back, holding her close as his heart beat returned to normal. His hand smoothing up and down her back, eliciting contented sighs from her. He smiled and kissed the top of her head. Sleeping through the night with her wrapped in his arms was something he could get used to. Something he wanted more than anything.

When he woke, the rumble of thunder was far in the distance. The storm had moved on after providing an unforgettable backdrop to his and Angela's first time together. Remembering their lovemaking sent a jolt through his system, short-circuiting his ability to think of anything other than the passion she'd sparked in him. What he hadn't expected was discovering a sensual temptress beneath her calm and shy exterior. If it weren't for the nagging complaints of his stomach he'd be happy to stay in bed with her for the rest of the day. He couldn't wait to step into the fire again and feel her flames envelop him.

The house was quiet, slumbering as if in deference to their rest. Their lovemaking had seemed not of this world. It crossed his mind, they'd been lovers before in past lives, but the only life that mattered to him was this one. All he knew was she'd made every part of him sing with satisfaction.

Angela slept secure in his arms as he studied the faint, dark circles shadowing her eyes. He'd been demanding, exhausting her with a craving that seemed to have no end. He'd finally let her sleep in the early hours of the morning. Even now he was tempted to awaken her with his hunger. He'd have to be patient and content himself with holding her for a few moments more.

Angela opened her eyes and tried to orient herself to her surroundings. She was in her room, technically Alex's guest room at Casa del Sole. Kicking free of the sheet, she realized she was nude. A flood of sensual images bombarded her, of Alex and her doing things she'd never thought herself capable of. They'd loved each other in every way possible and each time he'd brought her to bliss. Was it all a dream?

She shifted in bed and the sweetest ache she'd ever experienced tingled between her legs. No, not a dream. Dreams don't leave your body feeling as though it's been through a sensual marathon. A sleepy smile and a purr of contentment escaped.

She stretched, her back arching like a cat, and then peered over the side of the bed. Scattered about the floor was their clothing. Clothing that had been tossed without care as to where it might land. The evidence was clear, as were the vivid visions of yesterday and last night. History had repeated itself. Lovers in past lives, she and Alex were lovers once more.

She didn't want to think about how those two past lives ended in tragedy. Right, now her foremost concern was Alex.

What do I say when I see him? How should I behave?

She was so absorbed in figuring that out, she didn't hear the sound of rushing water coming from the bathroom. She sat up trying to recall what she said to him in the throes of passion.

This is a hell of a time to be having amnesia.

The bathroom door opened to a naked Alex vigorously towel drying his hair. She loved the deep, chestnut color of the thick waves, so incongruous to the rugged planes of his handsome face. Their eyes met and a huge smile spread across his face. "Well, good morning, beautiful."

"Good morning," she squeaked out. *I sound like an idiot.* She couldn't stop gaping at his gorgeous body. She must have been blushing because she could feel the heat rising up her neck to her face. But, wow, was he beautiful. It was the first time she'd gotten a good look at him.

Seeing him naked, freshly scrubbed, a man in the full sense of the word, was arousing. Suddenly she was having difficulty breathing and her body heated like a kettle on a stove. Any minute she expected steam to come out of her ears and her lips to purse together in a whistle.

He dropped the towel at the foot of the bed clearly enjoying her discomposure. Then, like a tiger, he pounced, pulling her beneath him, her body and his aligned in all the right places. "Shall we pick up where we left off?" He wiggled his eyebrows in a mock lecherous look.

She giggled at his antics. "I... I... need to use the restroom." She covered her mouth with her hand before he could land a kiss on her. She squirmed from his grasp, jumping out of the bed and taking the sheet with her. She wasn't about to kiss Prince Charming with morning mouth.

His laugh rumbled from his chest as he tucked his muscled arms behind his head and crossed his ankles. He was perfectly relaxed, naked as a jaybird. "Take your time, Angel, I'm not going anywhere."

As she fled, his words followed her. "No sense covering what I've already seen."

Blowing out a breath, she closed the door behind her, pressing her back against it. Her knees shook, and her heart beat *incalzando*, faster and louder until she sank dizzily to the floor.

Be still my heart.

Even the battle scars on his leg, arm, and ribcage didn't detract from his perfection, but rather enhanced her attraction to him.

In her art historian mind, she compared Alex's masculine beauty to Michelangelo's sculptures. Alex was lean and muscular, perfectly proportioned, but she'd already known that.

She needed to get her act together, regain her composure. One night does not a forever make. Forever?

Did I just presume that a permanent relationship with Alex was possible? Pull it together, girl. What you experienced was a mutual lust. We've been working shoulder to shoulder, infatuation was bound to develop.

Fact: The man is, for all intent and purposes, your boss.
Fact: Love affairs in the workplace rarely work out.
Fact: I'm scared to death of losing him.
Supernatural Fact: We were lovers in past lives.

Propping her elbows on her knees, she planted her chin on her palms and contemplated her delicious predicament. Alex clearly had his life ordered in a manner that worked for him. Single with no strings attached. Luxury apartment in Florence, fancy cars, country getaway. Exciting job that took him around the globe for a hefty fee and an extravagant expense account.

She, on the other hand, was just getting past the typical "starving" student mode. She'd already blown her first "real" career job. Well, that wasn't her fault since her boss was a lecherous snake. She had maybe a thousand bucks in the bank. And no place to live. She could move back home to her Dad's, but what would she do there, other than work at the local library?

Once the mystery is solved and we find the da Vinci... what happens after that? If we were lovers in our past lives, does that mean that solving this mystery will sever our connection?

She hadn't thought of that before. She had no idea what would happen after... She didn't want to lose him, but what if she did? What if everything fizzled out when the "excitement" of the mystery surrounding them was solved? Did the possibility of becoming an actual couple after this case even exist?

She shook her head and pushed her insecurities to the back of her mind. Hoisting herself up from the floor, she turned on the shower, needing to wash away her negative thoughts.

She emerged from the bathroom fresh from her shower with a towel snugly wrapped around her. Alex, as promised, hadn't moved. He just grinned at her. "Come here."

"Is that an order, boss?"

"Call it whatever you want. I just want you here." His sexy tone vibrated through her.

She sat on the edge of the bed and tried not to look below his waist. "Is there something I can get you?" *Jeez, you sound like a breathless Marilyn Monroe.*

"You can stop pretending that yesterday and last night never happened."

She sighed. "I know it happened and I loved it. We both did. There's been a fire burning between us since we met. Now that we've extinguished it, we can return to finding what we came here to find, a missing da Vinci."

She tried to read Alex's face. His eyes held a dangerous gleam. "I'm going to pretend I didn't hear that. I haven't extinguished a goddamn thing." He pulled her down to him and crushed his mouth to hers. He didn't let go of her until every muscle in her body went lax. When he broke the kiss, he held her firmly against him, nibbling on her lips.

"I'm starving, baby, and I need to replenish my strength. Get dressed and meet me downstairs for breakfast. We have a busy day. He punctuated his statement with one final kiss. He released her and jumped out of bed, scooping up his clothes from the floor. Without a thought to his nudity, he strolled out the door.

CHAPTER 13

Montefioralle, Italy
Present day
August 10

Angela pushed the swinging butler's door open to the kitchen. She was greeted by the fragrance of basil, marjoram, oregano, thyme, and freshly ground coffee. Maria stood at the stove, one arm wrapped around a large metal bowl, her other hand holding a whisk as she whipped the eggs into a frothy foam. Alex sat at the kitchen table reading a newspaper with a large steaming mug of coffee before him. The moment she walked through the door he looked up. His smile like sunshine bathed her in warmth.

"*Buongiorno,* beautiful."

"*Buongiorno,* Alex. *Buongiorno,* Maria."

"*Buongiorno, Signorina* Angela"

"Come sit, baby. I'll get you some coffee." Alex stood and pulled a chair out for her.

"Thank you. Can I do anything to help?"

Alex returned with the coffee pot and filled her mug, then set the pot on a ceramic trivet on the table. "You sure can. You can sit here, drink coffee, and keep me company. Believe me just looking at you makes the day better." His strong hands rubbed her shoulders massaging them, and he bent and kissed her neck, breathing her in. His breath in her ear sent a shiver down her spine. "You smell delicious. If Maria wasn't here, I might've had to make love to you on this table. Another time, perhaps," he whispered, shattering her composure.

There was no doubt about it, their relationship had changed... intensified. The pulse of energy when he touched her had only grown stronger, his gaze smoldered hotter.

She looked up, just in time to receive the press of his lips on hers.

"Hmm, now that's the best way to start a day." He pulled back from their kiss and sat beside her.

"You said we have a busy day today. Care to share what you have in mind?" She struggled to calm her racing heart.

"I've been thinking about that déjà vu feeling we have about Montefioralle, and that dream you had yesterday."

She shuddered. "It wasn't just a dream, Alex, it was real. I know it happened."

"I've been privy to your visions, they pack quite a punch. Although…" He grinned. "I kind of like what happened after you had the bad dream…"

"I do too…"

"That's what I hoped you'd say because I sure as hell don't regret one minute." He leaned in and growled in her ear. "I couldn't get enough of you last night, baby."

"Is it warm in here?" She fanned herself as a flash of heat crept up her shoulders, neck, and face.

"No, I think it's quite comfortable." His face broke into a wide grin, making her shift in her seat.

"I'm sure you do." She resisted the urge to reach under the table. Her impish side wanted to wipe the cocky look off his face with just one brush of her hand on his inner thigh. She heard the siren's call of her past life— Sophia—guiding her wanton thoughts.

"We've got a lot of footwork to do today," he told her. "First stop is the town hall. I want to check out the history of Casa del Sole, who owned it and when. We can also check birth and death records for Montefioralle in Greve. It's about a thirty-minute walk uphill from Greve to Montefioralle. The church of Santo Stefano, in the old village, is the highest point and I'm sure they have records going back hundreds of years. On the way back, we can check out the old cemetery. Then lunch and a bottle of Chianti."

She laughed, "You certainly know how to balance work with pleasure."

"I think you'll discover I'm an expert at that. And then…"

"And then… what?"

"And then I'm going to carry you upstairs to the bedroom, Scarlett, for our afternoon siesta." He winked and tweaked a pretend mustache.

Angela burst into laughter.

"Like my Rhett Butler impression?"

"I wouldn't quit your day job if I were you."

He chuckled, tapping her nose.

Maria arrived with a bright yellow frittata that looked as if she'd plucked the sun from the sky and offered it up for breakfast. It was layered with zucchini and cheese and crowned with fresh basil and parmesan. A basket filled with Italian breads, and a plate filled with an assortment of cheeses and a pot of plum preserves followed.

"*Grazie, Maria. La seconda cosa migliore al mondo è la sua cucina.*"

"*Signor Alex, sei proprio un diavolo.*" She left the kitchen shaking her head and giggling.

"What did you say to her? I think she called you a devil." Angela lifted a slice of the fluffy egg and set it on his plate then lifted a second slice for herself.

"Just that the second-best thing in the world is her cooking."

"What's the first?" She smothered a crust of bread with plum preserves.

"Making love to you."

"Alex!"

"What?" He stuffed a forkful of frittata in his mouth.

"I suppose she's used to you bringing strange women home for the weekend."

"She's not used to anything of the kind. I've never brought anyone here before. This place is sacred to me. I've never wanted anything to tarnish what I feel when I'm here."

A tingle ran up her spine, making her quiver. *Does he have any idea what he does to me when he says things like that?*

His expression grew serious and he leaned forward, clasping her hand in his. "For someone who can see her past lives, you sure can't see the truth of your current one. I want more than a brief affair with you."

"I guess I'm just worried that our past lives might be exerting an undue influence over our current feelings."

"Hey, where's that tough woman who didn't let a slimeball like Scordato get the best of her? The strong woman who, despite having these over-whelming visions, has the presence of mind to figure out what they mean? Where's the confident woman willing to risk all to solve a five-hundred-year-old mystery? Or is it that you just don't want me?"

Tears blurred her vision. "Stop it, Alex. What do you want me to say? That I can't live without you? That I'll give you my heart and if you break it, my bad?"

Alex stood abruptly, upending his chair. He pulled Angela out of her seat, causing her own chair to topple over, and wrapped his arms around her. She couldn't have escaped if she wanted to. Which she didn't.

"Look at me," he ordered in a low voice. She tried to look away, but he tilted her chin up, forcing her to look him in the eye. "The truth is, I'm in deep. Do you understand what I'm saying? You're the one who might break *my* heart. But I'm willing to risk it, because… Hell, I'm already in love with you."

Her eyes widened at his declaration and she trembled.

"And fuck the past and whatever happened before. If it brought you to me in this lifetime, then I'm grateful, but the past has nothing to do with how I feel about you."

Her throat constricted, swallowing whatever words she wanted to say. A single tear made its way down her cheek.

He cursed again and kissed the tear away, and then he kept going, planting kisses across her forehead, cheeks, chin, until he claimed her lips with a kiss that made the ground give way beneath her.

When they broke apart, she found her voice. "I'm so crazy about you— it takes my breath away."

"Good. Because you do the same to me." He dove in for one more quick kiss then righted her chair. "My lady, please sit and let's finish eating. Although I could feast myself on your lips and body for days, right now, I'm in need of another form of sustenance."

She nodded. It was all she could manage, she was still wobbly from his kiss.

They dug into the frittata with gusto. The melding of sautéed onions with the eggs, zucchini, basil, and cheese elicited moans of delight from Angela that made him regret choosing food over sex. He'd have to remedy that later.

"I'll have to ask Maria to give me this recipe. Maybe even I could master this one." Angela wiped her plate with a small crust of bread. Her phone vibrated on the table. She glanced at it. "Darn it! It's my dad. I forgot to call him after we left Florence."

"You better answer it."

"Hi, Dad." She listened. "I'm fine. I'm sorry I didn't check in." She nodded. "Yes, everything's great with my new job…"

Alex watched her intently. She blew him a kiss. "My boss is amazing."

He grinned.

"Scordato contacted you?" She glanced at Alex, her eyes filled with worry. Alex had already been attacked by the bastard's minions in Florence, and that was one time too many. If Scordato was trying to hurt Angela's dad, Alex would do everything in his power to protect him and Angela, painting or no painting.

She listened for several protracted minutes, her hand gripping the phone. "If he calls again, tell him nothing about where I am... yes, just have him mail the check to you." She nodded. "I'll email you and fill you on what's been happening... I know long distance calls are expensive... Give Misty a big hug from me... I love you, too, Dad," she said in a thick voice.

Angela laid the phone on the table and looked at Alex.

He didn't say a word, just searched her face and waited.

She took a deep breath. "Scordato called my dad, said I'd quit and left on bad terms. Just to worry him. Even though I'd already told Dad about working with you."

She stood and began to pace. "He played the big man and told my dad he wanted to send me my last check and asked him where he should send it. My dad said he didn't know, that this was all news to him. I told him... well, you heard the rest. Dad is no fool, he would never say anything to Scordato."

She continued pacing. Alex got up from his chair and stood in her path. "It's okay. I'll contact the local authorities in your hometown to keep an eye on your dad. The board fired him. He just wants to fuck with us. He knew we were in Florence and he probably knows we're here."

"Why are you so calm?" Her lips were trembling, her eyes teary. "He already tried to hurt you once. What if he tries again?"

"If he tries again, I'll deal with him. I have resources, too, Angela." Alex enfolded her in his embrace, holding her tight, he kissed her cheek. "The sooner we find that painting the sooner we can move on with our lives and be rid of that bastard."

"They're in Montefioralle, at the detective's vineyard."

Scordato opened an app on his phone and tapped a telephone number. He waited while the tracking technology updated. In less than a minute, a map popped up with a blinking red dot indicating the approximate location of the cell belonging to Angela Renatus. Scordato was holed up at his cousin Enrico's farmhouse in Castellina, a perfect base for their operations.

"They haven't moved from the house since they got there."

A lewd grin spread across Enrico's face. "I'll bet my new rifle, he's riding her hard. *"Non mi dispiacerebbe proprio fotterla!"*

"All in due time, *cugino.*" The cousins were as different as night to day. Whereas he'd pursued fame and notoriety in the art world, Enrico had risen through the ranks in the underworld. But they both shared the same appetites when it came to women.

Scordato sipped his coffee, frustrated that the two goons they hired in Florence had failed. No matter, they were in familiar territory now, where he'd spent his childhood. He knew the area like the back of his hand. Soon he would implement his plan.

"Tell me, Alberto, have you figured out how we keep the painting without the Uffizi making claim to it?" His cousin stood at the stove frying pancetta and eggs.

"Six months from now, when this has all blown over and Caine and the girl are just a distant memory, you and I will find the painting in an old farmhouse somewhere in Tuscany," Scordato replied, taking another sip of coffee.

Enrico set two steaming plates down on the table.

"Hmm, smells good, I'm starving." Scordato dug into the hearty breakfast, slicing into the crisp pancetta.

"But, what about the Uffizi? Won't they make a claim?" his cousin asked, sitting across from him.

"No. During my research at the Uffizi, last summer, I discovered that when Gerhard left with the painting, he either took or destroyed the records that listed it as part of their collection. They can't make a claim. They have no proof or records and the only people who ever knew of its existence are dead." His eyes glimmered with malice. "Or soon to be dead. Of course, none of this would be possible without Lorenzo Medici's cover-up."

"What do you mean?"

"Medici took the secret of the painting's provenance to his grave as did Leonardo Da Vinci."

"Why do you think they did that?"

"Family alliances. Giuliano had been promised in marriage to someone else. Why rock the boat with a broken promise and an announcement of marriage to someone else when Giuliano was dead? As for Leonardo, that's easy. Lorenzo must have agreed to guarantee Fioretta and Giuliano's son would be raised a Medici if Leonardo kept his silence about the painting. It must have been gratifying to the Maestro to see Fioretta's son become a Pope."

"But why wouldn't Lorenzo just burn the painting and erase it from history?"

"A sacrilege in Lorenzo's mind. Besides, he'd witnessed Savonarola's bonfire of the vanities and seen enough things of beauty go up in smoke. He was a collector of art not a destroyer of it."

Enrico dragged his bread across his plate sopping up remnants of yellow yolk. "And what about the German industrialist?"

"Your connections are good?"

"*Si*, always."

"I think a terrible accident will soon befall my German friend. I take it the price to make it happen is negotiable?"

Enrico sipped his coffee, his eyes hard as steel. "Only death is non-negotiable."

CHAPTER 14

Montefioralle, Italy
Present day
August 10

Alex drove the Ferrari over a dusty winding road, his fingers confidently maneuvering the gear shifts. He easily accelerated through the curves, putting the muscle car through its paces. Angela stole a glance at him. He wore aviator sunglasses and a cocksure smile. He was undeniably attractive, and his self-assurance buoyed her. Pulling into a small parking structure, he zipped the car into a space between a concrete pillar and a wall. He set the parking brake and turned to her. "You can breathe again."

"Smart ass," she grumbled, unclicking her seatbelt. "I swear you enjoy seeing me scared to death. You drive like an Italian… crazy."

"I was hoping you'd grab hold of me, squeeze my leg or something." He looked at her over the rim of his sunglasses and winked.

She loved his playfulness. He had a *joie de vivre* that was contagious, especially to a bookworm who'd never stepped foot out of the United States until now.

"If I squeezed your leg, you probably would have crashed your shiny new toy."

"Yeah, but it would have been worth it." He swung his tall frame out of the car, walked to her side, and opened the door. "Come on, let's go find Sophia and Gerhard."

The main square of Greve, in Chianti, wasn't square at all; it was oddly triangular shaped. The central marketplace, the Piazza Matteotti, was filled with tourists, easily identifiable by their cameras and backpacks. On all three sides of the square was a portico where artisan shops, boutiques, and restaurants were open and bustling with shoppers. They passed a window where hundreds of dried salamis, legs of prosciutto, and other aged meats temptingly swayed overhead. The heady scent of the spiced meats wafted through the door.

"Antica Macelleria Falorni is the oldest butcher shop in all of Tuscany. They've been in this spot since 1729," Alex said proudly, as if he and the butchery shared a common history.

"Oh, I could definitely get into trouble in there." Angela sniffed the air as if in a perfumery.

"We'll stop on the way out of town and load up. I gave Joseph and Maria the night off. I thought it would be nice to have the house to ourselves. We'll have lunch in Montefioralle and for supper we can snack on wine, salami, prosciutto, and cheese, in bed if you like." His teasing grin promised pleasures beyond salami and cheese.

There he goes again. Making my heart race as fast as that Ferrari of his.

She couldn't see his eyes behind his sunglasses, the best thing to do with his flirtatious teasing was to give as good as she got. "That sounds like a great idea. I love the idea of getting cracker and cheese crumbs on my ass."

He leaned in, his lips to her ear. "Don't worry, I'll be happy to lick them off."

Alex had quickly become an expert at throwing her off balance. His words travelled through her like oil through an engine. "You've put my fears to rest."

He laughed wholeheartedly. "Come on, baby, you're stealing all of my fun. Getting a rise out of you, seeing you blush, makes me want to slay dragons."

"I guess you'll just have to get your jollies elsewhere."

"Nah, I'll figure out another way to get to you."

"You just work on that, boy scout, maybe you'll come up with something. Try rubbing two pieces of flint together."

"Oh, rest assured, I will. I can think of a couple of other things I can't wait to rub together…"

That hit the mark. She was glad she was wearing sunglasses too.

Alex led them to a Romanesque building. Climbing the steps, they entered the offices of the mayor. While Alex questioned the receptionist about where they could find official land transfer records for the Chianti region, Angela studied the vaulted ceiling with its groin arches that rested on square piers. The piers were frescoed with everyday scenes of workers hoeing the fields and picking grapes.

She walked to the mullioned windows and gazed out, contemplating how quickly everything in her life had changed. The nightmare visions from yesterday and the day before had crossed the line between reality and dream.

The past was catching up with the present and it scared her. Watching the men she'd loved in her past lives get murdered wasn't something she wanted to witness in this lifetime. Alex might believe he was invincible, but she was scared for his life. Both Giuliano and Gerhard had been murdered just when love and happiness were within reach. Now, she and Alex were treading the same ground and following in their footsteps. She took a deep breath, calming her racing heart.

"Let's go babe, we're heading to the public library next."

"What's at the library?"

"They built a new state-of-the-art database uploaded with the public records from all the surrounding regions."

The building sign read *Biblioteca Comunale*. In her wildest imaginings, Angela couldn't have imagined the modern structure that had been built in this most ancient of towns. The library was architecturally stunning, built solidly on travertine blocks on which rested a terracotta structure wrapped in parallel grooved lines that appeared to emulate grape vines.

Alex presented the librarian with a note from the mayor requesting that he and Angela be allowed to view the post-unification municipal records. Alex's friendship with the mayor and contribution to his campaign had paid off. Normally it would have required permission and an appointment made with the Soprintendenza Archivistica di Firenze to access the computer system and records. Alex was an expert at getting around red tape. He brushed off Angela's amazement. "In my business, the less trail of inquiry you leave behind, the better."

"But avoiding government protocol and sidestepping procedure can get you in trouble."

He grinned. "I won't tell if you don't."

Sitting shoulder to shoulder, they booted up a computer in the technology center. Alex clearly had experience in trolling government records. In minutes they were looking at real estate sales records going back two hundred years.

"I'm going to go right for the target, Casa del Sole." The computer whirred and instantly produced everything pertaining to Alex's property. His brows knit together. "It looks like I bought the property from Fioretta Rossi. I knew I didn't recall the surname Caro being in the transaction. But the name Fioretta has to be more than a coincidence."

Angela couldn't hide her disappointment. "Something's wrong, I feel it. Go back further. Can you access property taxes?"

Alex's fingers danced over the keys. "Wow!"

Angela moved closer to the screen. As far back as records were kept, the taxes had been billed and paid by various heads of the Caro family. "So, who's Fioretta Rossi?"

"That's easy to find out." He opened the contact list on his phone and dialed. Angela studied his face while he talked to someone on the other end of the line. When he hung up, he surprised her with a kiss on the lips. "Fioretta Rossi is Sophia Caro's daughter. She lives in Rome. My realtor's texting her phone number to me. He looked at his watch, we can call her after dinner."

Angela swallowed a lump in her throat. "It's all true then. Sophia had a baby girl and named her Fioretta after the painting. She must have done it in honor of Gerhard. My visions and the nightmares are all true. In 1944 you were murdered, and I killed the man who shot you." She reached for his hand and laid it against her face.

"Alex, what if we're on a collision course and history intends to repeat itself? The thought of me being the cause of something happening to you…" Her voice broke, she couldn't finish the sentence.

"We need to find the painting, baby, can't you see that's what stops the top from spinning? If we find the painting, the dead will be satisfied, and we'll be free."

"You don't know that. Maybe this is all a cosmic trap and you and I are just pawns. Besides, I haven't a clue where the painting is."

"It's going to come to you—you're going to remember."

"I'm afraid to remember."

"I don't think you have a choice." He leaned in and kissed her, softening the truth of his words.

His forehead touched hers. "I know it's hard baby, but we're so close to finding that painting. Once we find it everything will be all right. I know it."

She nodded, desperately wanting to believe him.

He stood and pulled her up with him. "Come on, next stop the church of Santo Stefano and the old cemetery."

The well-used trail wound through groves of trees where sunlight dappled the ground. Alex and Angela wandered in and out of light and shadow. When the trail was wide enough, Alex walked beside her and held her hand, otherwise, he led, and she followed. It was about a twenty-minute hike to the ancient hilltop village of Montefioralle. Surrounded by stone walls, they entered through one of the original four Medieval gates into narrow alleys lined with tiny stone houses. Flower-filled pottery graced the entrances and window boxes exploded with red geraniums. The streets were paved with stone that had been polished by nearly a thousand years of footsteps.

Angela couldn't help but think about a pregnant Sophia making this climb with Gerhard and walking these same cobbled stones. At the highest point of the village was the Chiesa di Santo Stefano.

Arriving at the top of a stone stairway, they paused to catch their breaths and looked up at the edifice. It wasn't impressive from the outside, in fact, it was rather plain.

"It looks new. It echoes Gothic architecture, but without the pomp and circumstance." Angela's brows lifted with curiosity.

"It burned down at some point and was rebuilt in the seventeenth or eighteenth century. Not exactly new. Wait until you see the inside, it's really quite charming."

Alex pushed open the wooden door and they entered the empty church. Recessed into a niche high above the pews were three, stained-glass windows. The central panel depicted Saint Stefano, to his left a second window portrayed the images of Mary and the baby Jesus, and the panel to the right portrayed Joseph. From the windows, jeweled-colored light flooded the wide nave in an iridescent glow. It was quiet as a tomb and Angela remembered that Sophia and Gerhard's dream of marriage in this church never materialized. Instead, Gerhard's funeral most likely was held here. She imagined the weeping Sophia and her brothers sitting on these pews with a small support of neighbors and friends sharing their grief.

A painting caught the corner of her eye and drew her. She studied the Virgin Mary and the baby Jesus, flanked by two angels. "Thirteenth century I'd say." She moved closer to the identification plaque. "It's attributed to either the Master of Bagnano or the Maestro of Greve. It's always difficult to make a clear attribution from the Medieval period. Quite an important piece for such a small village."

Moving to the presbytery, they found other notable works, paintings of the Virgin Mary and John the Baptist and Saint Stephen from the fifteenth century, and an anonymous "Trinity of four Saints."

"Very impressive," Angela said admiringly.

"Montefioralle was a fortress town owned by four very powerful families, one of which was the Vespucci. You probably recall the name of Amerigo Vespucci, the explorer."

Angela's brow furled as she contemplated the name. "Vespucci? That was Simonetta's married name."

"Simonetta's husband was Amerigo Vespucci's cousin."

"How do you know all this?"

He smiled. "Did my homework and Googled it before we left. Thought I'd impress you."

She couldn't help but laugh. "Well, it worked."

An elderly priest entered the presbytery, his robes billowing around his frail, bent posture. His olive-skinned face etched with lines smiled as Alex approached him. Several times the priest stared at Angela as if recognizing her. She was disconcerted by his attention but couldn't help watching their exchange. She wondered if the priest could possibly remember Sophia and Gerhard. She calculated that he couldn't have been more than a boy in 1944.

After a few minutes, the priest and Alex shook hands. As he turned away, the priest nodded shyly toward her. She fought to ignore the eerie sensation that climbed her spine. "Did you learn anything? Why did he keep staring at me? It was strange, like he knew me."

"He knew Sophia and the Caro family well, but he didn't remember Gerhard. He also knew her daughter but couldn't recall her name. The reason he couldn't take his eyes off you was he thought you bore a remarkable resemblance to Sophia when she was young. I think he was as freaked out by you as you were of him."

"How about any birth and death records? Do they have them."

"No, he said they were lost in a fire a few years back."

"That's unfortunate. So now what?"

"He says many members of the Caro family are buried in the old cemetery. I've never seen it or been there. Apparently, there's another trail through one of the other village gates that returns to Greve. It's less used and you can't see the cemetery from it unless you know where to look. I think we should check it out."

"Let's go."

A hot, dry wind had begun to blow as they made their way down the trail. They walked in silence, the only sounds intruding upon the quiet came from the twittering of birds or the occasional buzz of bees and flying insects that darted across their path. Alex was focused on finding the spur that would lead to the cemetery.

The humidity was high, and Angela felt a trickle of sweat run between her breasts as she fanned a pesky fly away. The way the priest had looked at her had disturbed her. It was as if he knew more about her than she knew of herself. The past and its history of death and murder were sucking the life out of her and she had to make it stop. She was seeing the world through a filtered lens, through someone else's eyes. And now she was feeling it again, each curve in the path felt familiar. She stopped abruptly and Alex turned.

"We're here." She pointed ahead. "Just beyond that tree."

Alex studied her face. "How do you know? I don't see a thing."

"I don't know… but I know." She took his hand and they continued onward.

Only when they'd covered the distance and peered around the bend did they see the stone archway. Angela sailed past him, taking the lead. She relinquished control and allowed herself to be led forward by an invisible force. Beyond the arch was a gate that creaked so loudly when she pushed it open, it scattered a flock of pheasant—or maybe it was grouse—into the sky. Their squawks shattered the peace and quiet, reminding her of *The Birds*, one of Hitchcock's most famous films. She'd taken a film theory course in her undergraduate program and had become a fan of the master of suspense.

When all of this is over, I just want to hang out with Alex and watch old movies and eat popcorn and make out. If that's selfish of me then so be it.

Hundreds of gravestones in uneven rows decorated the hillside, surrounded by tall cypresses that bent in the wind. The cemetery was well maintained, although the priest told Alex that for the last twenty-five or so years it was no longer used for burial purposes. It was more a contemplative destination for hikers.

She shivered. It was eerie how the air seemed to change when she stepped through the gate. Cool fingers swept through her hair, and she wrapped her arms around herself trying to hold on to the heat. One foot in front of the other, her eyes focused ahead, she walked swiftly past the headstones.

Abruptly she turned and halted. She didn't need to look to know what she'd see. The simple white marble stone read *Sophia Caro, Beloved Mother and Grandmother, Born 1919, Died 1987.* All around Sophia's grave were other graves of the Caro family, including Sophia's brothers, Stefano and Roberto, who'd died years before. She shuddered. *I'm standing on my own grave.* Had Alex not caught her, she'd have tumbled to her knees.

"Babe, are you, all right?"

"I want to see the other side."

"The other side of what?"

"The gravestone." Her voice pleaded. "Please, help me."

Alex supported her, his arm firmly around her waist as they circled the grave. Alex read what was written out loud: "Giorgio Bandini (G.J.), Beloved of Sophia Caro and loving Father of Fioretta Caro, Born January 12, 1917, Died September 30, 1944."

"Giorgio Bandini has to be Gerhard Jaeger. They were buried in the same plot. She kept his identity a secret."

Angela lifted her face into the gusts of wind that stirred the cypress trees with a mournful cry. The wind carried the scent of dying flowers and laughter. She turned her head and time fell away from her like sand through an hourglass.

Montefioralle, Italy
August 10, 1944

A young man chased a woman whose breathless laughter spurred him on. She was as agile and spry as an antelope, and each time he was about to catch her she managed to escape his grasp. He stumbled to his knees laughing. His size and strength appeared no match to the woman who fleetly evaded his capture. He rose and this time he charged with his head down and his hands and fingers mimicking the horns of a bull. She froze, bracing herself for the impact, but at the last second, she whirled, furling her pretend cape and he passed without making contact. He turned and this time approached at a slow, deliberate pace. She yielded, opening her arms to embrace him and he gently tackled her. They rolled as one in the grass, coming to rest against an obelisk grave marker.

"Ouch," she cried, but when she lifted her hands to push him off, he pinned her hands above her head.

"Now I have you. Tell me where you hid it?"

"No, it's better if you don't know." She stuck her chin out defiantly.

He tickled her. "Sophia, you have to tell me."

Tears of laughter ran down her cheeks, but she shook her head no. Finally, he relented. Releasing her hands, he rested his forehead against hers. The laughter was gone from his face.

"Why? Don't you trust me?"

Her hands caressed his cheeks. "Of course, I do. But for our safety, it's better that only one of us know where it is. When the war is over we'll both decide what to do with it. I promise you, it is in a safe place where it won't be discovered."

"A ridiculous argument, but nonetheless I will surrender to your will. Graciously."

"Thank you."

He looked around the cemetery and shook his head. "I can't believe the only place we can be alone is in a graveyard." He bent pressing his lips to hers. She eagerly responded, pressing her body fully against him. He growled. "I'm not making love to you in the middle of a cemetery, it would be a desecration."

"You made love to me in every nook and corner of the Uffizi, and you're worried about a cemetery where only the dead can see?"

"The Uffizi was a joyful place to make love. Love among the dead seems a heresy."

She laughed. "Love can never be a heresy. What would be cruel is for all of these poor souls to witness the pleasures of the flesh that they are missing."

"You are so irreverent, Sophia. Where is the well-behaved Catholic girl?"

"I have never been well behaved, just ask my brothers. Perhaps you will punish me." She playfully teased.

"Once we're married and you are my official chattel, perhaps I will."

She pummeled his chest in mock anger. "You will never tame me, Gerhard Jaeger."

Now it was his turn to laugh. "I would never change a hair on your head, I swear by the sun and the moon."

"Careful," she admonished. "*O, swear not by the moon, the fickle moon, the inconstant moon, that monthly changes in her circle orb, Lest that thy love prove likewise variable.*"

"That one I know. Shakespeare's *Romeo and Juliet*. Don't compare us to two doomed lovers when we have a lifetime of love ahead of us." He silenced her reply with a kiss...

A heavy mist rolled in and the young lovers disappeared. Before Angela could react, she was silenced by a woman's weeping. When she turned toward the sorrowful cry, she saw a group of mourners huddled together. Two men supported Sophia, who wept uncontrollably. In front of them was a simple pine casket draped with flowers and a freshly dug grave surrounded by rich, dark earth. The resounding emptiness of Gerhard's last words of love to Sophia brought tears to Angela's eyes and she wept in sympathy with her heartbroken past incarnation.

Sophia looked up and locked eyes with her. They both stood staring at the other. For a heartbeat, two separate lifetimes, the past and the present collided and merged. As if in protest of the unnatural confluence of the principles of time, Sophia slowly faded into nothingness with her gaze on Angela. Angela called out, "Don't go."

CHAPTER 15

Montefioralle, Italy
Present day
August 10

Someone was shaking her, calling to her and when she looked into his eyes with their different colors, the spell was broken.

"What did you see, Angel? Come back to me." She watched his face fill with shadow as a cloud passed, blocking the sun.

"I can't... please... take me away from here."

He picked her up and carried her out of the cemetery, through the gate and arched stone entrance to the trail where he set her down. "Let's go find some lunch and a glass of wine."

"Thank you for putting up with me. You must think I'm a loony bird."

"You're not a loony bird." Alex lifted her hand and kissed her palm.

They were sitting at a small table at La Cantina, on the Piazza Trento, with a bottle of Chianti between them, sipping wine and waiting to order.

When the server presented the menu to her, she smiled but shook her head. "Just order for us, Alex. We can share whatever you decide."

After a lively exchange, the waiter hurried off to place their order. Angela's gaze drifted around the room. Alex was familiar with the restaurant, but Angela was, no doubt, examining everything with her art-historian eye.

The stone walls and barrel-vaulted ceiling enclosed them in a cocoon of stone, brick, and mortar. It was cozy and cool at the same time, with tiled floors, and floor-to-ceiling racks displaying regional wines. Each table was set with a vase of wildflowers and candles that glowed, casting shadows on their faces.

"Tell me what happens when you have a vision. One minute you're with me, and the next you're in a trance and I can't reach you."

"That's what's so extraordinary. I don't disappear, it's just that they appear."

"Gerhard and Sophia?"

She nodded and then everything poured from her. She told him every detail until he felt as though he'd seen it too. What they said to each other. What they did. She described the impossible sadness that filled her when time flashed forward, and she stood at the open grave. "I was a witness this time, not a participant, but then something weird happened. Sophia looked up and I swear she looked right at me. We were staring at each other, she recognized me, and she knew who I was—and then you called me back."

All he wanted to do was protect her, and he was failing miserably at it. She was being haunted by ghosts, but not just any ghosts. The ghosts of their previous lives. He gulped his wine. "We both know this is happening for a reason, Angela. Slowly you're being given the keys to unlock the door."

"And at least I now know that I'm the only one who knows where the painting is hidden. If I could just tap into that knowledge, we could end this now." She snapped her fingers, her eyes reflecting her frustration.

The waiter returned with a pizza that could only be considered a work of art. She closed her eyes and breathed in. "Mmm, smells good. What kind is it?"

"*Pizza con tartuffi bianchi.*" Alex grinned with satisfaction. *Nothing like food to change my girl's focus.* "Pizza with white truffles, sinfully good." He lifted a slice and placed it on the plate in front of her. "*Mangia, mangia.*"

Alex poured more wine, loving Angela's moans of pleasure when she bit into the crust. He wanted her to relax, to let go. His guilt over pushing her too far too fast was overwhelming. Indirectly, he brought this on. He was responsible for the black cloud that had settled over her life. He'd driven her into the lion's den by bringing her to Florence and Montefioralle, and by placing her in situations that were bound to trigger visions.

He took no satisfaction in the fact that she'd been in danger all along, that Scordato was a threat even before he came into the picture. *I'll make it up to you, baby, I swear. Once we find the painting we can close the book on this case and get on with our lives.*

Alex drove the Ferrari home at a more moderate speed because Angela was woozy, and he had other plans for their afternoon and evening besides nursing a sick puppy. He pulled up in front of the house, jumped out, and was immediately surrounded by the welcoming committee, Zaba, Ama, and Misu. Their tails wagged like three metronomes in counterpoint rhythm as they followed him around the car to Angela's side. "Take it easy, guys." He tried to block the dogs, protecting Angela from their exuberance, as he handed her from the Ferrari.

"Alex, they're just happy to see you." She crouched and the dogs lavished her face with wet kisses. She vigorously rubbed them, giggling at their enthusiasm.

"Correction. They're happy to see you. Me, I've just become the intermediary that delivers their favorite new toy."

"That's not true." She rose a tad shaky on her feet and stumbled into his arms.

His arms tightened around her. "Good, right where you belong. Let them know who the boss is. The one you come running to."

"You're not jealous of the dogs, are you?"

"Not anymore." He kissed her. "I've been wanting to kiss you all day long. Not those little pecks that don't begin to convey what I'm feeling. Truth is, I want to kiss you all the time."

She met his gaze. "Kiss away."

"Oh, I intend to." He nibbled her neck. "But maybe we could get more comfortable first." He steadied her. "Are you okay to walk?"

"I'm fine." She pushed her finger into his chest. "Don't you worry about me."

Like I'm not worried about you every minute of the day. "Okay, I'm just going to grab the groceries."

He felt like the pied piper. Angela followed him into the kitchen with the three dogs in a single line behind her. He emptied the bags and put everything away as she watched him with a goofy smile on her face. The dogs gathered around her.

She leaned on the counter. "I love spending time with you. You've been so good to me—" She hiccupped and covered her mouth. "Oh, excuse me." She began hopping on one foot while holding her breath.

He erupted in laughter. "What are you doing?"

"I'm trying to cure my hiccups." She continued bouncing up and down.

His laughter must have been contagious because she burst into giggles in between hiccups. He grabbed her. "Come here, you. I love spending time with you, too. I think you're becoming a habit I don't want to break. Your laughter is part of it. I keep thinking if she can laugh so readily with what she's going through, imagine the laughter that will fill your world when all this crap is behind us."

She wrapped her arms around his neck and pressed herself seductively against him. "Soooo, you want me for my laughter?"

"Hey, look at that, I cured your hiccups." Her face was turned up, her lips inches from his. Her hair tumbled down her back and he ran his fingers through it. "Mmm, not just your laughter. Let's go upstairs, I have a surprise for you."

"Come on, you can find a better line than that to get me in your bed."

"No, really. I have a surprise for you." Taking her hand, he led her out of the kitchen. The dogs who'd patiently waited, tails wagging, followed. Alex called over his shoulder, "Give it a rest, buddies, I'm not sharing." He lifted his hand. "*Fermi, a cuccia!*" They stopped. Their master's command to stay understood.

Angela wasn't nearly as drunk as earlier. The drive had cleared her brain. She knew exactly what she was doing. She wanted Alex, wanted to feel every part of him. Every time he touched her, sparks ignited her to the point of frustration. He pulled her down the hallway, past her bedroom door. "Alex, I really want to shower. I'm all grungy."

"Yeah, me too."

"You passed my room." She looked back toward her door.

"I think you're mistaken." He flung open the double doors of his bedroom suite. "This is your room. I hope you don't mind, but I had Maria move all of your stuff in here."

Angela's mouth gaped open. Over her head a coffered, barrel-vaulted ceiling rose nearly thirty feet in the air. Floor-to-ceiling bookshelves lined one wall. A skylight in the ceiling rained afternoon beams of light, accentuating the dust motes dancing like snowflakes, trapped in a prism.

She stared at a wall covered with paintings, which had to be copies. Had they been real, their value would have been countless of millions of dollars. She knitted her brows.

"Don't look so perplexed. They're all copies of paintings I've recovered. I spent so much time searching for them that I became very attached. Hence, the wall of disparate art. As for the books, I collect them. I'm always in some far-off corner of the world. It's a pleasant hobby and a distraction."

"It's an amazing room, Alex. Breathtaking. You have a lot of hobbies."

"I do. But I have a new one that I can't get enough of. One that makes the others pale in comparison."

"What is it?"

"You."

"Me?"

"Yes, although I'd place you more in the obsession category."

She laughed. "You know this library is incredible."

"Oh, you haven't seen anything yet." He clasped her hand and led her through a set of carved wood Baroque doors. The master bedroom was spare, again the incongruous modern theme in an old traditional house. The centerpiece was the bed with its winged attached nightstands that seemed to float against the back wall. The bed was placed opposite a wall of floor-to-ceiling windows, beyond which lay an endless expanse of vineyards that terraced up the hill. In the middle of the windows was a gas fireplace. Alex hit a switch and flames shot up out of the purple jeweled stones.

"It looks like the fireplace is floating above the floor. It's so strange, all of this modernity in a country home."

Alex hit another switch and the first movement of Beethoven's *Pathetique* surrounded them. It's melodic tones floating throughout the suite.

"I like the juxtaposition. The rest of the house conforms, but this sliver is my own personal rebellion. I like simplicity but the high-tech kind." His brows lifted with his challenge. "Wanna see the bath?"

"I can't imagine it topping the bedroom, but then you do continue to surprise me."

He winked. "Good answer." He swung open the door and she gasped.

"It's... it's... I don't know what to say." Her eyes flitted from one end of the bath to the other. It was all white Carrera marble and chrome, but it was the shower that was like no other. A glass cube, one wall and the ceiling marble with the remaining sides glass. What she found perplexing was the outside wall, a floor-to-ceiling window opened to the vineyards and backyard. "You want people to watch you shower?"

He laughed. "Not hardly."

"But... I don't understand..."

"It's one-way glass. You can't see in, only out."

"So, what do you see from the back of the house?"

"You see a curtained window, an optical illusion."

She shook her head in disbelief. He pulled her into the shower. "Lift your arms." She did as she was told, and he pulled her shirt over her head. Then he slid his lips down her neck and continued to undress her until she was completely naked. He turned her to the view of the vineyards and stripped. He threw all their clothes out of the shower and pressed a button on the wall.

He pulled her back against his chest. She could hear a slight hiss and then the water from the waterspout and faucets on the wall came on at the perfect temperature. She closed her eyes and lifted her face upward, losing herself in the sensuous feeling of his lips and the pulsing water touching her skin.

"This is the sexiest shower on the planet."

"I know," he murmured in her ear, "and I assure you we're going to make good use of it in the future, but..." He separated his body from hers and she felt the loss of his heat.

"I have this craving to wash you. To soap you up and touch every part of you."

The deepness of his voice travelled through her like an electric current. "You do?"

"I do, baby." He poured shampoo into his hand and massaged her scalp. She closed her eyes, concentrating on a sensation she'd never experienced before except in a beauty salon by a stranger. Minutes passed. Then he moved her under the water and rinsed the soap out. He filled his hand with conditioner and coated it through her hair.

Tears sprang to her eyes. Without meaning to, he'd touched on something deep inside of her. She was motherless and all the things that mothers do were alien to her. A heartache she'd never come to terms with. Alex's gentleness brought back those feelings of loss. It was as if he was psychically tuned in to whatever had hurt her in life and he was on a mission to heal her.

"What's wrong, baby, did I do something wrong?"

"No, Alex, everything you do is right. I didn't have a mother... who washed my hair as a child... I... I don't know what to say."

"Don't say anything. Just let me please you. If you want to moan, don't let me stop you." He winked.

Everything he did felt like heaven. He poured liquid soap on a loofah and turned her around. Rubbing the sponge in a circular motion down her back, over her bottom, he lathered her in the lavender-and-rosemary-scented soap. She sighed with longing, her desire for him mounting. Standing behind her, his soapy hands massaged her breasts, travelling down her belly and farther down to her inner thighs. She moaned as he swirled the rich lather between her legs, making her gasp with pleasure.

He whispered in her ear, "Now, it's my turn."

Seeing him standing there naked and aroused, ignited her even more. "Can I help?"

"I was hoping you'd ask."

She ran her hands over his soapy body. His muscles tensed beneath her fingers. When she touched his shaft, he groaned. "Jeez, baby, you're making it hard for me not to take you right here."

"This is so much fun, I don't want it to end. I can't decide which I like better, bathing you and feeling your hard body, or looking out the window and watching the sun sink below the ridge line of the mountain." She realized she was getting pretty good at teasing him the way he teased her.

"Why choose?" He moved in front of the window, giving her a view of both the sunset and his silhouetted body. Her hands, again, sought his manhood. She loved watching him close his eyes and fight not to succumb to the pleasure.

Her lips traced a path on his neck and whispered, "Okay, that's just too much of a good thing."

He pulled her under the rain spout and kissed her, his hardness poking against her stomach. Water poured over them and rivulets of soap and conditioner glistened on their skin before disappearing down the drain.

He murmured against her lips, "Shall we finish this here or in bed?"

She moaned. "Bed. My legs are buckling."

Smiling, he turned off the water, opened the shower door and grabbed a thick towel off the suspended towel shelf. He gently dried her from head to toe. "I don't know who's enjoying this more, me or you."

"I can't speak to your pleasure, but mine's off the charts."

"Good answer." He wrapped her snug in the towel and grabbed another, quickly drying himself. Then he picked her up and carried her to the bed.

Maybe it was the shower and the long, slow lead up to their lovemaking, but every nerve ending in her body felt alive and responded to every touch, every kiss, every beat of his heart, every press of his body on hers, every whispered word of adoration. He made love to her as if it were the only thing on earth that mattered. She rode a sea of passion until she crested like a wave, shattering into a million points of light.

He rhythmically thrust through her orgasm until her trembling stilled, then stiffening he came, his groan of pleasure filling her ear. "Angel, I've never felt like this before," he breathed, still inside her.

His words launched another round of fireworks, her eyes fluttered closed and a moan escaped her as she tightened around him and climaxed once more.

"Every time you shatter like that, I want to feel it again. Like an addiction I never want to stop," he groaned.

"I can't help it, it's you, my reaction to you."

"Don't stop whatever you do, baby. I can't get enough."

"A part of me is afraid where this might end. I'm afraid that, like a candle burning from both ends, the wax will melt and there will be nothing left to burn."

"You've got to trust that this is more than a fleeting moment, believe that it has roots that run deep. Don't you understand that those roots are wrapped around my heart?"

She nestled closer into his arms. "I'm trying, Alex. More than anything I want to believe this is real."

"It is real." On the nightstand the buzz of his phone drew his attention. "Hang on, let me check this." He picked up the phone. "Okay, I've got Sophia's granddaughter Lucrezia's number in Rome. I should call her now before it gets too late."

He dialed and Lucrezia picked up. He explained to her that he was the buyer of Casa del Sole and he had some questions he'd like to discuss with her mother, Fioretta.

Angela watched his face as he listened to Lucrezia. After what seemed an eternity, Alex asked. "I understand your mother's condition, and I know you don't think she'd be of any help to me, but I think that talking to me and my girlfriend might trigger something in her memory. I'd like to give it a shot."

He listened, drawing his brows together. "I know you think I'm wasting my time, but I'm willing to take that chance. If you agree, my girlfriend and I will fly to Rome in the next few days and call on your mother whenever it's convenient. I promise we won't do anything to upset her."

Again, he listened.

"Thank you. I'll text you our itinerary and you can let me know what time would be agreeable to you."

Pause.

"Very good. I look forward to hearing from you." He hung up and turned to her.

"I don't get it. What did she say, and what's this about going to Rome?" She was still trying to still her pulse after hearing him call her his girlfriend.

"Fioretta has Alzheimer's and Lucrezia doesn't believe her mother will be able to answer any questions, but I have a feeling about this. Call it what you want, a detective's intuition or whatever, but I think when you and Fioretta meet, another window of memory will open."

"So just like that, we drop everything, leave Montefioralle and go to Rome on a hunch?"

"Yep. That's what investigators do, and this is an investigation isn't it? Besides, what's so bad about you and me taking a side trip?"

"Nothing, but it's a lot of time and money to spend on a hunch that might not pan out. Especially since we're making so much progress here."

"You let me worry about the money. I'm only sorry we can't stay longer. This is going to be a get-in-and-get-out-fast. Three days at the most. You've never been to the Eternal City. I think we'll have enough time to see a few of the sights."

She didn't know why it bothered her to leave Montefioralle, but he was probably right. Sophia's daughter might hold some key to the mystery. "Do we tell her about the reincarnation stuff and the painting?"

"I don't know. Best to play it by ear, see if she remembers the cave or whether she ever heard her mother speak about the da Vinci. I'm curious to know what she knows about her father, too."

"I was Sophia in my past life... It feels insane to think I'll be meeting my own daughter." Her heart rattled in her chest, imagining what their reaction to each other would be.

"How about me? She's my daughter, too, even if she never knew me."

"I just don't understand why this is happening. Why am I remembering things that are better left unknown? There's a reason why most people can't remember their past lives. It's too upsetting to watch yourself and people you love grow ill or die. Not to be able to change things is heartbreaking. What's the point?"

"The point is there are lessons to be learned. The point is you and me were meant to find each other."

"It certainly would be easier if you could remember, too. When is the veil going to lift for you?"

"Besides my marching orders from Giuliano at the Getty and then that stunt he pulled in the sacristy, I don't think it's going to happen. For some reason you're the conduit. It's unexplainable and, from what I've read, rare. It's clear there's a reason. It's not accidental. At least I don't think it is. I'm just hoping that finding the painting will bring closure and we can move on."

He gathered her into his arms. "Speaking of moving on, how about we get back to where we left off." He kissed her until she surrendered all argument, and then just to finish her off, he added, "And then let's put together that picnic with all the goodies we bought. I'm hungry and can't get past the thought of licking the crumbs off your body."

How does he do that? How did he kindle a flame in her when she was having doomsday visions? One kiss and she couldn't think of anything else. How did someone who'd spent most of her life alone, suddenly become attached to a man to the point that all reason was blown away like a pile of leaves in the wind?

She tried to rally around caution, to prepare herself for whatever might come, and then he swept in like a hurricane, razing her barriers and leaving her open and vulnerable. Her cautious side worried that what was happening between them was due to unusual circumstances. What if it didn't last? It was happening too fast and at too great an emotional height. If it all came crashing down, what would sustain them?

She was a historian who analyzed the past, to open the doors of discussion. She hypothesized about possibilities, while he was the detective working feverishly to reach a definitive conclusion. Alex's temperament was mirrored in his love for fast cars, he was in a race to the finish line. They were polar opposites.

He kissed the tip of her nose. "You're thinking too much."

"It's what I do."

"Think about this." He pinned her beneath him filling her with a passion impossible to ignore. She was lost in his feverish need, the thrust of his body inside of her, and she couldn't see beyond it, nor did she want to. All she wanted to do was climb to the dizzying heights of sensuality and shatter like glass beneath him. Sex, which had never played an important role in her life, was suddenly taking center stage. For the moment, she locked away her worries and let her heart and body rule her head.

CHAPTER 16

Rome, Italy
Present day
August 12

The chauffeured Mercedes Benz sped away from the Hassler Hotel and headed to Il San Lorenzo, on the Via dei Chiavari, near the Campo de'Fiori piazza. Alex held tight to Angela's hand in the backseat. She looked out the window taking in the sights. They whizzed past the Coliseum, ablaze in lights and he heard her audibly sigh. His gaze was locked on her and had been since she'd emerged from the bathroom dressed and ready to go.

"Did I tell you how beautiful you look?" The thought of her luscious, red-lipsticked lips on him made him squirm.

She noticed his discomfort. "Penny for your thoughts? And yes, you've told me at least five times. But you can say it again, I'm not tired of hearing it."

She wore a simple white blouse and the gray pencil skirt. The same outfit she wore when they first met. Actually, it was the second time they'd met; the first time she'd been in a trance at the Getty. He knew her wardrobe choices were limited. A tight budget meant few frivolities. He wanted to take her to every fancy boutique in Rome and adorn her in an array of outfits that would do justice to her beauty, but he knew she'd never allow it. *One day*, he thought.

They were seated by the Maître d' at a white linen-draped table. The dining room was intimate, with cream-colored walls hung with modern art and photographs. The recessed vaulted brick ceiling displayed a crystal chandelier reflecting rays of sparkling light that imbued the room with a magical glow. From their table, they could see out the glass doors to the terrace and the fading afternoon light.

"It really is the Eternal City, isn't it? A place where elegance and decay inhabit the same time and place," Angela said.

"That's Rome, crumbling antiquity and unparalleled luxury."

"Where does Lucrezia live?"

"On the outskirts of the central city. It's a very upscale neighborhood."

"Well, I'm looking forward to seeing how the well-heeled in Rome live."

"Speaking of the well-heeled, I've been thinking that after we find the painting and put this case to rest we might spend some time travelling."

"Travelling?"

"Yeah, maybe you'd like to meet my mother and father. I know I'd sure like to meet your dad. Any man who could have raised a daughter like you is tops on my list."

Her mouth gaped open.

"That supposes, of course, that you and I were to become a couple." He smiled, enjoying the look of dumbfounded disbelief stamped on her face.

She closed her mouth and took a long swig of her Bellini. "I think you're jumping a little too far ahead, don't you?"

"Would you mind allowing me a little wishful thinking?"

She took his hand and leaned in to kiss him, to thank him, he supposed. He knew she'd intended to just brush her lips on his, but he grabbed her behind her head and delivered a slow, deep, lingering kiss.

"That's better," he murmured against her lips. Kissing her was an adrenaline rush. It made him think of things he'd never considered. What would it be like to wake up every day of his life with her, to have a child with her?

The idea of trusting her, protecting her, dedicating himself to her seemed natural. His parents' marriage had been a disaster, but that was because his father cheated, and his mother wasn't the most nurturing woman in the world. Neither he, nor Angela were like that.

The waiter cleared his throat and they broke apart laughing. He, of course, didn't care who saw him kiss her. *Hell, I'd kiss her in Macy's front window.* "Do you want to step outside your comfort zone? Live a little dangerously," he asked her, with a lift of his brow.

"And do what?" She bit her lip and lust rippled through him.

"Be careful what you wish for," he whispered. "I was thinking of ordering the degustation menu." Her eyes lit hungrily, and he suddenly wished they'd stayed in their room and ordered room service. He'd lived thirty-two years in this world, survived unparalleled danger in Afghanistan, experienced his share of meaningless relationships, seen it all and done it all, yet nothing and no one had ever affected him like Angela. She made the simple and the mundane special.

Angela applauded when the waiter set the first course, a colorful presentation of three different fish tartare, on the table. The waiter's eyebrows raised as if he was in the presence of an alien from outer space. Then he bowed in deference to her childlike appreciation. Alex knew at that moment that she had a gift she wasn't in the least aware of. Her infectious *joie de vivre*, the way people reacted to her positive energy, made her a magnet. Normally wary of people's motives, it wasn't a characteristic he possessed. But just like the waiter, he'd fallen head over heels and trusted that she was without affectation and real. Or maybe it was just one of the mysteries that enabled her to connect with the past. For a twenty-seven-old academic, she appeared to be completely oblivious of her power.

He'd stifled his laughter when Angela's face screwed up with disgust as the waiter set down a plate of grilled squid served on a bed of mint flavored artichokes. But like the trouper she was, she tentatively nibbled on a tiny morsel. Rapture filled her features and his heart pounded in reply. He'd bragged about this restaurant and seeing Angela's face when she took that first bite was vindication that he'd made the right choice. If paradise lay on a plate, he'd sent her there.

By the time the spaghetti *alle vongole*, a specialty of the house, arrived, she was making such exuberant moans of delight, his pants tightened. "Do you really think it's fair for you to show the same amount of ecstasy here as in the bedroom?"

"That's not true and you know it. It's just so good." Her face flushed, as she reached for her water glass.

Her embarrassment is priceless.

"Besides, you're the one who says you love watching me eat. I'm just showing my appreciation." She tore off a chunk of bread and dunked it in the broth, popping it in her mouth. She chewed, her exaggerated moans making him shift in his seat.

"I guess I'll just have to test you when we get back to the room. See which produces the most response, sex or food."

"You do that," she added, "You might have to work a little harder though, these clams are going to be hard to beat."

Damn. Just when I think I can't fall in deeper... "We don't have to be at Lucrezia's tomorrow until one o'clock. Do you think you might be up for a walk in the morning?" *That's if you can walk after I'm done with you tonight.* "I want to show you one of the best views in Rome. It'll give us a chance to see a lot of the city and work up an appetite."

Her eyes widened. "That would be amazing. Where are we going?"

"You'll see when we get there. A guy has to have a couple of surprises up his sleeve."

"Alex, you surprise me at every turn. Sometimes I feel like a country bumpkin. You're so well-travelled, you've been everywhere."

"Yeah, but I've always done everything alone. So, sharing it with you puts a whole new spin on it. It's like discovering everything all over again. It gets me high seeing things through your eyes."

When they finished their meal the sun was down, and Angela yawned.

"I better get you to the hotel or I won't be able to test my theory."

"Your theory?"

"I'm dying to see what makes you moan more: clams and spaghetti or me."

First class travel wasn't anything Angela was used to, but for Alex it seemed to be the norm. Their suite at the Hassler Hotel was so luxurious, so beautiful, she couldn't stop herself from walking around admiring each room. Alex had booked the Medici Suite in honor of their search for the wedding portrait. The stunning views from the terrace overlooked the Spanish Steps and the heart of Rome. The opulent suite was a golden jewel box with red-suede upholstered furniture and bed. She felt like a kid in a candy store.

Alex sat on the sofa waiting for her to stop her pacing. Finally, she plopped down next to him.

"Do you always live like this?"

"Pretty much."

"I don't get how recovering art could be so lucrative." She crossed her legs and settled back against the plush sofa. "It doesn't seem possible."

He stood and poured two glasses of champagne from the bottle he'd ordered up to the room and handed her one. "I haven't been entirely honest with you." He raised his glass. "To us."

She clinked her glass lightly against his and took a sip. She couldn't hide the worry in her voice. She couldn't handle the thought of him lying to her. "You haven't?"

"No."

"Why? What are you hiding?" Was he going to confess to having used her to get to the painting? Was all of his interest in her based only on getting his hands on the da Vinci? A spasm of pain gripped her heart.

He scrubbed the back of his neck. "The art recovery business is good, but my real money comes from a trust fund."

Angela tried to process what he was saying. He was avoiding looking at her. She didn't know what to feel first, anger or hurt or both. "Why? Did you think I'd turn out to be a gold-digger? Were you afraid you couldn't trust me? How wealthy are you?"

"Have you ever heard of Crawford Oil?"

"Vaguely. Do you want to elucidate?"

"My mother is a Crawford and I'm the only heir. We have a rather strained relationship. She doesn't acknowledge anything I've achieved on my own as important. The only thing that matters is my becoming the man she and my grandfather groomed to take over the helm of Crawford Oil. If my grandfather had his way my last name would be Crawford. I've been fighting what they believe is my preordained destiny for most of my life. I'm sorry, I should have told you right off."

She couldn't breathe. Her hand flew to her chest. She stood and began to pace. She didn't know what else to do. Her heart was breaking. "I trusted you with my life and you couldn't trust me with your family history?" If she didn't keep moving she was sure she'd explode.

"I've spent my whole life avoiding entanglements. I learned early that, when it came to me, women were after my money and what they could game from me."

She flung her hands up in a dismissive gesture. "Well, you don't have to worry about me. Once we've found the painting you can go back to your playboy ways. I want nothing from you." Tears were streaming down her face now, but she didn't care. *He said he loves me, but he doesn't know what that means. Love is about trust.*

He stood and grabbed her by the shoulders, forcing her to look into his eyes. "You don't understand. I've kept this a secret from you because I was afraid of losing you, Angela, afraid you wouldn't give us a chance. I keep telling you, I've never felt like this before, but it doesn't seem to sink in."

She pulled away, breaking his hold, she was having trouble breathing between the lump in her throat and the tightness in her chest. "You certainly didn't put much faith in me. And why should I believe you when you lied to me?" Her hands covered her mouth as she fought back a sob. She lowered her hands and took a deep breath. "Y-you didn't tell me about our interactions in front of the Botticelli painting at the Getty when I was having a flashback. You didn't tell me that Giuliano Medici spoke to you from the painting and told you who you were in a past life and who I was before I even fully knew."

"I explained to you why I waited to tell you. I just wanted to get you safely away from Scordato."

She shook her head, her vision blurred from tears.

"I meant to tell you sooner about my background; to level with you, but with so much going on, I just didn't want to add to everything." He reached out for her, but she stepped back.

"That's what you said before, Alex," she was in full ugly cry now, but she didn't care. "T-hat y-you didn't want to add to my burden, but maybe you're not being entirely honest with yourself. M-maybe you're not really ready for this... whatever this is?"

He stepped closer to her, his eyes laced with anguish. This time she didn't move back. He cupped her shoulders with his big, warm hands. She stiffened, wishing his touch didn't awaken every nerve ending in her body. She wished she was better at resisting him.

"I d-don't think this can work, Alex," she breathed, willing herself to stop crying. We're too different." *Oh God, this is so hard.* "I don't know how to act on this stage you live on, but now I see I'm totally out of my league. You're a master at deception." She was sobbing again, and she couldn't stop, couldn't say anything else. Could barely get a breath in because of the tears.

He wrapped his arms around her and pulled her in tight. "It's you who's out of my league, Angel," he croaked in a broken whisper. "I don't deserve you. I've always had everything I've ever wanted, or at least I thought I did. That all changed in a bar in L.A. I tried to fight falling for you because of the case, but the more we were together the more deeply I fell." He leaned back, wiped her tears with gentle fingers. "I never expected to find anyone like you. Please forgive me. I want this, want you more than I've ever wanted anything in my life. I swear there'll be no more secrets between us."

His striking, different-colored eyes swam with his own tears. The same eyes of Gerhard Jaeger, Sophia Caro's lover. He was telling the truth. She felt it to the depths of her very being. Felt it flow back five hundred years, to Fioretta and Giuliano. Loving the same man through different lifetimes. She cupped his face in her hands. "Alex, I have to know that you believe I don't care about the money. It doesn't matter to me. What matters to me is us. Sharing our hearts, bodies, and souls. We can't move forward until we promise no more secrets."

"Baby, please forgive me, no more secrets. I promise."

"Here we are in one of the most beautiful rooms in the world, in one of the most beautiful cities in the world. I'm with the only man in the world I've ever wanted to share myself with. Hold me, Alex. Make love to me." She wanted to forget all the things that were against them. She wanted to lose herself in him.

"You'll never have to ask twice for that, Angela." He took her hands and held them behind her back, his lips claiming hers.

She told herself that everything would turn out fine. They could stop fate from repeating itself. They had to.

Alex stepped onto the terrace and took in the breathtaking views. The sun rose over the Trinita dei Monte church towers, burnishing the city in a golden glow. He sipped an espresso and gazed at Janiculum Hill and the dome of St. Peter's Cathedral.

Returning to the room, he sat on the edge of the bed and watched Angela draw even breaths in her sleep. The scent of lovemaking clung to their skin and the sheets. Last night his need and passion had been desperate in its desire and divine in its fulfillment. He'd put his heart and soul into loving her and when her last sighs of contentment faded into silence, he'd wrapped himself around her and held her through the night.

He'd never craved to just lie with a woman before, never wanted to listen to her heart beat or hear her even breaths when she rested in his arms. He'd never delighted in the press of a woman's skin on his, but with her he did. His was a simple need and she satisfied it just by being.

He wanted to spend every minute with her. He woke her with a kiss. "Good morning, beautiful."

An impish gleam sparkled in her eyes as she stretched her limbs. "Mmm... Good morning, *Stud*."

He threw his head back and laughed. "Baby, I aim to please."

Giggling, she pulled him down beside her and snuggled into his embrace.

He ran his fingers through her hair, loving the thick, dark waves. "How did you sleep?"

"I slept well. No dreams or nightmares."

"That's great, sweetheart. See, how good I am for you?"

Resting her chin on his chest, she caressed his face. "You *are* good for me, Alex. Are we going on that walk you promised?"

"We are. Unless, of course, you'd prefer staying in bed for another ride through Stud Town." His eyebrows did the wiggle she found so amusing.

"Oh, no…" she said between fits of laughter. "This girl needs a little rest from your stud-like ways."

He chuckled. "Don't think you're going to dissuade me from my favorite task."

"Are you kidding? I would never think of depriving *myself*, you gorgeous hunk of man."

Exchanging teasing banter, they showered together, dressed, and grabbed some coffee and cornetti in the Palm Court restaurant, surrounded by ancient walls covered with ivy. An abundance of flowers perfumed the garden.

Leaving the table, they walked toward the exit. Angela looked up, shielding her eyes and watched the platinum clouds float across the dappled blue sky. "It's such a beautiful day for a walk." She linked her arm through his. "How about telling me what our destination is."

"Come on, admit you like it when I surprise you."

"Mysterious as ever. What sign are you?"

"Scorpio."

"Of course. No match for my Cancer sixth sense."

"Don't know about that, but whatever you are you've gotten under my skin."

They took the Spanish steps, where already people had begun to gather and sit. By the afternoon it would become difficult to navigate the steps because of all the tourists congregating, snapping pictures and shooting videos on the most famous stairway in the world.

Holding hands, they strolled to the Piazza di Spagna and paused at the Baroque fountain created by Bernini. Alex read the reference plaque translating that the Fontana della Barcaccia, the Fountain of the Ugly Boat, was completed around 1629. "Recent history for a city that dates back to antiquity," he joked. "The waters that feed this fountain come from a 19 BCE aqueduct built by the Romans called the Acqua Vergine. Now that's what I call old."

They continued down the bustling Via Frattina where shops and restaurants were beginning to open, past the Basilica of Saint Lorenzo with its pale orange façade. When they got to the Napoleonic Museum, they turned right on the Lungotevere tor di Nona where they strolled along the Tiber River. The weather was warm, and Angela removed her sweater and tied it around her waist.

"Everywhere you look it almost feels like time has ceased to pass."

"That's Rome. An old woman who refuses to die. She's seen conquerors and civilizations come and go, yet she remains eternal."

"Hence the name, Eternal City."

"I forgot who it was that said, Rome will exist as long as the Coliseum does; when the Coliseum falls, so will Rome; when Rome falls, so will the world."

She smiled. "See, there you go surprising me again."

"Hey, I'm not all about fast cars."

They crossed the mossy green waters of the Tiber River at the Ponte Principe Amadeo Suavoia Aosta, and a short while later they arrived at the Passeggiata del Gianicolo. Alex followed behind her, enjoying the sway of her hips as she climbed the stairs to the top of the Janiculum Terrace. He thought about Angela's description of Sophia and her resemblance to Sophia Loren. He remembered the priest in Montefioralle saying how much Angela looked like Sophia. *He sighed and thanked fate for bringing them together in this lifetime.*

They circled the statue of General Giuseppe Garibaldi on horseback, the man acknowledged to be responsible for the unification of Italy. Holding hands, they strolled across the terrace to admire the view.

Alex pointed. "From here you see the historical center of Rome. The Pantheon, the Altare alla Patria—a monument celebrating the unification of Italy—the Castel Sant' Angelo, and St. Peter's Basilica."

"Breathtaking, a patchwork of color." Angela sighed.

"I knew you'd like it." He wrapped his arms around her and she leaned back against him. They stood in silence, taking in the rooftops and domes.

"My life has been so topsy-turvy, so out of control. It's nice to have just a few hours of living in the present without our past lives interfering."

"I want to make all your dreams come true."

"Just hold tight to me, Alex, and don't let go."

Alberto Scordato tapped a number on his smartphone.

Enrico answered on the first ring. "*Ciao, come vanno le cose a Roma?*"

"Uneventful. Rome is Rome. I've been receiving regular updates thanks to our friend, Madame X." Having a relative in the mafia certainly came in handy. Enrico's mysterious hacker had kept close tabs on the duo. "The two are behaving like lovers on their honeymoon. What's going on there?"

"I'm getting things in order for our big party."

That meant Enrico was making arrangements for the unfortunate demise of Scordato's German friend, Max Jaeger. *Collateral damage. All for a good cause, though.*

Alberto couldn't stop the rush of adrenaline that surged through his veins when he pictured the moment when he first would lay eyes on the elusive painting.

Soon, he thought. Soon it will be mine.

CHAPTER 17

Rome, Italy
Present day
August 13

Their driver from the Hassler Hotel pushed the call button and the gates swung open to a contemporary villa in the XVth Municipality. Alex held tight to Angela's hand as they walked up a flowered path to the front door. The three-story home was all white stucco and wood and opened to expansive views of the city skyline and the mountains that surround Rome. The gardens were filled with wildflowers and lavender that scented the air. Tall Cyprus trees lined the street. The house faced the city, and in the distance, they could see the towering cupola of St. Peter's Cathedral.

Alex eyed the modern structure. "This house must have cost Lucrezia and her husband a pretty penny. He's a lawyer and she's a psychologist. It probably accounts for them selling the vineyard. This looks like new construction."

"It's a beautiful home, but I wouldn't trade it for Casa del Sole."

He squeezed her hand. "Neither would I."

Alex rang the doorbell and a petite woman with dark, almond-shaped eyes and a wild mane of black curls answered the door, greeting them with a kiss on both cheeks. He calculated her to be in her early forties, but her olive skin made her appear younger. She was very pretty, but Alex didn't see much of a resemblance to Angela, who, if they went by the priest at Santo Stefano, was a ringer for Sophia Caro.

Fioretta's daughter, Lucrezia Conti, greeted them, her eyes widening when they landed on Angela. "Excuse me for staring, but are we related? You look like my nonna, Sophia Caro."

Angela hesitated, her face blanching, then shook her head.

Alex stepped in smoothly, "Angela keeps getting that a lot here in Italy because of her dark hair and eyes." He smiled and shrugged.

Lucrezia smiled as well. "I suppose that must be it. My mother just finished lunch and is in her room. I have some errands to do so I must run, but Ana, my mother's nurse will be in the next room should you need her. I'm going to be honest with you, my mother isn't responsive. She rarely knows who I am. Sometimes she talks to herself or to my dad, who's deceased, but she's completely out of touch with reality."

"I'm sorry about your mother," Alex said. "But I want you to know Casa del Sole is in good hands. I cherish it and plan on carrying on the tradition of wine making that your family started. You and your family will always be welcome there."

"That's very kind of you, Alex. I'm glad to know the vineyard is in such caring hands. It was a very hard decision to give it up. We sold Casa del Sole when Mama got ill. She couldn't maintain the vineyard anymore and we lived too far away to take care of her and the place. My husband's law practice is here, our lives are here. It didn't make sense. Unfortunately, Mama took a drastic turn for the worse when we moved her here." Lucrezia ran her fingers through her hair. "My grandmother and mother loved Casa del Sole. They had a great affinity to the land, which I'm afraid I never shared. All I ever wanted to do was escape from that constrictive society and old-fashioned world. We all have to follow our own path, I suppose. It's taken me two years to get over my guilt about selling the vineyard."

"We'll do our best not to upset your mother," Angela assured her.

"Thank you. By the way, I forgot to ask, what are you trying to find out from Mama?"

"Angela and I have heard some rumors that there's a cave on the property that was once used to store wine. I'm interested in finding out if it really exists."

"Oh, that cave." She waved her hand. "I've been hearing about it my whole life. My grandmother died with that secret. She never shared it with my mother or me. Frankly, I think it was a figment of her imagination. I loved my grandmother, but she was *pazza*, crazy as you say." Lucrezia emphasized her point by twirling her index finger around her ear.

"She never recovered from my grandfather's murder. She was a total recluse and a terrible mother. I don't think there ever was a cave. It was just one more way for Sophia to control us all. She loved creating the mystery that there was this secret cave filled with hidden treasures. I guess she hoped we'd never leave, never desert her precious vineyard."

Alex nodded agreeably. "You're probably right, but who knows?"

"Certainly, not my mother, but you can try. Actually, I think she'd love to hear about Casa del Sole even if she doesn't know what you're talking about. I'll introduce you to Ana, who'll show you out when you've had your visit with Mama."

Angela clutched Alex's hand for reassurance and they followed Lucrezia to a wing on the left side of the house. She knocked on the door and opened it. The room was filled with sunlight shining through floor-to-ceiling sliders that led to a private garden patio. The room was cheery and decorated with antiques that had probably been brought from Montefioralle. Filling the shelves of an etagere were framed family pictures. Angela strolled closer to take a better look. She picked up a photo in an old frame. "Is this Sophia?" The woman was laughing, her eyes locked on a handsome, blond-haired man.

"Yes. That's the only picture of her and Giorgio Bandini, my grandfather. He was killed a week before they were to marry. She's only a couple of months pregnant with my mother in that picture. According to family lore, it was a terrible tragedy that devastated my grandmother."

"Very sad," Angela whispered. She couldn't believe Giorgio Bandini's real identity of Gerhard Jaeger had disappeared as completely as he had.

Lucrezia called out in Italian, "Ana, Mr. Caine and Ms. Renatus are here to see Mama."

A voice answered. "We're just finishing up, and then I'll bring her in."

"Thank you." Lucrezia stared out the window and smiled. "This is my happy place. My husband and I built this house with the proceeds from the Casa del Sole sale. For us, it was the right thing to do. We built this suite specifically for my mother and filled it with personal items from back home, but none of that could stop the Alzheimer's from erasing her memories."

The door from the bedroom opened and a nurse in scrubs pushed a wheelchair with a tiny, old woman into the sitting room. The disease that had stolen her memory could not erase the last vestiges of her great beauty that showed in her delicate cheekbones and bob of gray-blonde curls. The woman stared vacantly ahead.

"Mama, this is Alex, the man who bought Casa del Sole, and his *fidanzata*, Angela. They've come a long way to visit with you."

The woman showed no reaction to her daughter's words. Her eyes drifted to the garden, she blinked rapidly from the bright sunlight.

Angela's heart skipped a beat. She moved closer to Fioretta Rossi. "Her eyes—they're two different colors."

"Yes, apparently my grandfather had that odd trait…" Lucrezia's gaze landed on Alex and her brows knitted in thought. "How odd…" Her eyes shifted from Alex to Angela and back.

"My eyes are different colored," Alex stated the obvious.

"Yes… I just realized that." Lucrezia shook her head as though dismissing an outrageous notion.

"Well you can blame my mother and father for that, they couldn't get their genes straight." He grinned, his charm easily captivating.

Lucrezia chuckled and turned to her mother.

Alex and Angela exchanged a look. *Close call*, Angela mouthed. Alex nodded in reply.

Lucrezia crouched in front of the wheelchair, laying her hand over her mother's. "Mama, I have to go out for a bit, but you have a nice visit with Alex and Angela. Ana is here if you need her."

Fioretta just stared straight ahead, as if looking right through her daughter. Lucrezia kissed her mother on the cheek and shook her head. "I'm sorry, but this is exactly what I warned you would happen."

"It's all right, Lucrezia, we knew this was a longshot," Alex said. "I want to show my appreciation by sending you a case of our new vintage from Casa del Sole. I think you'll be pleased."

"That would be wonderful. It's the one perk Giovanni and I miss, although we have a cellar filled with Casa del Sole wines." She reached out and grasped their hands in each of hers. "Enjoy your time in Rome."

Lucrezia left and Ana excused herself, telling them to call her if they needed her.

Fioretta stared out the window, oblivious to their presence.

Angela pulled up a chair in front of Fioretta and took her hands. She looked into Fioretta's eyes.

"She looks like her father, Gerhard, doesn't she?" Alex whispered.

"Yes, she does. She must have been a real beauty when she was young; she still is. She has Gerhard's blonde hair and Sophia's thick curls." Fioretta looked straight at Angela, but it was as if she wasn't there. There was no cognitive awareness, no sign that she was even aware of her presence.

"Maybe if you talk to her about the vineyard or her mother you can spark a memory in her mind. There has to be something left of the woman she once was."

"I'll try." She caressed Fioretta's cheek, the skin beneath her fingers as delicate as crepe paper. "Fioretta, Casa del Sole is so beautiful you must miss it terribly. My boyfriend, Alex, bought your vineyard and home, and I've fallen in love with it. But since I got there I've been having dreams... dreams that leave me so sad."

Alex translated for her and they watched as Fioretta blinked rapidly and sighed. Alex and Angela exchanged glances. Maybe Fioretta was listening and understanding.

"I dreamt about a cave and the two people who loved each other very much in that cave. I think I saw your mother and father. I'm sorry you never got to meet your father, he was so looking forward to your birth. In my dream, your parents were very much in love."

Angela waited while Alex translated what she said. She looked down at her hand. Fioretta was squeezing it so tightly that her knuckles turned white. She glanced at Alex who nodded at her to continue.

"Alex and I went to the cemetery in Montefioralle and I prayed at Sophia and Giorgio's graves. I was happy to see they were buried together. I had a vision at the cemetery—Sophia and Gerhard—" Angela's voice faltered in mid-sentence. A flash of light blinded her, and she was forced to close her eyes. Her heart pounded in her chest. The vein in her temple throbbed. Fioretta's bedroom dissolved into a gray mist, Alex and Fioretta fading away in a heavy fog. A hand pulled her up. A voice whispered in her mind. *It's time...*

Montefioralle, Italy
September 30, 1952

She was walking up a steep hill in the middle of the night. Silvery streams of light lit the trail, slipping in and out of the shadows whenever the clouds passed in front of the moon. The wind rushed around her, scattering leaves and howling through the branches of trees along the path. She carried a lantern and moved with purpose, surefootedly. When she reached the top, she strode straight to a massive slab of rock that rested against the mountain. Placing the lantern on the ground, she pushed her weight against the stone until the slab moved aside, revealing an opening in the mountain.

Picking up the lantern, she took a last look around before slipping through the opening and sliding the rock back into place, sealing herself inside. Turning, she pressed her back against the wall and caught her breath. Lifting the lantern, the flame created dancing shadows on the walls.

Sophia studied the cave. It was a long time since she'd last been here and so much had changed, not in the cave, of course; here nothing had changed. Time stood still. This had been her refuge from her older brothers who'd taunted her as a child. Now those same brothers were no longer alive. Roberto had been killed, fighting the Germans as a partisan a few months after Gerhard's murder, and Stefano in a car accident six months after that. Tragedy after tragedy had befallen the family—had befallen her. She was the only surviving Caro, the only one left who knew of the cave's existence.

Bottles lined the walls in racks. There were vintages that hailed from the earliest years of the vineyard's existence in the 18th Century. One day she'd move these priceless bottles to the new wine storage facility she'd begun building when she inherited the vineyard. She shivered, it was cool in the cave.

She walked deeper into the back where there was a bed. Laying her hand on the musty mattress she remembered falling back on the bed in the arms of her love. Tears blurred her vision as she sat on the bed and wrapped the frayed, musty blanket around her shoulders. She sat there for a time and allowed the memories to sweep over her like the hands that had once caressed her. The loss of him sent anger thundering through her and she threw the blanket off. "Why?" she cried aloud. Her voice bounced off the walls in the empty cavern.

She retraced her steps back to the main cave where a row of large barrels lined a wall. It had been years since they were used for their intended purpose of aging wine. The barrels were raised off the ground, their spigots rusted useless by time and neglect. She got down on her hands and knees, turned onto her back and, brushing cobwebs away, she slipped under one of the barrels. The barrel was so large that only her feet extended out. Then she inched her way out from under the barrel clinging to a backpack. She wiped the dirt from her face and sat up. She clutched the backpack to her chest as if it were the most precious object in the world. Standing, she brushed her clothes off and went back to the bed.

Her breath was labored when she opened the backpack and pulled a cardboard tube out. She removed a rolled object from it. Carefully, she unwrapped the tissue paper, revealing a rectangular canvas, paint side out. It was perhaps thirty-six by thirty-two inches and had not been touched since the day at the Uffizi when she and Gerhard had fled from Florence.

Tears fell from her eyes as she spoke to the painting. "I know you're the reason this nightmare befell us. How could a painting of such beauty have taken him from me? There's some kind of curse on you. Whomever possesses you dies. Why did he take you? Tell me why?" She cried. Her tears fell on the canvas and she gently wiped them away. Leonardo da Vinci's painting gave no response. Beautiful but silent, its history known only to the dead and to her. A wedding portrait of two accursed lovers. Not so different from herself and Gerhard.

Sophia sat staring at the painting in silent misery. "Giuliano Medici and Fioretta Gorini are no more, and my Gerhard is no more. One day I will be no more, and you'll remain forgotten and no more. I can't destroy you because he loved you. What I can do is make sure you never see the light of day. I can make sure that you disappear from history. I will not profit from you, nor will anyone else." With that she rewrapped the painting and stuffed it back in the backpack. She returned the painting to its secret hiding place inside the barrel, reachable only through a concealed trap door underneath. No one knew this cave or its secrets other than Sophia. When she died its secrets would die with her.

Sliding the slab open, again, she squeezed through the crack and slid the boulder back in place. It had begun to rain, and she tried not to think about another day when two lovers had found refuge from the rain, only to have their happiness destroyed by two murderers. She clenched her fists and pounded them on the boulder, crying, "No!"

"Mama," a frightened voice called to her. She whirled around, her eyes wild with anger and pain.

"Fioretta? What are you doing here?"

"I'm sorry, Mama. I saw you leave the house and I followed you. When you disappeared, I was so scared. Where did you go?" The child wore nothing but a nightgown. She was soaking wet and shivering.

Sophia forgot her anger and rushed to her daughter, picking her up. "Tesoro, you should not have followed me."

"I'm sorry, Mama, please don't be mad at me."

"I'm not mad, but you must never do this again. Promise me."

"I promise, Mama."

"You must forget this place and what you saw. Never, never come here again."

"Yes, Mama."

"I will punish you, Fioretta, if you ever come here again. Do you understand?"

"Yes, Mama."

Fioretta clung to her mother's neck, her legs tight around her waist. "Mama, I love you."

"If you love me, you must never come here again. I love you, too, my darling."

Water streamed down their faces, whether from tears or rain, Sophia didn't know. She held Fioretta to her chest, whispering words of comfort as a sudden wind began swirling around them like a mini-tornado. Round and round it went, lifting them up off the ground as mother and daughter clung tightly to each other...

Angela gasped as she plummeted back into her own body. Her eyes flew open and she stared at the elderly Fioretta who gazed back in anguish. Angela's arms were wrapped around the frail form.

Fioretta repeated over and over, the volume of her cries rising. "Mama, I love you. Mama, I love you."

Alex couldn't believe what he was seeing. Fioretta and Angela were clasped to each other crying. From what he could tell, they were both in the past together reliving a traumatic memory that had taken place more than sixty years before.

Fioretta's childlike voice repeated over and over like a needle stuck in a record groove. "Mama, I love you." Her two-colored eyes were locked on Angela while her pleas grew louder and more fervent. "I love you, Mama. Please forgive me."

Angela embraced Fioretta, rocking her back and forth, smoothing her hair with gentle hands, consoling her with whispered endearments in Italian. "*Shhh... Non fa niente. E' tutto passato. Stai tranquilla. To voglio bene, ti vorrò sempre bene.*"

Whatever was happening had nothing to do with Angela. It was Sophia speaking through her, reassuring Fioretta about something that had occurred many years ago. He assumed it was karmic, something that had stood between them in life.

Fioretta grew calmer. Angela's last words in Italian had soothed her. "I love you, Fioretta, I always did. Whatever happened between us is forgiven. You are my child and I love you. We both know it was better you forgot what happened. One day soon we will be together again." She kissed the old woman's cheek. And then as if the effort of what had occurred had drained her of life, Angela collapsed in a dead faint. Alex caught her in his arms.

The nurse ran into the room her eyes wide. "*Dio mio*, what is going on in here?"

"It's all right," Alex glanced up at the nurse and asked her to fetch a glass of water. Cupping Angela's face in his hand, his heart wrenched in his chest. Once again, he'd been unable to protect her, unable to keep her safe from the past. It was tearing her apart and he felt helpless. "Baby, talk to me," he pleaded. "Come back to me." How many times was he going to have to utter those words?

Ana returned with a glass of water and handed it to Alex. Then she checked on Fioretta.

A few moments later, Angela's eyes fluttered open. "Where am I?"

Alex held the water to her lips. "Drink, baby. You're safe. I've got you."

"What happened? I've never seen Fioretta react to anyone like this." The nurse held Fioretta's hand.

"I'm not sure," Alex lied. "Angela was talking with her and then she had a fainting spell. We were sight-seeing this morning and perhaps she became dehydrated. I'm sorry. We didn't mean to upset Signora Rossi."

"It'll be fine, but I think it would be better if you leave now. I can't imagine what could have set her off like this."

"Yes, of course. Angela, baby, do you think you can stand."

Tears filled Angela's eyes and she brushed them away. She sat up, and he helped her to her feet. The old woman was calm and watching the two of them. She reached a trembling hand out to Angela.

Angela grasped it and bent to kiss the blue-veined fingers. Fioretta's eyes grew watery. Angela wrapped her arms around the frail woman and brought her lips to her ear. She whispered, "I love you, Fioretta, I always did." She kissed her cheek and gazed at the old woman, her eyes lingering, then she turned and walked out of the room.

"Please tell Lucrezia, thank you. Tell her I'll be in touch." Alex hurried out, after Angela. He found her clinging to the staircase bannister. Her body heaved with silent sobs. He took her in his arms and she burrowed into his chest.

"Do you think you can walk to the car?"

"Yes."

He didn't ask anything else of her until he got her safely in the Mercedes. He secured the seatbelt around her. "Okay, I think you've been through enough today. Alfredo, take us back to the hotel."

Angela was scared. The twenty-minute ride back to the Hassler gave her too much time to ruminate. The episode with Fioretta had drained her and shaken her to her core. All of her other past life experiences had either been visions or dreams. But what had occurred just now with Fioretta was different. Somehow Sophia had followed her into the future, inhabiting her body in the present day.

I became Sophia. How can that be? Is it possible that the deeper I go, the more my past lives can take hold of me? Am I losing myself?

No matter how she tried, she couldn't get Sophia's words about the painting out of her head, *there's some kind of curse on you. Whomever possesses you dies.* Her fears for Alex's safety drained her of whatever strength she had left.

The more she thought about the painting and the inherent danger it posed to Alex, the more she worried that it was a sign that they weren't meant to be. Once her fears took hold of her she couldn't shake them.

After they got back to the hotel, Alex insisted she take a nap and she agreed. She kissed him on the lips and lay down on the bed. He covered her with a blanket and sat beside her, sweeping her hair away from her face.

No words passed between them.

She loved him. She loved him, and she feared for his life.

As her eyelids grew heavy she glimpsed the worry banked in his eyes. Worry for her because he couldn't stop the past from pulling her back into its shadowy depths. She had to retrieve the painting and maybe then, she could break free. But for now, Morpheus was calling to her and she answered, falling into a deep, dreamless sleep.

When Angela awoke she was lying in Alex's arms. She gazed into Alex's extraordinary eyes. They were filled with remorse.

He cupped her cheek. "Today, when you disappeared into the past, I realized how helpless I am. I couldn't protect you and it ate at my gut. I've talked this big game of keeping you safe and every time I fail you. I'm worried that this damn painting is going to cost me too much. That I'm going to lose you."

His words reminded her of what Sophia had said, *I know you're the reason this nightmare befell us. It's because of you he was taken from me. Whomever possesses you dies. Why did he take you? Tell me why?* "You aren't failing me. But I'm failing you. Your involvement with me can only bring disaster." Her voice was raspy from sleep and emotion. "I don't belong in your world."

"You are my world." He bent his head to kiss her. A delicate, tender kiss that moved her to tears. She couldn't stop the force of nature that drew them together. She was conflicted, being with her endangered his life and living without him meant a life without love. She could only hope that whatever happened, Alex would be safe from the fate that befell him in his past lives.

He peeled back the blanket and pulled her up to her knees. Kissing her with a fevered intensity that brought her walls tumbling down. Frantically, they unbuttoned, unzipped, unclasped, letting their clothes fall where they may.

She was an arid desert, craving the storm that promised to quench her parched earth. Her arms clasped his neck, the soft skin of her breasts pressed against the rough hair of his chest. Her breath escaped in a rush of exaltation. She'd never known what unbridled passion for another meant. The dream of satisfaction and the fear of losing herself threatened to obliterate who she was. It frightened her, but she could no more refuse the promised pleasure than she could forego food and water. Each was indispensable and Alex was becoming indispensable to her.

Is this what Fioretta felt for Giuliano, what Sophia felt for Gerhard? Were they, Alex and her, just the continuation of what had been? Neither with a will of their own, but part of a cycle of destiny written in the stars.

He was kissing her everywhere, intent on claiming her. The heat between them threatened to consume her. The past exploded in her mind, blinding her, bursting like the flashbulbs of an old-time camera. It was as if Giuliano, Gerhard, and Alex were making love to her at once. Giuliano's loving endearments, Gerhard's bold passion, Alex embodied them all, which made his lovemaking otherworldly and without equal. She couldn't resist, she couldn't pretend indifference. She belonged to him…

The way he loved her was a gift, a plea, a total relinquishment of his heart. He belonged to her and she to him. With a groan of passion, he took her, and she cried out drenching him in her ecstasy.

Afterward, he whispered in her ear. "I'll take one of your beautiful orgasms to start, but my love, one is just the beginning. I don't think you can resist me any more than I can resist you. I'm never going to let you go. I'm going to keep you close to me whatever comes. I'm going to prove to you every day and night that we belong together."

His words ignited her, she craved every part of him. When he poured himself into her again, she opened the floodgates taking everything he had to give. She held tight to him as if there was no tomorrow.

CHAPTER 18

Montefioralle, Italy
Present day
August 14

Tomorrow came and they flew back to Florence and then drove back to Montefioralle. Alex focused on the shifting gears as he pushed his speed machine through its paces. He was determined not to let Angela out of his sight. Her fears had only reinforced his desire to keep her safe.

When they returned to the house, he swept her off her feet and carried her to their bedroom. Making love to her kept her in bed where he could be there should her past lives come calling. Their bed was safe. He knew he couldn't keep her there indefinitely, however, his own insecurities were wreaking havoc. He was afraid of losing her. Afraid that she would choose logic over love.

He woke up, tangled in sheets, legs and arms entwined with Angela's, the scent of their lovemaking a heady perfume that lingered in the air. Alex fingered a strand of Angela's dark hair and buried his nose in it, inhaling her intoxicating scent. He was tempted to wake her by nestling himself inside of her. To begin the day by making love to her would be heaven. He couldn't get enough of her. He refrained only because he'd made love to her most of the night and he was afraid she might be sore.

It occurred to him that they hadn't been using protection. *She's probably on birth control, but maybe not.* Why didn't that bother him? He was thirty-two years old, and having a child wouldn't be the worst thing that could happen. With her, it might be the best thing ever. Marriage. He tried to picture them as a family. *Not in the Ferrari, that's for sure. A nice, safe Range Rover.* He shook his head at his musings. *I want this with her. But I need to get us to the finish line. Solve the mystery of the painting.*

He snuggled against Angela's back. Her purr affected him like a mating call. He was loaded and ready in an instant.

"Good morning," she whispered.

"Good morning, beautiful. I hope you got enough sleep."

"Well... not really. It seems someone was determined to steal most of it."

"Can I steal some more?" He pressed into her. She gasped and he growled, sizzling from the rush of sparks bursting into flames. "Baby, the more you give, the more I want."

"Don't stop." She was breathless.

"Mmmm, never." He entered her from behind, his hands cupping her breasts, his fingers circling her nipples drawing gasps from her. Then cries of pleasure as he trailed his hands down to her moist core.

Alex knew when flames burn this hot they quickly consume everything in their wake, and this was no exception. When she melted with a cry of "Alex," it drove him crazy, the world ceased to exist, time stopped, and the past, the present, and future merged into one heart-stopping moment. She was definitely his kryptonite.

Spent, in a world of their own, they lay as one. Their hearts beat in rhythm, their breaths slowed in time, neither wanted to break the spell.

He kissed her ear. "You're mine, baby. You've given up that ridiculous notion that we aren't meant to be, haven't you?"

"How can I even consider leaving a man who hasn't let me out of bed for over twelve hours?"

"I'm considering keeping you here for another twelve," he pressed against her molding himself to her curves.

She turned in his arms. "Are you afraid if you let go of my body I might disappear?"

He nodded sheepishly. "Maybe. It seems I'll go to any length not to lose you."

"You win. You're not losing me, Alex. What woman doesn't welcome being worshipped by the man she loves? I'm not sure why I'm the lucky girl who stole your heart, but I'm so happy that it's me."

"Are you saying you love me?"

She reached up and laid her hands on his cheeks. "Let me clear up any mystery. Yes. I love you. I love you. I love you."

He grinned like he just won the lottery, "I'm satisfied with that answer."

"I'm not." She ran her fingers over a battle scar on his shoulder from his tours as a Navy SEAL. Then, slowly, she delicately trailed them down his chest, brushing the fine line of hair on his abdomen until she grasped him, sliding her hand lightly over him. Her breath became uneven, it was the first time she'd initiated sex with him. His body stiffened in anticipation. Her lips sought his and he let her lead, loving every minute of her laying claim to what she wanted.

Rolling on top of him, she pushed him inside and rolled her hips against him, rocking to her own inner rhythm. He could barely breathe, it was so erotic watching her dance with him inside her. Her parted lips so sweet and tempting. Unable to resist, he reached up and massaged her breasts and then pinching one nipple with one hand, his other hand dropped to her clitoris and he gently rubbed it until it was swollen and hard. "Alex... it feels so good."

Her heat engulfed him, and he couldn't hold back. He bent his legs and thrust up into her, driving up as she fell into him. They cried each other's name as they exploded. She tumbled onto his chest trembling.

"Angel, that was the most sensual thing I've ever felt." He groaned. He knew this was a breakthrough for her. Sexually she was exploring and that's something you only do in a relationship of trust and love. His heart pounded in his chest. It was a gift he'd cherish forever.

The beginning of their life together.

Angela rubbed her hair dry and strolled into the bedroom. Alex sat on the bed working on his laptop. He'd offered to shower with her, but she'd begged off, she needed some time to think and to refresh after a day and night of lovemaking. She was tired. She seemed to be getting more tired all the time. There was a price to pay for travelling backward and forward in time.

"Do you feel any better? I'm worried about you." Alex set the laptop aside.

"Yes, nothing like a hot steamy shower to wash away your troubles. I'm sorry about not wanting to shower together. I needed some quiet time to think. So many unanswered questions."

"I know. We'll find the answers, baby. I promise you, we'll get to the bottom of this and move forward." He patted the bed for her to sit. "None of this is going to matter a month from now."

"I hope you're right. I don't think I can take much more." She wrapped the towel around her head and sat beside him.

"Babe, I haven't pressed you, but what exactly happened between you and Fioretta?"

She'd made up her mind on the flight home; she wasn't going to tell him that she knew where the painting was. She felt terrible about it, considering she'd made him promise no more secrets and here she was keeping the biggest secret of all. But she had no choice. She had to protect him. She wasn't going to risk the possibility that history might repeat itself. She wasn't going to endanger him. He was in more danger than she was; he was murdered in two past lives, she wasn't. Even as scared as she was, nothing was worth risking his life. No matter what he said, the possibility was real that this was some cosmic repetition of what had already occurred. She knew she could never convince him of her fears, so the best thing to do was keep him in the dark.

On the plane she'd devised her answer and was prepared when he asked. "What I experienced was a tragic moment in Fioretta and Sophia's lives. I found myself as Sophia walking up a steep trail. It was a rainy night and I was on my way to the secret cave. I wanted to look at the painting that Gerhard had loved so much. It was so important to him and I knew it would bring me closer to him.

"I never got there because Fioretta followed me. I was so afraid she'd catch a deadly cold and I'd lose another person I loved. I sternly reprimanded her and scared her. The child begged for my forgiveness. I didn't mean to be so harsh, but my heart was breaking. It was the anniversary of my engagement to the only man I would ever love, and she'd spoiled it. I don't think Fioretta ever forgot that night or the feeling that her mother didn't love her" *Good. I didn't lie, I just omitted a bit of the truth.*

She inwardly squirmed as Alex studied her face with shrewd eyes. She wasn't a card player, so she hoped she'd managed a good poker face.

"So, you're saying she never actually got to the cave and the painting, which means you have no idea where the cave is?" he asked.

She sighed. "Not yet, anyway."

"Maybe we should just start combing the hills above the vineyard?"

"I don't think that's productive. The one thing I'm certain of is that the cave is well concealed. I don't think we'd get anywhere."

"I see…" His brow furrowed. You had a pretty strong reaction to what you saw."

"It was so heart wrenching hearing Fioretta cry *Mama, I love you*, over and over, just as I'd heard it in the vision. I wanted to bring her some peace."

"What did you whisper to her?"

"It was strange, but the words in Italian came to me—I said—*I love you, Fioretta, I always will. Be at peace. You are my child and I love you.*" Her voice cracked and tears trickled down her cheeks. "I'm not sure whether I hurt her or helped her."

Alex wrapped his arms around her. "Angel, don't cry. You did the right thing. You gave an old woman peace. People get twisted sometimes by what happens to them. Sophia lost her way after losing Gerhard, Fioretta suffered. That's life I'm afraid."

"Did that happen to you with your mom after your parents divorced?"

He stiffened. "My mother is another story entirely."

"She may have failed you in many ways, but I'm sure she loves you. You do believe that, don't you?"

"When it comes to Faye I've never known what to believe. I wish I had your gift to see into my past lives. Maybe Faye and I are just working out our karma. Maybe I was her father or mother in a past life and I let her down." He laughed. "Who knows? Wow, I'm becoming quite the psychic spiritualist."

Angela smiled. "Yeah, next thing you know you'll be wearing a loincloth and meditating in the wilderness."

He pulled her closer. "The quicker to get to you with just a loincloth on. I can be your guru, so long as it doesn't entail abstinence." There went his eyebrows again, and she burst into laughter.

"The quicker I'll know if I get a rise out of you."

"Delicious little potty mouth. That beautiful ass of yours might need a paddling."

"Are you sure you're up to the challenge?" *Just what I needed to distract him, sexy banter. Men and their one-track minds. Although, I'm not complaining. It's distracted me too.*

"Trust me, I'll leave my mark."

"Looks like my shower was prescient."

"Looks like you might need another one."

"Are you ever satisfied?"

"Not with you around. Hot shower and hot sex is the best way to start a day."

He might as well have plugged her into a socket. Warmth travelled through her body like a power surge of electricity, lighting her up. She hoped she didn't short circuit and blow a fuse.

"What's so funny?" Alex asked.

"I'm trying to figure out how Angela the academic transformed into Angela the sex goddess."

"My guess is you were a dormant volcano just waiting to erupt. All it took was the right man to awaken you."

"And you think you're the right man?"

"I know I am. In fact…" His hot breath filled her ear. "I sense the lava building now, barely able to contain itself." His lips travelling along her collarbone made her breath catch. "See what I mean?" he whispered in her ear. Your response tells me all I need to know."

"Is this what you call chemistry?"

"Yes, this is what you call a full on chemical reaction."

"Hmmm…"

"All I need to do is add one more ingredient." He rolled her onto her back and pinned her beneath him.

"Ouch, your laptop!"

"Oops, sorry about that." He pulled it out from under her. "Forget the shower. Now, where were we?"

CHAPTER 19

Alberto Scordato's cell phone vibrated in his pocket. He swung his rifle over his shoulder and answered.

"Enrico, *come stai*? Have you made the arrangements for Max's send off?"

"Yes."

"Are you sure there will be no trace, no questions?"

"For all intents and purposes, an unfortunate accident."

"I see." Scordato knew to be cryptic on the phone even though Enrico had acquired satellite phones, safeguarding their calls so they couldn't be traced. Enrico was a good foot soldier. Scordato knew he'd make sure their plans went off without a hitch. Max's demise was a loose end that could not be avoided. He knew too much and was after the painting and Scordato didn't believe the only reason was to clear his family's name. In his mind everything came down to money.

Enrico interrupted his thoughts. "Did you find out what they were doing in Rome?"

"Yes, thanks to Madame X." One day, he would ask Enrico about meeting this mystery woman who was making their plan virtually effortless. His cousin had never met her either but had connected with her through a network of intermediaries. Everything was going according to plan. Between his cousin's mafia connections and his own brilliant mind, they were well on track to locating the painting. "They were visiting a woman named Fioretta Rossi."

"Does she have a connection to the painting?"

"I did some digging through the public records and Fioretta Rossi sold the vineyard to Caine two years ago. She's the daughter of a woman named

Sophia Caro. I did some research and I learned that Caro coincidentally worked at the Uffizi in 1944 when Gerhard Jaeger was there. The link is undeniable."

"Which means the detective and the intern are edging closer to the painting."

"*Si.* But the thing I find particularly interesting as an art historian is that her name is Fioretta. Fioretta was Giuliano Medici's mistress and the mother of his only child Giulio. The Medici ties to Leonardo are unquestionable." He peered around a cypress tree, spotting a stag in the distance. "Tell me, Enrico, why would Sophia Caro name her daughter after Medici's mistress?"

"I take it you think it's because of the painting."

"The *pièce de résistance* is that Fioretta, probably with the encouragement of her mother, named *her* daughter Lucrezia. Lucrezia Tornabuoni was Giuliano Medici's mother. None of this is coincidence."

"When do we make our move?"

"Soon, Enrico, very soon. It is all about the timing. I want the situation with the German settled simultaneously with our plans for Caine."

"The German's jet is now accessible, and my men will make the modifications when you give the green light."

"Good. By the way, plan on eating venison for a while." Scordato disconnected and stuffed his cell phone back in his pocket. Swinging his high-powered hunting rifle off his shoulder, he slid the bolt open, loaded five bullets, and closed the bolt. He lifted the rifle, aligned his eye with the telescope and panned until he sighted the stag about one-hundred yards away. He slid the safety lever off, took a deep breath, released a bit of air, and held it. Slowly squeezing the trigger, he fired. The stag stumbled and fell motionless.

He grinned and walked back to the truck, setting the rifle on the backseat. "Dinner."

CHAPTER 20

Montefioralle, Italy
Present day
August 17

After Rome, Angela needed a break from the case. They'd made love, walked and played with the dogs, cooked spaghetti and meatballs, and made love again. She should have been physically spent, but Angela had tossed and turned, mumbling in her sleep, and Alex spent a sleepless night worried about her.

At one point she'd flailed, fighting an invisible demon and pounded on his chest. Italian and English intermingled in her tortured mind as her dreams seesawed her from the past to the present. He had to shake her awake until he finally got through to her that she was safe in his arms.

He was worried, the nightmares were getting worse, and no matter how much he soothed and held her, he couldn't chase them away. The search for the painting was taking its toll; she was sinking into the quicksand of the past.

After a few fitful hours of slumber, he woke up and gazed at her sleeping face. Dark circles rimmed her eyes. Maybe he should take her away, go somewhere away from Montefioralle and Florence and the ghosts that stalked her dreams. He considered it, but he knew it wouldn't help. The only thing that would end the nightmares was finding the painting. Only then would she be free. Only then would they both be free.

Regretfully, he slipped from beneath the sheets and left the warmth of her body. He wanted her to sleep as long as possible. She needed to recover.

He was besieged by nagging thoughts, something about her story about Fioretta didn't connect. Was she keeping something from him? Not telling him everything about what had occurred in her last episode. Would she do that? He was certain she trusted him, so why would she hold back information? Then it hit him full force.

She's protecting me. She's afraid the past will repeat itself.

The thought of it made him want to punch his fist through a wall. Didn't she understand the danger she was in?

He dressed, determined to act. He needed to protect Angela.

Maria and Joseph hadn't returned yet from their weekend away. Their son had to work, and they needed to babysit their granddaughter. Alex was glad for the extra alone time with Angela. He would press her to reveal the complete truth of her vision with Fioretta.

He strode to the library and opened a secret wall panel. Inside was an assortment of firearms and ammunition. He began loading and checking to make sure they were all in firing order. *If that bastard even tries to get anywhere near Angela, I'll kill him first.* When every firearm was loaded and ready, he began stashing them around the house in hidden lockboxes. He put his favorite Glock in the glove compartment of the Ferrari, just in case they had to make a quick escape. Feeling better that he'd prepared for any eventuality, he returned to the kitchen.

He'd just finished laying out ingredients for breakfast on the counter when the phone rang. Max Jaeger's name popped on the screen. Alex had kept his texting to Max at a minimum, however, he'd mentioned the side-trip to Rome. Max was probably checking in for an update.

"Good morning, Max. How're things in Munich?"

"*Guten morgen.* I feel like a rat on a wheel, always running. Are you back from Rome?"

"Yes."

"How did it go?"

"It went well. We're getting closer. But if you're asking if I know where the painting is, I don't. Not yet, anyway."

"I see. I have some disturbing news to share with you later."

"What's wrong with right now? I'd rather not let my imagination run wild."

"We need to have this conversation in person. I have some business to take care of in Florence. I'm flying in today. I think we have to be cautious. Scordato has resurfaced and your suspicions were right, he's after the painting."

"He was fired from the Getty. And I know I'm right. He's in Europe, and he's after the painting. As I already told you in my previous briefing, I'm certain the two goons who attacked me in Florence were Scordato's men."

"Yes, who would have thought an art director could possess such criminal tendencies?"

"Scordato is a sociopath," Alex said in warning. "You need to be careful. I wouldn't put anything past him."

Max laughed. "Don't worry about me. I have a team dedicated to ensuring my safety. I don't trust him either, but it's you that needs to be careful. I'll call you when I land. I'd like to meet for dinner, with Angela of course."

"I have a better idea. Why don't we have dinner at my apartment in Florence? I'll make you a home-cooked Italian meal. It will be far more relaxing and give us some privacy. We can discuss everything then. I'll text you directions. I'm right in the city center, at the Palazzo Rucellai. Let's say 7 p.m. cocktails."

"That will work fine with my schedule."

"Good, I look forward to it. Max, I think it will be good for you and Angela to meet."

"Yes, I believe it's time I met your consultant. I have some questions for her. *Auf wiedersehen.*"

"*Ciao.*"

Angela woke to the mouth-watering aroma of eggs and bacon. She stretched and instinctively reached for Alex, but the bed was empty. *I guess Maria and Joseph didn't make it back and Alex is cooking.* It was easy to distinguish between Maria's Italian breakfasts filled with herbs and spices and Alex's purely American cuisine. Not that one was better than the other, bacon and eggs sounded great.

Her night had been a series of nightmares. Unfortunately, she remembered nothing. *I'm probably too exhausted to recall anything.* She'd come to realize that there was a difference between the past calling to her and her trying to see into the past. She couldn't get Fioretta's cries of *I love you, Mama,* or the despair in her eyes, out of her head. Why do people hurt the ones they love?

Poor Alex, he must be so frustrated. How was it that nightmares could be so physically punishing? The proof was her body, every inch of her ached. Of course, that could also be from all the delicious sex.

In the bathroom, she stared in the mirror and shuddered. She looked like a wraith. Purple shadows circled her eyes as if she'd been in a prize fight and lost. *Damn, you look terrible.* She jumped in the shower and turned on the tap. The enclosure quickly filled with steam while hot water from the rain shower head ran in rivulets down her body. *Heaven.*

As she lathered her hair, she gazed out the window at the artistry of Mother Nature. The fading greens of summer were transforming into the vibrant rusts and golden yellows of fall. Even from this distance, the grapevines appeared lush with fruit.

The passing of seasons reminded her that no matter what, life moved on. *Nature never lies. It always shows us her truth.* If Sophia had not hidden the painting, if she had not lied to Gerhard, would that have changed the trajectory of their lives? If Fioretta and Giuliano had told Lorenzo of their marriage and their child, would they have lived under the protection of the Medici household? Would Giuliano have survived the assassination? And in so doing, would Fioretta have lived through childbirth with no tragedy to weaken her spirit?

She remembered Alex telling her of the *vendemmia* when they first arrived. Had it only been a week ago? It felt like years. So much had changed. *I can't keep the truth from him. It's not right. We can't begin a life together based on lies.* Especially after she made him swear to honesty.

The truth shall set you free.

She stood under the showerhead, letting the warm water wash away her fears and cleanse her mind and heart.

She would surprise him. They could take a hike with the dogs and she would lead him to the cave. She smiled, anticipating his surprise when she pulled the infamous portrait out of its seventy-year-old hiding place.

She stepped out of the shower and wrapped a fluffy towel around herself, anxious to get downstairs, to Alex.

All their troubles would be over; they'd be free to be together without the specter of the past hanging over their heads. She imagined a future free of a five-hundred-year-old painting. A future where she and Alex could develop into something more. Maybe this crazy relationship wasn't wrong. Maybe Alex and she could find their happily-ever-after ending.

Alex whistled along to a recording of Pavarotti singing *Nessun Dorma.* Angela's laughter made him turn. As usual, she was followed in by her escort committee—Zaba, Ama, and Misu.

"Good morning, love. What's so funny?"

"You. Opera? You like opera?"

"Guilty as charged. Opera's the music of love and passion, and besides, this is Italy and it would be sacrilegious not to love the music of my adopted homeland."

"I would never have pegged you as an aficionado. I kind of figured you were heavy metal all the way."

"Remind me sometime to show you my pics from the Big 4 concert in Warsaw, in 2010—Metallica, Slayer, Anthrax, and Megadeth."

She rolled her eyes at him as he pointed the wooden spoon at her to make his point. "The things you don't know about me could fill a book. I'm afraid you're just going to have to stick around to know all there is to know about the mysterious Alex Caine. Besides, no way I'm going to be predictable. I hold your interest by surprising you."

"You've held my interest since the moment we met, and you continue to surprise me without even trying."

"Right now, I'm surprising you with an all-American breakfast of bacon and eggs."

"I thought Joseph and Maria were due back."

"Their son had to work, and their daughter-in-law is pregnant and due in a month. They stayed an extra day to help with their grandson. They won't be back until tomorrow."

Expertly he slid the eggs and bacon onto two plates and set them on the table. Returning to the stove, he opened the oven and grabbed thick slabs of Italian bread, tossed them in a basket, and added that to the feast. He leaned down and kissed Angela's cheek, joining her at the table. "How's it look, beautiful?"

"Like heaven." She crunched a rasher of bacon.

"You had a tough night."

She dropped her eyes. "I know, sorry. When I looked in the mirror, I scared myself to death. I look terrible."

"You're beautiful. I like that sultry-I've-had-lots-of-hot-sex-look."

"I wish it was from that. I mean it is, but it's not."

"Anything you remember from last night?"

"No. I think I was so exhausted that my mind just shut down." She broke her egg and sopped up the yellow yolk with a slice of toasted bread. She popped it in her mouth and closing her eyes, sighing with pleasure. "I heard a French chef on a cooking show say that the mastery of a perfectly cooked egg was a sign of greatness. Where'd you learn to cook anyway?"

"I've always cooked. That's what comes of having a mother who never set foot in a kitchen. But, when I moved to Italy I trained with top chefs at their homes. It's a great way to vacation and learn at the same time. Good food, great wine, and interesting people from around the world. We'll do it together, if you like. I've been wanting to take a cooking class in France."

He couldn't take his eyes off her as she continued to dip the crusty bread in the egg. It was amazing the pleasure he derived from watching her eat. He leaned in and ran his finger over her lip, wiping away a drop of yolk that she'd missed with her napkin. Before he withdrew his finger, she licked it, sending a super charge to his groin. His imagination, steps ahead, pictured her splayed on the kitchen counter. *Damn. No time for fun and games.* Which was a reminder that he needed to tell her about his call with Max and their dinner plans.

"Angel, I heard from Max Jaeger. He's flying in today and I've invited him to dinner at the apartment in Florence. I thought we'd drive up this afternoon, but we need to make a stop in town and pick up some ingredients, and the Ferrari needs gas. I thought I'd whip up a *zuppa di pesce* with garlic toast, and salad. We can pick up cannoli for dessert, and you can practice your sous chef skills." He winked.

Her eyes glowed with pleasure. "I'm so excited to do something normal, like being your sous chef."

"Me too. Once we've solved this case, I hope you don't get too bored with normal."

"Me? You're kidding, right? You're the jet-setter."

"The only jet-setting I'm interested in has to do with spoiling a certain lady." He took her hand and kissed her palm.

"Alex, I think we should tell Max what happened to Gerhard. It seems only fair. After all, his family has lived all these years never knowing the truth. At least, it will bring him some closure."

"There's something else I want to tell him."

"What's that?" Her brows lifted in question.

"I'm going to tell him that the da Vinci belongs to the Uffizi and not a German museum. It must be returned to them."

Her face lit up. "Really?"

"Yeah, I've given this a whole lot of thought. Max had floated a few ideas about selling it at auction through Christie's or Sotheby's or making a grand gesture and donating it to the Staedel in Munich. I'm sure Max will be on board. His primary motive was to clear his uncle's name. But I don't think he'll mind that the painting is returned to the Uffizi."

He reached for her hand and kissed her palm. "I know you believe returning the painting is the right thing to do. If that's what you want, then it's what I want, too. Besides, I'll still have the bragging rights."

She squealed and jumped into his lap, her arms wrapping around his neck. She peppered his face with kisses amidst exclamations of delight. That got the dogs barking and wriggling around his legs.

"Whoa, there's one more thing I plan on doing," he said between kisses, his voice laced with laughter.

"More, what more could you possibly do?"

"I can insist that a certain art historian get credit for the discovery, and make sure she's the one to write the seminal paper on the painting." She stopped kissing him, and leaned back, her eyes wide. His hands cupped her face. "Think of it, baby, no one understands its provenance and the mystery that surrounds it better than you. I shouldn't have much trouble convincing Celestine to give you the recognition."

"You can't begin to know what this means to me. It's a once in a life-time discovery."

"Maybe for some, but in your case, I think this is just the beginning."

"I do have a confession to make."

"That you love me?"

She scrunched up her face. "Of course, I love you!"

"Whew!" He wiped pretend sweat off his forehead.

"Ever since this whole hunt for the painting began, I was worried about the whole money side of finding the painting. Even after you told me that you're wealthy, I still couldn't imagine anyone being able to turn down that kind of money. I know you're going to say I'm crazy, but it was always in the back of my mind."

He traced the delicate line of her cheek and gazed deeply into her eyes. "Angel, I can't even remember when that changed. It probably started on that first night at the bar. Baby, I'm in love with you. There isn't anything I wouldn't do for you."

Tears filled her eyes. "I'm in love with you too, Alex." She met his lips. Whatever reticence he'd felt from her before dissolved in that kiss. He knew the difference immediately. She opened completely to him and he knew it would only get better from here. He ached to be inside of her.

He rose with her in his arms. "I see no reason to waste that sentiment. I think we have plenty of time to seal the deal before I put you to work in the kitchen."

CHAPTER 21

Castellina, Chianti, Italy
Present day
August 17

Alberto and Enrico loaded up the rented truck with supplies. Their hired hacker, Madame X, was monitoring Alex's cell phone calls and it was time to move. Both were dressed in hunting camouflage and boots. Enrico came out of the farmhouse carrying an ice chest, which he placed on the back seat.

"Alberto, I packed some food. I threw in a couple bottles of wine, just in case."

"Good thinking. I promise your efforts will not go unanswered. By the end of today the painting will be ours." Alberto patted Enrico on the back. "Is the rifle loaded?"

"No, I wasn't sure if you would want to load it yourself and take a shot or two."

"That's probably a good idea, although yesterday, when I bagged that stag, the Bergara handled smooth as silk. As I recall on our last hunting trip, I brought down a three-hundred-pound wild boar with one shot."

"Don't remind me. We had a sizeable bet going as to who would bring home the biggest prize."

Alberto rummaged through the duffel. "You packed the gloves and balaclavas, didn't you?"

"Of course, I'm a professional. Everything is with the ammunition."

"Just checking, we don't want to leave any fingerprints or hair follicles."

"Have you forgotten about boot treads? We'll have to make sure we don't leave any boot or tire treads."

"We'll burn the boots when we get back to the farmhouse."

Enrico looked at his boots and shrugged. "Not the first time I've done that."

"Come, help me. Let's do a last-minute check on everything." Alberto strode to the trunk and opened the green duffel bag. He pulled out a carton of cartridges and then unzipped the nylon bag covering the high-powered hunting rifle. Sliding the bolt open, he loaded five bullets, and closed the bolt. He lifted the rifle and aligned his eye with the telescope and panned until he sighted a hare about one-hundred yards away. He slid the safety lever off, took a deep breath, released a bit of air, and held it. Slowly squeezing the trigger, he fired.

Alberto laughed. "Too much rifle for such small game, but good target practice."

"You haven't lost your touch, cousin, nor your emotional detachment. A true hunter." Enrico grinned.

"This Leonardo da Vinci painting is the rarest and most important game I've ever hunted. We nab it and we're on easy street." He glanced at his watch. "We need to get moving. I want to give us enough time to find a safe place to observe Caine's house. Once we've positioned ourselves and we see him leave, we'll have to move fast."

"Precision timing is key," Enrico rubbed his hands together. "I believe the German should be leaving Munich very soon."

"His flight plan is listed for twelve o'clock," Alberto said.

"Have you come up with a solution to what we do if the girl refuses to take us to the painting?"

Alberto pulled a container out of his jacket pocket and opened it. Inside were three filled hypodermic needles. "I plan on drugging her with truth serum. Questioning her will be easy and she'll have virtually no memory of what happened."

"Does that include sex?" Enrico grinned lecherously.

"If everything goes to plan, you'll have time to satisfy your lust. We both will." He looked up at the sky and the dark clouds that lay on the horizon. "Good thing we packed those waterproof rain jackets; there's a storm coming. A blessing for our endeavor. Nothing like rain to extinguish any and all evidence of a crime."

Alex showered and dressed, sat on the edge of the bed. Angela lay curled on her side, a smile of contentment on her lips. "You smell delicious," she purred.

He brushed his lips over hers, feeling the spark of electricity that never failed to arouse him. "Come on, get up and get dressed. We need to go into town and pick up a few things and get gas."

"Please, can I just stay here with the dogs? I need to get myself together." She raised her hands in supplication. "Please?"

"Under one condition only. You need to know how to use the Glock. It'll only a take a few minutes."

Angela's eyes widened. "Now? You're going to show me now?"

He grinned. "It's either that or I'm going to jump back in this bed and make love to you again."

"If you do, I'll never make it through dinner tonight with Max."

"Then up you go." He stood, took her hands and pulled her up out of the bed. He ran his eyes over her naked body. "Put something on or I won't be able to concentrate."

"No worries there, I'm not too keen on the thought of shooting a gun in my birthday suit." She pulled on her jeans and a plaid red and black flannel shirt. "Better?"

"Not really, you could be dressed in a burlap sack and you'd still be sexy to me." He opened the drawer and pulled out a Glock 19, 9-millimeter Luger. "Okay, I've already changed the grip to better fit your hand and I've loaded the magazine. There are fifteen bullets in here and an extra magazine ready to load." He pushed the release and the magazine popped out. "Here you try it."

"Like this?"

He watched her execute the exchange.

"Perfect. Do it again."

Again, she deftly removed the magazine and reloaded it. "Okay, I think I've got it."

"Now this is the release that unlocks the safety. Once you press it you're ready to fire. Spread your legs so you're balanced and extend your arms out straight, locking your elbows." He got behind her and positioned her. "Look straight down the site and gently squeeze the trigger. Don't worry, the safety is on. When you actually fire, there's going to be a recoil and the muzzle will pop slightly. Just keep squeezing the trigger and breathe. Aim for the largest part, the center of mass, the chest."

"I can't do this Alex."

"Sure you can. I know right now it seems impossible, but if you're threatened, I know you'll do what's necessary. Hopefully, you'll never have to use it." He took the gun from her and placed it back in the nightstand drawer. "Okay, you know where all the panic buttons are, and you have the dogs. I'll be right back."

"Go. I'm going to make some coffee and shower."

He put his arms around her. "I'd much rather shower with you. Hopefully, you're going to remember where Sophia hid the damn painting and we can get on with our lives."

She tilted her head up and kissed him. "I have a feeling it's going to be soon."

Reluctantly, he let go of her. "Okay, I'm out of here. Hasta La Vista, baby. Back in a flash."

CHAPTER 22

Montefioralle, Italy
Present day
August 17

Alberto and Enrico, dressed in camouflage, watched the gates to Casa de Sole swing open. A red Ferrari revved its engine and exited, its tires crunching on the gravel. When the Ferrari had disappeared from sight, the two men ran from the brush on the other side of the road, through the gates. They crept close to the house. Enrico pulled his cell phone from his pocket and waited.

Alberto put his hand on Enrico's arm, stilling him. "Let's make sure the detective is far enough away before we set it off. Just in case. We want the authorities to be investigating a deadly crash and nothing else."

The Ferrari picked up speed taking the curves, tires squealing. If the newscaster's voice hadn't grown louder he wouldn't have heard it. "*German industrialist Maximillian Jaeger's private jet crashed in a field outside of Florence. Initial reports have confirmed there are no survivors. Jaeger, a world-renowned real-estate tycoon, was also the founder of TreeHouse, one of the most popular online vacation rental websites in the world...*"

The newscaster's report continued, but Alex's brain drowned out the report. He was reeling. His last conversation with Max playing in his brain—
Angela!

His foot hit the brake, but there was no response. *Fuck!* He couldn't think, his racing pulse pounded in his head. He fought to hold the out-of-control Ferrari on the road, but the steep incline and pull of gravity had him careening downward. In the back of his mind, all he could think about was Angela and the danger she was in.

Sweat poured down his face. He was going to die and there'd be no one to protect Angela. He automatically stomped on the brake hoping for some response, but there was none. The next turn was sharp, and the car swerved, losing traction with the road. The wheels lifted and the Ferrari nearly flipped. A momentary straightaway gave him a second of respite and he tried downshifting, but the gears were locked. The car dropped down on the road with a crunch and the squealing sound of metal scraping pavement made his stomach churn.

An eerie voice whispered in his head, in Italian. *Saltare dal cavallo.*

What the... fuck? Jump from the horse? On top of everything else he was hearing voices. Barely managing to keep the out-of-control Ferrari on the road, he unsnapped his seatbelt.

He knew the next turn would be his last. He fought to push open the door against the wind and force of gravity.

Taking a leap of faith, he flung himself out of the car, covering his head and tucking his body inward as he smacked the pavement like a rubber ball, bouncing and rolling to a stop. Laying for a few minutes, he tried to calm his racing heart and catch his breath.

Cursing, he stood on wobbly legs, a searing pain sliced through his left shoulder. A moment later, a massive explosion lit the sky. If he hadn't leaped from the car, he would have been toast. The world slipped away from him as a curtain of black enveloped him...

He and Andy, his best friend, were laughing as they drove their armored Humvee back to base. They were returning from a routine day on patrol, monitoring a village not far from Kandahar. And then all hell broke loose. The Humvee hit an IED and their vehicle flew into the air, exploding. Andy lay dead, pieces of him scattered all over the road. Alex had been thrown from the vehicle and lay in the dirt with a severely wounded leg, broken ribs, and a chunk of shrapnel lodged in his arm. They medevacked him to a hospital for emergency surgery. The last thing he remembered from that day was Andy's face just before the explosion...

Alex woke up with a gasp at the burning pain. It felt as if a soldering iron had been plunged into his shoulder.

Fighting against dizziness and nausea, he lifted himself to a sitting position and then pushed himself to his feet. Staggering to a tree for support, he glimpsed bits and pieces of his car littering the road. The debris made his mind flashback to the carnage of Afghanistan. He shook his head compartmentalizing the past. He knew, without a doubt, the explosion wasn't from impact. No amateur could have orchestrated such a devastating blast.

It was a bomb, set off by an electronic signal. Probably similar to what killed Max. This was a hit and by all accounts, he should be dead. He recalled the whispered voice warning him to get out of the car. *No, he hadn't said car, he'd said horse. Jump from the horse. Ferrari. Horse. It had to be Giuliano who'd warned him.*

I have to get to Angela. Struggling against the agony in his shoulder, he hobbled back up the road toward Casa del Sole, praying he wasn't out of time.

Angela ambled downstairs, the dogs trailing her heels, to the kitchen and made a cup of coffee. She stood at the sink and gazed out the window, noting the darkening skies. So much for her beautiful day, rain was coming. Finishing her coffee, she filled the dog bowls with food. A loud blast reverberated, rattling the windowpane. Wondering if a thunderstorm was approaching, she peeked out the window again, catching sight of a plume of smoke coming from the bottom of the hill. *Alex!* She raced from the house, the door slamming behind her.

Heavy arms grabbed her from behind, holding her in an iron grip. A beefy hand covered her mouth, muffling her screams. She kicked and flailed, digging her nails into his arm and elicited a yowl of pain as she managed to slip free. Off like a rocket, she ran as fast as she could, but was tackled and flipped over. The face leering down at her looked familiar.

"Keep her steady while I ready the needle."

She screamed as another man's face came into view. *It's him!* She began thrashing and wriggling as hard as she could, trying to break the hold of the man who held her.

"My dear Angela," Scordato said as though they were sitting down to tea. "Don't make this harder on yourself." Scordato pulled a hypodermic needle from his backpack and she kicked out, trying to stop him.

"Hold her still, dammit." He pushed up her sleeve and punched the needle into her arm. In seconds, she stopped thrashing, her body went limp as a rag doll. She fought to keep her eyes open as her vision blurred. *Please, God, save Alex.*

"Angela, meet my cousin, Enrico. He's been looking forward to meeting you."

She spat at them. Enrico slapped her and then squeezed her breast.

She whimpered in reply and cursed at them. Scordato was surprised by her profanity. The truth serum certainly had an interesting effect. He looked forward to how she'd behave when they took turns with her.

"Enrico, there'll be plenty of time for that later. I only gave her a small dose of the serum. We need to act fast. Now hold her steady." He lifted her face so she could see into his eyes. "Angela, my dear, it's so good to see you."

"Not good to see you."

"I need you to show me where the da Vinci is."

She scrunched up her face. "Where's Alex. I... I have to show him, too."

"I talked to him. He's going to join us there."

"He hates you. So do I."

"Believe me the feeling is mutual. Which way do we go?"

Angela's eyes rose to the mountain behind the vineyard. "Way up there."

"Take us there." Scordato's voice was mellifluous and encouraging.

Enrico and Scordato grabbed her under the arms, dragging her up the steep incline. They kept her from falling but their progress was slow.

The trail had steepened and begun to twist. Her gaze shifted from one man to the other. "I think we're here, I mean there." She frowned. "You shouldn't be here. You want the painting for yourself. Greedy!"

Scordato threw his head back and laughed. "I love how honest you are, bella, and yet you're as weak as a kitten. I've forgotten how charming you can be."

They broke through a thicket of dense growth and the trail ended abruptly. They halted. Ahead was a large granite slab that seemed to rest against the mountain.

"Is this the place?"

She nodded. "You have to press that slab of rock and it will open."

Scordato gestured to his cousin who did as Angela suggested. Enrico placed his fingers in the groove and the slab gave. He pulled harder and it slid open enough to allow them to slip through.

Dropping his backpack to the ground, Enrico unzipped it and took out a flashlight. He turned in a circle and the beam of light lit the cave.

Spying a lantern on a shelf, Scordato reached for it and handed it to Enrico who lit it and held the light aloft. Against one wall were floor-to-ceiling racks, which held at least a hundred bottles of wine. At random, Alberto pulled a bottle out and studied the label. 1954. "Too bad we can't take some of this wine with us. It would be nice to celebrate our successful discovery of the da Vinci with your fool detective's wine, but alas, I'm afraid we'll have to be satisfied with the painting alone. Now, Angela, it's time for you to deliver."

On the opposite side of the cave she spotted the wine barrels. Inside one of the barrels was the da Vinci. Her stomach did a backflip and the hairs on her arms stood on end. The world around her began to spin. Voices called to her; faces like a deck of cards tossed by the wind, flashed by. It was as if she was inside a whirling tornado, like Dorothy in the *Wizard of Oz* she spun downward. Just when her lungs were about to burst, she felt herself step once more into the past...

Florence, Italy
Uffizi Gallery
July, 1944

"Sophia, are you all right? You stopped talking mid-sentence and you look pale."

"I don't know what came over me. I suddenly felt as if I couldn't draw a breath."

Gerhard put his arms around her and kissed her forehead. "It's very musty in here. You might be allergic. Do you think you can continue?"

She smiled, taking his face in her hands. "Yes. I wouldn't think of depriving you of your adventure. I want you to experience the hidden treasures of the Uffizi."

His eyes drifted to the storage slats that climbed the walls to the ceiling. Hundreds of wrapped paintings beckoned. In the center of the room were canvas clothed sculptures. "Is all of this catalogued?"

She took his hand and drew him to a door. "Come see." Opening the door, she switched on the lights. The walls were lined with filing cabinets. "These files contain records of the entire collection. Each cabinet is labeled by year, starting from the thirteenth century. The Roman and Greek pieces that were in the Medici collection are catalogued separately. "Go ahead and take a look."

Like a child in a candy store, he eagerly opened the drawer labeled 1490-1512, the period considered the High Renaissance. While he thumbed through the folders studying their contents, she sat in a chair. *Perhaps he's right and I am allergic.* Queasiness assaulted her and her hands flew to her belly. *Or perhaps this bambino is to blame.* She hadn't told him yet that she was pregnant.

I have to tell him. It isn't fair for him not to know. One way or another, with or without him, she would have this child. She prayed he would be happy when he found out.

He interrupted her daydream. "Sophia, I'm interested in seeing this piece." He pointed to a catalogue number. "It's from Leonardo da Vinci's atelier. I'm sure it's something mediocre, but I'd like to see it."

"May I ask what makes this one so special?"

"Intuition?" He laughed. "Call it my insane obsession with the insignificant output of the greatest but least prolific artist of all time. I'm a treasure hunter at heart." He extended his hand to her, helping her rise from the chair, trailing behind her into the main storage facility.

She was familiar with the system, having worked on it for two years. "It's up there," she pointed. "Take the ladder and bring it down."

He ascended the ladder and carefully retrieved the painting. He laid it on a work table and unwrapped it. She watched his face light up and followed his gaze.

It was a wedding portrait consistent with the practices of the period. A particularly beautiful example, to be certain. She studied the groom with puzzlement. "That's odd. Giuliano Medici never married. He was murdered on Easter, in 1478, in the Pazzi conspiracy."

Gerhard studied the painting. "Clearly that's wrong. Or maybe the painting was done in anticipation of a soon-to-be wedding. Who do you think the bride is?"

"His mistress at the time was Fioretta Gorini. We know very little about her. She died in childbirth, a month later. Their son was raised by his uncle Lorenzo and later became Pope Clement the VII. I wonder if it's possible that they were secretly married?"

"Well, I can tell you one thing for sure, this is no apprentice's work. Look at the brush strokes and the way Fioretta captures the attention of the viewer by staring out from the painting. Does it remind you of any other painting?"

"It looks familiar, but tell me what you're thinking."

"Let me see the file, please." Taking it from her, he opened it and began reading and turning the pages. She peered over his shoulder. He came to a document. Excitedly, he tapped the page with his index finger. "How did the collection come into the hands of the state?"

"Anna Maria Luisa, the last of the Medici, signed the *Patto di Famiglia*, in 1737, willing all of the personal property of the Medici to the Tuscan state. It included a stipulation that none of the collection ever leave Florence."

He pointed, again. "This is an inventory from Lorenzo's household. Notice the notation of the wedding portrait? It says inherited from Lucrezia Tornabuoni, Giuliano and Lorenzo's mother, in 1482 and makes a point of saying "artist unknown." There's no mention of who the people in the portrait are. Isn't it strange that Lorenzo doesn't mention that the portrait is of his brother? Why do you think that is?"

She shook her head. "Possible problems with political alliances. Giuliano was promised in marriage to someone else."

"Exactly. Why cause trouble when both Giuliano and the bride are dead? What difference would it make to history?"

"None really."

"Unless the painting gained notoriety. Then it would be hard to keep under wraps, wouldn't it?"

"I suppose it would. But why would the painting gain fame?"

He whispered with reverence. "If it was painted by Leonardo da Vinci and not attributed to a minor artist in his atelier, then it would gain immeasurable fame."

"You think this is a da Vinci portrait?"

"I do."

"But that's impossible…" She couldn't finish the sentence as the possibility took hold in her mind.

"I'd like to study it and the file more carefully."

"Yes. Let's take it upstairs. I'll sign it out."

"No!"

"What do you mean, no?"

"Let's just take the painting and the file and decide later what to do with them."

"That's against policy, Gerhard. If we take the painting and the file, there is no record of its existence."

"Please, indulge me."

She didn't have the heart to refuse him. Besides, it was more important to impart her own news to him. "Gerhard, darling, I have something to tell you." He was so ebullient it seemed a perfect opportunity to tell him about the pregnancy.

He took her hands. "What is it, *amore mio*?"

"Gerhard, I'm pregnant. A couple of months."

"Why didn't you tell me sooner?" He took her into his arms, kissing her. "I'm so happy! I'm the luckiest man in the world."

"You want this? You're not upset?"

"Upset? The woman I love is bearing my child. Why would I be upset?"

"The war Gerhard. It's not the best of times to be delivering children into the world. Especially given that you're an occupying German soldier."

"We can't always choose when happiness comes. This is a child of our love, a reinforcement of what we both feel."

She leaned her head on his shoulder. "Thank you."

"What a day for me. Finding a long-lost Leonardo da Vinci and finding out I'm to be a father. Come, let's go upstairs and celebrate…"

Angela felt the pull of time dragging her back… Stumbling and swirling with the power of a gale strength wind at her back, she plummeted back into her trembling body. Her eyes opened, disoriented, fuzzy.

Slowly, the world around her came into focus. She was on the bed in the cave, in Montefioralle. Scordato and another man were arguing a few feet away.

"You must have given her too much of that damn truth serum, Alberto. And what the hell has she been going on about?"

"Calm yourself, Enrico. The dose was minuscule, not enough to put her under. As far as her ranting goes, if I had to guess, she's experiencing visions from a past life. That's the reason she knows where the painting is in the first place. At least we know there won't be any interference by the detective. He's most likely nothing more than a burnt ember by now. We're so close, cousin. We're going to be rich beyond our wildest dreams."

The drug had completely worn off, and Angela knew that the vision she'd experienced had nothing to do with the effects of the serum. The two men had no idea she was fully awake and clear-headed, listening to their every word.

She fought the tears that threatened. *He's not dead. He can't be dead.* She understood why Sophia blamed the painting for Gerhard's murder. *History will not repeat itself.* She would not let these monsters win. *I can't let it happen again. Alex is not dead. I would know if he was.*

Then, like a wind chime in her mind, she heard Giuliano speak. *Alex is not dead. We are all here, Angela. Here to help you. Stay strong. This time they will not win.*

She opened her eyes and blinked. Scordato's face morphed from one of his incarnations to the next. She recognized the hate-filled face of Francesco de' Pazzi, and then she saw Franz, the German deserter who'd threatened to rape Sophia and murdered Gerhard. She couldn't bear to look at him.

The same was true when she looked at Enrico. His features transformed before her eyes and she could see her enemy for who he truly was. Bernardo Bandino Baroncelli, the man who'd struck his dagger through Giuliano's heart, and in another life, seventy-three years ago, she'd shot and killed him. He was the other deserter, Dietrich, the man who ended Gerhard's life.

As impossible as it was to believe, she realized this moment was her opportunity to right the wrongs and be the instrument that exacted their karmic debt. She could change the future result and stop the circular nature of cause and effect, and the rebirth of pure evil.

She pretended to still be under the influence of the truth serum. "Director Scordato, what happened?"

"Angela, I've been so worried about you. You had some kind of seizure. Are you feeling better?"

"Yes, I am."

"Do you think you can help us find the painting?"

"S-shouldn't we wait for Aleshhh?" She intentionally slurred her words.

"By the time you retrieve the painting, Alex should be here."

A warmth surrounded her. A diaphanous cloud settled over her vision. Sophia and Gerhard stood next to the bed wrapped in each other's arms. Their skin glowed with the freshness of youth. They kissed, and the honesty of their love tore at her heart. When they broke the kiss, they both looked at her and smiled. She thought she heard movement and turned to look. On the side of the bed, Fioretta stood with Giuliano, his arms secured around her. They, too, smiled, encouraging her.

"Alex will come, won't he?" she asked the ghosts.

"Of course, he'll come," Alberto answered.

The ghosts nodded in unison, yes. A single tear made its way down her cheek and dripped onto her hand. In that instant, the ghostly apparitions faded, dissolving like morning mist on a lake after the sun rises. A burden lifted from her shoulders and, taking a deep breath, she knew what she must do.

Alex made it back to the house. Sheer will and adrenaline spurred him on. He ignored the stabs of pain from every breath he took and every step forward.

"Angela, where are you?" His voice echoed back at him. He hadn't expected to find her there, but still, the reality felt like a punch to his gut. The dogs jumped on him, whining and growling. He patted them. "*Dov'è Angela?* Where is she?" He knew the dogs would die to protect her. It didn't make sense.

When he checked the kitchen, he found her coffee cup near the sink. There was no sign anywhere of a struggle, so he had to assume Scordato had lured her outside somehow without the dogs. He looked out the window just as he knew she would have.

Shit! The explosion. She must have panicked and run from the house, not thinking about anything other than getting to him.

Alex drove all thoughts of her being harmed out of his mind. He had to stay focused on one thing and that was finding her. He ran upstairs and checked the nightstand next to the bed. The Glock was where he'd left it. Grabbing it, he stuffed it into his waistband. She was unarmed. But she was smart and resourceful. He prayed her psychic ability would include knowing that he would come for her no matter what.

He ran to the lockbox and pulled out extra magazines for the Glock and stuck them in his backpack along with a medical kit. He changed into hiking boots and strapped his sheath and combat knife to his leg. He hurried downstairs with the dogs on his heels.

It had begun to rain, and he grabbed his hooded anorak and Angela's raincoat. He held it to the dogs' noses. The scent of her made their tails wag commensurate with their love for her. His command to the dogs was succinct. "*Trova Angela. Silenzio e caccia!*" he ordered. Trained to hunt, they ran off ahead toward the mountain, their noses to the ground. The command to find Angela and hunt in silence completely understood. He knew the dogs would find her. In his gut, he knew she was all right. She had to be.

He tried to keep up with the dogs, but the jarring pain in his shoulder impeded his progress. His thoughts raced in tandem, fear and guilt vying to overwhelm him. If anything happened to her he'd spend the rest of his life seeking vengeance.

He thought about Angela's worries for him, how she feared history was repeating itself. In his mind he replayed what had occurred when Fioretta and Angela had met. How they'd locked in on each other and travelled together back to the past. That's where the needle got stuck in the groove. Her behavior had significantly changed after that. She said she would tell him everything about her vision with Fioretta when they were alone. But what had she told him? She'd denied ever getting to the cave, claiming Fioretta had been the cause.

His anger rose, quashing his ability to think. The veins in his neck corded, echoing the knot that swelled in his gut. It was the first time he consciously understood that she'd been lying to him. *Jesus, she knows where the painting is.* Pushing beyond the pain, he began to jog up the trail.

Angela had done everything she could to delay the inevitable. Scordato was losing patience with her.

"This conversation has grown wearisome, Angela. Show us where the painting is hidden."

Reluctantly, her gaze shifted to the barrels.

Alberto's face broke into a smile. "Very clever. Is it inside? Where's the opening?"

"Beneath the center barrel there's a panel that opens." The look of avarice on Scordato's face sickened her. Not only was he a disgusting pig, but a greedy bastard.

"Tell me something, Angela. I'm curious, how did you find out the whereabouts of the painting?"

"It came to me in dreams." She had no intention of explaining her connection to Fioretta and Sophia.

"Why do I think there's more to this story? Are you psychic?"

She didn't answer him.

"It's interesting that the mystery of the painting was revealed to you in dreams."

She shrugged. "There are things that are beyond any explanation."

In the meantime, Enrico had gotten down on his knees to examine the barrel. "Alberto, it's too small a space, neither of us can fit under here."

"Don't be foolish Enrico. We're not crawling underneath that. Angela is." He turned to her. "I believe, that's your cue, Ms. Renatus."

Angela felt as if she stood before a wall in front of a firing squad. Trembling, she knelt and began to drag herself beneath the barrel. She took one more glance toward the two men. What she saw made her shake her head. *I must be hallucinating. It isn't possible.* Neither the director or his burly accomplice knew that on either side of them stood the grim-faced apparitions of Giuliano and Gerhard. For once, she prayed the ghosts from the past were real. In her head she heard Giuliano whisper, *the past will not repeat itself.* His words enveloped her in a sense of peace, giving her courage. She was not alone.

Angela held her breath as she wriggled beneath the barrel. She brushed aside the cobwebs and shuddered, hoping the spiders who had made them had abandoned their webs for more fertile ground. This was absolute yuck, but if Sophia could do it, then so could she. Shuddering, she ran her hand over the surface beneath the barrel. It was crusty and uneven. "I can't see."

"Enrico, shine the flashlight under the barrel."

A beam of light lit the bottom of the barrel and she saw the outline of an opening. She scooted farther in and pushed on the slat. It popped open and she reached inside. Blindly she felt around trying not to think of what else might be in there. Then she felt it. She pulled it toward the opening and grabbed onto a strap. Tugging the backpack out, she dragged it with her as she slid out from beneath the barrel.

She lay still for a minute trying to catch her breath and still her pounding heart. It seemed impossible that inside this old backpack was one of the most priceless works of art in the world. The thought made her head spin. Her whole body trembled. The backpack weighed nothing but for some reason, it felt as if it was filled with rocks. Her fear was getting the better of her. She had to reel it in.

She sat up clutching the backpack and stared into the muzzle of a shotgun. Her heart pounded erratically in her chest. Would death claim her first, before Alex, in this lifetime?

"Hand over the backpack, Angela. Give it to Enrico."

"Are you going to kill me, now, in cold blood?"

"That won't be necessary."

"Why not?"

"I'm going to administer a large dose of LSD and Ketamine. Three or four hours from now, when you wake, you'll have no memory of what happened."

"What's ketamine?"

"It's a date rape drug," Alberto said.

Enrico ogled her. His look of lust made the color drain from her face.

"It won't hurt Angela, but more importantly, it won't be necessary to permanently silence you." His leer matched Enrico's. "You might even enjoy it."

"You'll never get away with this." Her only hope was to keep him engaged in talking. She'd die fighting before she'd let that evil beast, Enrico, touch her.

"We already have. Your detective is dead. Police will rule it as an unfortunate accident. The painting is ours and you'll remember nothing about us drugging you and taking the painting; nothing about us killing your precious boyfriend; nothing about the demise of the noble Max Jaeger." She gasped at his admission. "And of course, nothing of what we're about to do next…" His words hung in the air as both men leered at her.

She fought the urge to gag. *Alex is not dead. I would know if he were.* Anger boiled inside of her. She wished she had the gun Alex had left for her back at the house. If she did, she'd have no trouble killing them.

Enrico grabbed the backpack from her, removing the tube. "It's here Alberto. I can't believe it, but it's here."

"Be careful with it, Enrico." He kept the rifle aimed at Angela.

Enrico removed the layers of tissue and lamb's wool protecting the precious work of art. For the first time in seventy-years, Leonardo da Vinci's masterpiece saw the light of day.

Angela gasped; the wedding portrait was exactly as she'd seen in her visions. The unmistakable hand of a genius was in every brush stroke… the way Giuliano looked at Fioretta with complete and utter love and devotion, and the way Fioretta gazed out from the painting with the mysterious allure of a timeless beauty… Angela's eyes filled with tears. The painting was a masterpiece, every bit as intriguing as the Mona Lisa.

The eeriness of the moment wasn't lost on her. Even the two murderers stared in awe at the five-hundred-year-old painting by the hand of the greatest genius the world had ever known.

No one spoke. The reality of what they were looking at made words superfluous. While the men gaped at the painting, Angela realized what she had to do.

A pounding rain drenched them, but Alex and the dogs continued to climb the trail. He'd slipped and fallen twice and was slathered in mud, but nothing was going to stop him from getting to Angela.

He jogged to the top of the trail and emerged from the dense brush. The three dogs silently sniffed the ground and came to a halt. Exactly as they'd been trained to do when they hunted and located prey, they sat before a wall of rock, their tails wagging. His heart was bursting from his chest and it wasn't from the climb. Sophia's cave, the cave of Angela's visions was behind that rock slab.

How did it open? He ran his fingers over the smooth slate. An eerie sensation took hold, as though unseen hands were guiding him. He pulled the slab, it moved a few inches. His heart pounding, he peered in. His stomach lurched when he heard voices. Carefully, he drew the Glock from his pocket and released the safety.

His thoughts were racing. If he plunged in with his weapon drawn Scordato might kill Angela, and there had to be an accomplice in there with him. He'd seen two sets of larger shoe prints on the trail.

It was too risky. He stuffed his gun back in his belt and whispered to the dogs to stay. Then raising his hands in surrender, he entered the cave. His best bet was to surprise and disorient the two criminals.

Scordato whirled toward him, a rifle in his hands. "Well! I'm afraid this changes everything."

Misu had run after Alex with the other two dogs close behind. All three dogs growled, poised to attack.

"Call them off Alex, or I'll shoot them. Enrico and I will kill them and the two of you."

"Alex!" Angela's scream echoed in the cave. The terror in her eyes unnerved him, but he breathed a sigh of relief knowing she was unharmed.

"It's okay, Angela." He turned to the dogs. "*A cuccia subito!*" All three dogs sat. They remained still, their eyes locked on their master.

Angela was not to be silenced. "No, it's not okay. History is repeating itself. Why did you come here? Can't you see your life is in danger?"

He heard the panic in her voice and knew she wasn't thinking rationally. This whole past life stuff had clouded her vision. He was relieved that the barrel of the gun was pointing at him and not her.

"Take it easy, Scordato." He glanced at the other accomplice who had his gun aimed at the dogs. The man was in his element, comfortable, which meant he was a professional. Alex knew the odds were against them. There was little chance of him taking out both Scordato and the other man. He also knew there was no way they'd leave Angela and him alive. He was going to have to make a move and risk everything. But before he could...

What Angela saw was otherworldly. The cave shimmered, the past and present converging before her eyes. The apparitions of Giuliano and Gerhard held her gaze, their gestures, encouraging her to act. There was no way Scordato would allow her and Alex to live. He would finish it here, kill them here, leaving their bodies to rot in the cave. He'd kill the dogs, too. Ama and Zaba's eyes flitted back and forth from Alex to Scordato. Misu's fur was raised and his back bowed, poised to strike.

If time had caught up with them and history was repeating itself, so be it. She would not go down without a fight. *Now! Do it now!* Her enraged scream pierced the air as she sprinted toward Scordato.

Alex ordered, "Angela don't!"

Scordato spun around, his rifle swinging back to Angela. But she kept going, charging like a lioness knocking him over. The rifle flew out of his hands. Snarling, she clawed at Scordato's cheeks, scraping skin as he howled and flung her off.

At the same time, Alex lunged at Enrico unbalancing him before he could fire. Alex and Enrico rolled in the dirt with the dogs viciously circling around them. Alex slammed his fist into the criminal's jaw, knocking him out cold. "*Attacca e sottometti.*" Misu leaped on Enrico's chest, snarling, holding him in place.

Alex yanked the gun from his belt at the same moment as Scordato reached for his rifle. Like an old western standoff, they fired at the same time.

"No!" Angela screamed. Then something unbelievable happened. Everyone and everything shifted into slow motion around her. The ghosts of Giuliano and Gerhard appeared, their hands gripping the rifle and pushing it upward. Then with a whoosh, they disappeared, and everything sped up again.

Instead of hitting Alex in the chest, the bullet grazed his shoulder, knocking him to the ground, and ricocheted to the back of the cave, shattering a bottle of wine. She scurried to Alex and picked up the fallen Glock. It was surreal and impossible, but with what she assumed was something beyond the perception of human knowledge, the ghosts had managed to cross the boundaries between the afterlife and the living world. They'd intervened purely through the force of their will.

Scordato had been knocked off his feet, as well. His arm oozing blood, he cursed and scrambled for his rifle. "This time I'll finish it."

Filled with a blinding rage, Angela pointed the Glock at Scordato. Fioretta and Sophia appeared beside her. Their voices echoed in her mind.

You must end it, Angela, for all of us. Their ghostly fingers covered hers. Together, they pulled the trigger.

The gunshot blast reverberated throughout the cave. Scordato's eyes widened in disbelief as he fell to his knees. He clutched his stomach, blood seeping through his fingers, and toppled over.

Alex rolled to his feet and, reaching for Scordato's rifle, trained it on Enrico, now moaning on the ground. Misu and the other dogs formed a circle around him, their growls echoing around the cave.

"Alex," Angela dropped the gun and wrapped her arms around him. Her chest heaved with her sobs. "You're bleeding."

"Baby, I'm okay, it's just a graze. I'll be fine. His fingers were gentle on her cheek, but she couldn't help wincing. "I'm so sorry, honey," he said, his voice cracking.

"I'll be fine, bruises heal. I'm just so happy you're okay." She covered his hand with hers.

"If Scordato wasn't already dead, I'd take great pleasure in killing him."

"I know, but we won. It's a miracle. We changed destiny. We broke the curse."

"Angel, you were amazing." His eyes glowed in the dark cavern, making her breath catch at the love that shone from his gaze. "I don't understand how Scordato could have missed me. He was just a few feet away."

"It was them—Giuliano and Gerhard stopped time and shifted the rifle." Angela wrapped her arms around Alex's waist.

Catching a flash of movement behind Alex, Angela's arms tightened around the man she loved as Giuliano and Fioretta appeared beside Gerhard and Sophia.

The ghosts embraced each other, united in death as they once were in life. With a last look at Angela, they dissolved into nothingness. She wasn't sure, but she thought she glimpsed a smile of satisfaction on their lips.

Alex kissed her cheek, then bent to pick up the Glock. "Here, hold the gun on that bastard while I grab my backpack."

He returned to the cave a moment later and pulled a zip-tie from the bag. Enrico was still unconscious, but it didn't matter, Misu and the other dogs stood ready to pounce if he made a threatening move.

Alex patted Misu on the head. "*Seduti.*" The dog backed off and sat. Alex rolled Enrico onto his stomach and bound his hands with the zip-tie. Standing, he returned to Angela, taking the gun from her trembling hand.

"We weren't alone, Alex. They were all here in the cave, including Fioretta and Sophia.

His eyes darted around and returned to her. "Ghosts can't change the trajectory of bullets—"

"But that's just what happened. I saw them as clearly as I see you now. Giuliano and Gerhard somehow managed to push up the barrel of the rifle when it fired. But even more bizarre is that Fioretta and Sophia's fingers were on mine. We pulled the trigger together."

Alex looked around. "Are they still here?"

"Why, are you afraid of ghosts?" She smiled.

"Why would I be afraid of my past lives? I just want to thank them."

"They've moved on, Alex. I don't believe we'll see them again. But I'm pretty sure they know your sentiments."

Cupping her face with his hand he grinned. "Good. I'm happy they can finally rest in peace because I was getting tired of them hogging your time. From now on, I want you all to myself."

"Won't you get bored after a while?"

"Angel, something tells me that life with you will never be boring." His lips claimed hers and for the second time that afternoon, time stood still.

CHAPTER 23

Paris, France
Shangri-La Hotel
Present day
September 1

Alex held Angela snug against him, his body still quivering with pleasure from their morning sex. It didn't matter how many times they made love, he only knew that every time made him profoundly happy. He still couldn't quite believe she was his, or that the nightmare was over. Enrico confessed to everything, including the murder of Max Jaeger. With his sworn statement, the police investigation was neatly wrapped and closed within a couple of weeks. Angela and Alex were cleared of any wrongdoing. The memory of how close they'd come to death was beginning to fade like an old scar.

The painting was returned to Celestine Marchesi at the Uffizi. Gratefully, she agreed Angela would be given full credit for its discovery and would be granted the honor of bringing her discovery to the attention of the world.

For the third time that morning his muse jumped from the bed.

"Alex, I'm sorry." She opened the French doors that led to the terrace. "But I can't stop looking at it." He had to admit that their view of the Eifel Tower was spectacular. Even he, who'd grown up with every luxury imaginable, was impressed. The suite was comparable to the most elegant *pied à terre* on the Avenue Montaigne. *Worth every penny.* Indulging Angela turned him on. Her delight put a fresh spin on the world. It was impossible to suffer from tedium in the face of her inexhaustible enthusiasm and joy. *Loving her is like being reborn.* He laughed aloud, realizing that's exactly what they were, reborn lovers.

"What's so funny?" She peeked her head back through the door. Her bed-mussed hair spilled around her shoulders.

"You're so beautiful, baby. But if you don't stop prancing around nude on the terrace we're going to have every Peeping Tom in Paris out on the rooftops with telescopes."

She looked down as if realizing her state of undress for the first time. "Oops, it never occurred to me that anyone could see me." She ran back in pouncing on top of him.

He rolled her over and balanced above her. He kissed her soundly. "Mmm, I'm glad that one thing didn't change after finding the da Vinci."

"And what's that?" She lifted up on her elbows, pressing her breasts into his chest.

"Every time we touch I feel fireworks."

"It doesn't bother you that we returned the painting to the Uffizi?"

"Not a bit. I got something worth a whole lot more to me than money." She laughed. "That's because you've got plenty of money."

"It's true, I do, but I don't think you can ever understand how much more important you are to me."

She caressed his face with the back of her hand. "Maybe I'm going to let you prove it to me for the rest of our lives."

He claimed her mouth with a blazing kiss. Then, pulling away, he rolled out of the bed.

"Hey, you can't just kiss me like that and leave."

"Yeah, I can. You just provided me with the opening I've been looking for." He disappeared into the closet and, a minute later, returned and sat on the edge of the bed.

"What's this about, and what are you hiding?" She playfully poked his arm.

He cleared his throat. "I've got something serious to say."

She sat up and pulled the sheet over her breasts. "Okay."

"Angel, I've never met anyone like you and I've never done anything like this before. I'm hopelessly in love with you and I want to be with you forever." The hand behind his back came forward bearing a velvet jewelry box. He set the box in her palm and opened it. "Please say you'll marry me, baby."

She gasped, the dazzling light from the ring reflected in her eyes. "Alex, it's beautiful. When... how... is this really happening?" Her eyes filled with tears. "I don't know what to say."

He plucked the diamond ring from the box and slipped it on her finger. "Just say yes, Angela. We belong together. We've always belonged together. Before in our past lives and now in this one."

"I love you so much, Alex."

"I love you too, baby. And I have another proposal to make to you."

"Another proposal?" A curious smile chased her tears away.

"Work with me, be my partner. Permanently."

"You mean in the winery?" She grinned.

He shook his head. "Well, you'll be a de facto partner in that, anyway. What I mean is, you and me solving art crimes. Restoring stolen and missing art to their rightful owners. You're a natural, Angela. It's a worthy cause for your talents."

Her brows knit in thought. She glanced at the ring on her finger and then into his eyes. "Partners. I like the sound of that." She wiggled her eyebrows the same way he always did. "Shall we seal the deal with a kiss?"

He laughed, pulling her down on top of him. "Angel, a kiss is just the beginning…"

EPILOGUE

Montefioralle, Italy
Present day
September 15

Angela stood at the sink in the kitchen staring out the window. The *vendemmia* was in full progress. The grapes, having reached their peak, were ready for harvest. Alex was busy supervising the picking in the vineyard with Joseph. The dogs were running to and fro, enjoying the excitement. Maria was gathering fresh herbs from her garden. She was going to teach Angela how to make a proper tomato sauce that she could use as a base for a variety of dishes.

Angela glanced down at the sparkling engagement ring on her finger. Paris had been everything Alex had promised. The beginning of their "once upon a time" fairytale. A dream come true. Her love for Alex was like the grape harvest, sweet and ready to be plucked, the taste of it satisfying and fulfilling. She pictured their future together and wanted nothing more than to run out to the vineyard and plant her lips on his.

After the harvest, they would travel to Chicago, and drive up the coast of Lake Michigan to her hometown of Lake Bluff, where Alex would formally ask her father for her hand in marriage. Then they'd fly to San Francisco to meet his mother and his step-father. After what Alex predicted would be a series of parties celebrating their engagement, they would fly to London where she'd meet his father.

Her heart fluttered at the thought. *Please let them like me and bless this marriage.* She sent up a silent prayer, remembering that Fioretta had once made that same prayer for her marriage with Giuliano. It seemed nothing could stop the forward motion of time and love.

Since the climactic events in the cave, she had only one small episode, one loss of herself when she'd slipped into the abyss of the past. Standing before the Mona Lisa at the Louvre, she'd once more found herself travelling through time to the studio of Leonardo da Vinci. He'd begun the portrait of a woman with an enigmatic smile and she could see him delicately applying paint with his brush. It was the Maestro's thoughts of Fioretta that had drawn her back in time. For a brief moment, she felt Leonardo's fond remembrance of her. *I miss you, Fioretta.*

Alex had squeezed her hand and she was herself again. She'd said nothing to him. She was afraid that even acknowledging her loss of the present would somehow make it recur, and she would be taken by the vortex of history and once more dragged from her body to witness the past playing over again. The thought of that happening made her shudder.

Now, of all times, she was feeling it again. A strange tingling took hold of her and her vision blurred. She rubbed her eyes, trying to clear them. When she opened them, she shook her head trying to see through the mist that clouded her vision. A young woman with long blonde hair ran through a field. She clutched a package wrapped in burlap. Frantically, she looked behind at her pursuers. Two men armed with AR-15s and dressed in military fatigues were closing in on her. Angela didn't recognize the woman or the men, but she felt the woman's fear as if it were her own.

The men grabbed her, and the woman screamed. Angela clasped her hands over her ears trying to drown out the woman's terrified cry. Her vision cleared and everything disappeared in an instant. She jumped, startled by the press of someone's hand on her arm.

"Signorina Angela, are you all right?" Maria asked.

A feeling of peace washed over her. She gazed into the warm, brown eyes filled with concern.

"Maria, I'm sorry, what did you say? For a minute I wasn't myself."

"Si, I understand. You have a rare gift."

"A gift? More like a curse."

"No, signorina, it is *the sight*. I sensed this gift in you from the moment you arrived. But I knew you needed time to understand it. After dinner, we will have a cappuccino and some amaretti, and I will tell you what I have learned in my own life." Maria took Angela's hands in both of her own. "You must learn to embrace it. You must not fight the visions." Maria hugged her and walked back to the sink to rinse the fresh herbs.

A wave of panic drenched Angela in a cold sweat. Could Maria be right? Was this so-called gift going to plague her for the rest of her life? She wanted no part of any second sight. Glancing out the window, she spied Alex walking toward the back door. He looked ruggedly handsome, unshaven, and bronzed by the sun. Love mingling with fear flowed through her veins. Should she tell him? Would he, too, encourage her to embrace this gift? What would it mean for their future?

The door opened and Alex's eyes lit up when he saw her. Two steps brought them together. His arms held her, and his lips pressed to hers. "How's my baby?"

"She has a story to tell you."

ALSO AVAILABLE

OUT OF TIME THRILLER SERIES

The Girl Who Knew da Vinci
BOOK 1

The Girl Who Loved Caravaggio
BOOK 2

The Girl Who Adored Rembrandt
BOOK 3

The Girl Who …(Coming in 2021)
BOOK 4

TIP OF THE SPEAR THRILLER SERIES

Escape
BOOK 1

Vengeance
BOOK 2

Ransom
BOOK 3

Exposed (Coming in 2021)
BOOK 4

THE ONLY ONE ROMANTIC SUSPENSE SERIES

The One
BOOK 1

The One and More
BOOK 2

One More Time Is Not Enough
BOOK 3

SIGN UP FOR BELLE AMI'S NEWSLETTER AT
BELLEAMIAUTHOR.COM

FOLLOW BELLE AMI ON BOOKBUB AND AMAZON

ABOUT THE AUTHOR

Belle Ami writes breathtaking international thrillers and compelling romantic suspense with a touch of sensual heat. A self-confessed news junky, Belle loves to create cutting-edge stories weaving world issues, espionage, fast-paced action, and of course, redemptive love.

Belle is the author of the ongoing international espionage thriller series *TIP OF THE SPEAR*, which includes the highly acclaimed *Escape*, *Vengeance*, and *Ransom and Exposed*.

She is also the author of the ongoing bestselling *OUT OF TIME* thriller series, which includes the #1 Amazon bestseller—*The Girl Who Knew da Vinci* and #1 Amazon bestseller—*The Girl Who Loved Caravaggio* and *The Girl Who Adored Rembrandt*.

Belle is also the author of the romantic suspense series *THE ONLY ONE*, which includes *The One*, *The One & More*, and *One More Time is Not Enough*.

Recently, she was honored to be included in the RWA-LARA Christmas Anthology *Holiday Ever After*, featuring her short story, *The Christmas Encounter*.

A former Kathryn McBride scholar of Bryn Mawr College in Pennsylvania, Belle, is also thrilled to be a recipient of the *RONE*, *RAVEN*, *Readers' Favorite Award*, and the *Book Excellence Award*.

Belle's passions include hiking, boxing, skiing, cooking, travel, and of course, writing. She lives in Southern California with her husband, two children, a horse named Cindy Crawford, and her brilliant Chihuahua, Giorgio Armani.

Belle loves to hear from readers—you can contact her at: belle@belleamiauthor.com

Connect with Belle Ami online:
belleamiauthor.com
BookBub
Amazon
Twitter: @BelleAmi5
Facebook
Instagram
Newsletter Signup

Made in the USA
Las Vegas, NV
27 April 2021